MW00884146

The Devil in Polo presents the
Evil Angel Series

A Beautiful Lie

By
Shawn Wallis

In loving memory of Katie

In the beginning
Good always overpowered the evils
Of all man's sins...
But in time
The nations grew weak
And our cities fell to slums
While evil stood strong
In the dusts of hell
Lurked the blackest of hates
For he whom they feared
Awaited them...
Now, many many lifetimes later
Lay destroyed beaten down
Only corpses of rebels
Ashes of dreams
And blood-stained streets...
It has been written
"Those who have the youth
Have the future"
So come now children of the beast
Be strong
And shout at the devil
                                    - Motley Crue

Table of Contents

Introduction

In the small town of Topsfield, Massachusetts, lies a quiet neighborhood amongst the hills of Route 1. The Nike Site and its miraculous military history will help bury the secret that has been kept hidden for over 30 years. Welcome yourself to the story of one teenager's fight within himself to endure tragedy amongst those of the wicked at Masconomet Regional High School. The horror to face an evil consequence will test the bravery of one soul to enact the kindness deep inside his own heart. The paradox between evil and good will test the gall of one teenager determined to right his wrongs and save the souls of those affected. The fate of the town will depend upon this journey and he must face the spirit that has chosen him above all.

Inspired by
True Events

Chapter 1
Tourniquet

The silent morning began like any other in the life of one teenager who felt he had escaped a burden of irony with all that had occurred the previous few years. The feeling of countless measures released from his shoulders bringing him to this moment of truth. This was the solace he deserved for everything that bestow upon his grace became an anxiety like no other. Removing the dampened baseball cap from his head to wipe the sweat dripping from his nervous brow, Shawn would create a recourse for every reason to stand on a mound of horrific consequence.

Staring into the bluish sky of indigent clouds, his vision fell beneath the nervous eyes of a beautiful resilience. His buckling knees supporting his thin seventy-one-inch frame frightens all that watch in support of this hyped boy with the golden arm. It is the first game between the Slidell High Tigers and the Mandeville Skippers in the rural town of Slidell, Louisiana. On this beautiful April afternoon in 1991, the smell of fresh cut grass and the feel of the warm clay placed upon this field would become an isolated heaven for one specific angel.

The hype that had coveted the teenager from a small town outside of Boston, Massachusetts invited a large community of eyes to witness an unfolding event. The baseball field chiseled with perfection set the stage for the unknown to reveal itself with ridicule and years of scrutiny. Shawn's cheap black cleats covering his feet and saggy baseball pants were all on display as each warm up pitch would strike the catchers glove with a whopping loud sound. The excitement filling the warm Saturday morning air would spread throughout the crowd like a tidal wave.

The previous year would set the stage for this exact moment as the hype of one man's will, would attempt to carry the baseball team upon his back. Shawn would fill the void the Slidell High School baseball team had been looking for and the feeling was reciprocated by all the coaches and teammates. The past years were merely a success for this community and it was all coming down to this moment when the baseball team needed a hero. Slidell High School became the talk of the surrounding towns with all the mysterious hype about a student transferring from a small Massachusetts town. Officially arriving with a magic curveball and a live cut fastball, the rumors were swirling that Slidell High found the complimentary piece to win another state title. Reality crawled into the eyes of the unknown town with an article written in the Times Picayune. The local newspaper out of New Orleans would pin the hopes of the upcoming baseball season on the premonition that a stranger would save them from obscurity.

The town of Slidell had a long tradition of great baseball teams and the drought to fulfill the earlier years of success weighed heavily on Coach Abney and his Tigers. Earlier that previous August, everything would change with a delivery of a bulky letter addressed to the Coach of the Baseball Team for Slidell High School. With the grip of a bear, Coach Abney tore open the letter with the strength of fifty men and falling onto his desk was a short-paragraphed letter addressed to himself. Unfolding the contents of the letter, it began to reveal electric words striking ideas in his mind. His worthy smile that had been absent the previous few years was back. Alone by himself in his office, he immediately began to unveil his plan to field a baseball team worthy of what Slidell had deserved under his tenure. Rejoicing over and over in his mind the will to bring back what his town longed for would consume him for months to come. The dialing of the buttons on his phone rang out the number of this new student's previous baseball coach at Masconomet Regional High in Topsfield, Massachusetts. Unable to pronounce the name of the High School, Coach Abney could care less as his thick fingers pressed hard enough to mash the buttons through the floor.

The anticipation to speak to the man responsible for creating a new life for his team began to peak and the line suddenly picked up. The conversation between the two coaches surrounded the arrival of a stranger with a golden arm and perfect statistics. Shawn was the answer Coach Abney was looking for and with each word inside of his ear spoken, the stranger on the other end became clearer. His team was inheriting a perfect scenario of wildness and nothing was going to keep this secret from becoming revealed. The conversation between the two men would last over an hour and as fast as he could whisper, the phone was back into his ear.

The Times Picayune had left the coach last year for dead with an embattled article calling for his dismissal after a horrendous season. It was the perfect moment of redemption for Coach Abney and no hesitation existed with the unkind words for the editor of the paper. It was a plight of angriness and purity that spoke of a new season that he was predicting to be his greatest accomplishment. Coach Abney invited a chaotic circle of envy to his card game and he was dealing queens. It was up to the world to beat him at his own game and he was up for the challenge with the ace coming to town.

Quick words and innuendos were spreading like wildfire that a senior from another town was registering to become a pupil of Slidell High. He was going to be the player that the town hadn't seen in many years and was going to lift a championship for the city to glorify. The perfect circle constructed an enormous chance to reveal the luck that Coach Abney was finding himself as a gift from the Gods. The hype was enormous throughout the senior year of Shawn Lee and he was more than willing to handle it all. Fading forward, he brought himself back to the moment on this mound as if it became a reflection of haunting memories. The cool breeze whistling freedom into his daunting blue eyes, his wondering mind recollected a higher reason for his sanction. It was his letter that brought the attention facing him and the thousands of eyes witnessing the call for a hero to save them.

The setting upon the mound appeared familiar to Shawn as he previously endured a vicious battle of irony. The stage was different, but the thoughts were reminiscent of everything he was willing to fight for and the absence of evil became special. Placing the ball cap upon his head, the hollowing moment was front and center and the town and its community were now witnessing a revelation. All the talk and its meaning were now at full circle and this was the moment. The seventeen-year-old phenom was about to deliver a resuscitating fastball proven to wake up the deadening silence surrounding him.

Positioning both feet upon the hill of clay, his awkward stance would face the catcher a little over sixty feet away. His fate just twenty yards between the mound and home plate, he would lean away from the rubber and begin to wind up like a clock tower over looking the town. The beautiful magic of a perfect windup was on display for all to see and as graceful as a perfect cloud in the sky.

Dancing forward with a jolted thrust, a darkness soon began to fall as he leaned forward. Upon release of the baseball from his hand, an enormous pain swarmed down his shoulder and into his elbow. At that same exact moment, a thunderous lightning bolt from the cloudy sky shook the ground and all those in attendance. The Devil's brilliant disguise hiding the popping noise from Shawn's arm while the baseball traveled midflight towards its destination. Reflections of the eerie clouds hovering gracefully over this once graceful hero. The golden arm of their charmed warrior was now in peril as the travelled ball became insignificant.

Beyond the backstop separating the path of destruction was a digital reading indicating the fastball had reached a signal of ninety-six miles per hour. The historic moment meant nothing while the fate of this beautiful stranger was facing another direction. Gasps and whispers rang silent as those who witnessed the fastball shattering the brazen silence would fear the worst. Standing on top of the mound with a daunting pain inside of his elbow, he kneeled to one knee. Catching the attention of his coaches, it was the footsteps of those that struggled to reach their destination in the sudden fog that covered the field. The crowd in awe seemingly gazing at a fallen god, the one pitch that produced a strike was the last one heard around town.

The pain unbearable to feel within his soul, Shawn never imagined that he would become a victim of his own gall. He placed himself on this pedestal and it was a mere fact that he was kneeling to surrender everything he stood for. With the support of his coaches and the thousands in attendance in the stands, it was the fear of fading that bothered Shawn and all he wanted to do was hide.

"I'm done Coach", Shawn replied to his coach's questions of being alright. His arm feeling thirty pounds heavier on his body, it was a mere revelation that he found himself broken and bent. It took this moment to shape a reality that the power to feel invincible all these years was now over.

Simply dejected and unaware of his surroundings, Shawn stood up and began to walk over to the dugout. Holding his arm, he would look down in horror as to hide his emotions from the crowd that wanted to believe their hero was alright. Each step away from the mound was grueling and it represented how far from grace Shawn would fall. Each imprint left in the grass on his way to exile would further represent the moment of grace that would never become his. The silence of the bench at his team's dugout welcomed him as he sat by himself and focused his eyes towards the same sky that shared its beautiful color.

The dark clouds existing over the evil that graced the presence of a hidden evil had soon faded.

Asking his coaches to leave him quiet for a while was easily accepted as the game had to move forward. While they would continue without him, nothing felt lonelier at that moment than sitting alone and pretending everything never happened. Could it be a mere possibility that something else was controlling the fate of this teenager? That question would roll inside of his head and while the town had lost all control of its destiny, the future was just beginning. Unknow to this town was the past of the stranger that had given them all hope. Not one person who became enlightened by the kindness of this hero was aware of where he came from and the uneasiness he suffered. The previous five years before this moment were of a biblical tale of good versus evil and Shawn was just beginning to understand his purpose in life. The same sky that supplanted itself among the eyes of this beautiful stranger were now giving away to something else.

With regret in his eyes, misery found itself next to his peripheral vision in the shape of a dark figure. Standing tall and wreaking of cigar smoke, Shawn knew that his presence was a surprise. The clouds shifting in opposite direction to where they once stood, the shadow covered the sudden darkness. Without acting in doubt, Shawn's eyes remained focused away from reality as to ignore the evil that had found him again. The ground became unstable and the temperature began to drop in the thick air surrounding the ballfield. The small hairs on his neck rose away from his skin and the voice came without hesitation.

A slight laughter ensued as temptation met fate in the eyes of the unforgiven.

"Didn't expect to see me again so soon?" the familiar voice asked.

"Son look at them all. Watching you celebrate something that isn't truly yours. Enticing each moment as if the Gods prepared this day for eternity", he stated.

A slight chill in the air embracing the heat from Shawn's body, he tried hard to ignore his presence. Sitting on the wooden bench with his hurt arm pressed up against his body, Shawn kept his eyes gazed upon the game.

"Did you think that this was going to last forever? These people don't deserve what you are giving them. Are you seriously kidding me?" it asked.

The darkened spirit drew closer to his face and began whispering in his ear.

"Look at them all Shawn…Look at them! They are not worthy of what we are allowing them all to witness. Each breath a gift from his holiness and it sickens me. This sickens me to the core and you are feeding into their hopes," the dark figure stated.

15

"You were chosen by me to supplant my beliefs into this world and you broke your promise. Did you ever imagine Sir what would happen if you betrayed me?"

"Did you?" The deep angry voice stated.

"I pleasantly sat back like a sheep in disguise planting the seed for you to endure. I truly never thought I would end up back here amongst these chains you placed upon me. I balanced this distance among us to watch you build all of this up only to see it all fall-down. This is the blind faith in my eyes and the balance between Heaven and Hell will never relinquish our fate. With or without you, I will seek others to serve what I was placed into this world to do. Do you remember what I told you a few years ago?" the dark figure asked.

The hesitation was perceived loudly by Shawn, but he refused to acknowledge what was being said. Each word spoken would climb its way beneath the surface of his skin, but he was withdrawn from showing how much it bothered. Staring into the sky and its beautiful purpose, the moments of the battle a year earlier began to soften the heart of this gentle teen.

Slowly tearing up in the corner of his eye, Shawn slowly turned his head away from the dark figure and slowly murmured, *"Wherever, whenever and however you choose to roam with your wicked ways, I will be there. If I must dig*

up everything in the ground that surrounds you, I will
unbury your secrets. Are we clear?"

Each breath of fresh air passing in his lungs allowed Shawn
to bravely stand up to the same apparition that helped
bring him into this world. The same air regurgitating
through his body was the same the dark figure would
surround itself with and the reminder of the war
previously quickly subsided. Turning his head around as he
stood on his feet, Shawn looked into the eyes of the
apparition.

"I may be free from you, but I choose to keep this within
me so that you can never be free of who I really am.
Whoever you choose, whoever you call out to, let them
know, let them all know that I am coming for them,"
Shawn boldly stated.

Shawn whispering to his buried soul the vendetta that
became his purpose in life. It was the realization that the
gift given to Shawn all those years ago as a child began to
make him realize something. This exact moment was
crucial to disallow evil to bully the innocent. It was his
comprehension that the demon lost control over him.

Listening to his strong words, the figure remained silent
with his deadening stare and began to reply.

"I once told you that nothing is more relevant than
honoring those who have showed you the path. I gave you
purpose in understanding what you are capable of and

pulled your worthless body from beneath the ground. You owe me Shawn, you owe me more than just these countless months of hiding from who you are. I promise that I will see you again my young friend, you can count on it", the demon angrily replied.

Shawn again looked into the eyes of the mass of grey before him and the demon spoke his name, *"Shawn"*.

The teen quickly replied, *"Vincent",* as if they had greeted each other at a formal dinner.

Stopping briefly to relight his cigar, the apparition turned around and began walking away into the clear air. With each step, the face of evil would crack a smile. The fading silhouette slowly disappeared into the air and the eyes of the hero would begin to reveal that he wasn't broken. He had a purpose and it would define everything that he was born for and it was clear to him that he had a reason to live.

Misery decided that on this day the long and lonely road Shawn would choose captivated the lost for many years to come. Representing the faith during their confrontation provided a paradox of steps for this fallen hero. He understood that nothing was going to protect this planet more than he could. Shawn had done it once before and those fateful words would create a hidden destiny to subdue the evil tempting to entice him.

Chapter 2
Red Cold River

Four years removed from that eerie day on the baseball field in Slidell, Louisiana, the scrawny teenager found himself staring at the clock in detention hall at South Weymouth Junior High School. The large hand was moving ever-so slowly while the short hand wasn't moving at all. The time was quarter past three and it was literally minutes away from a journey with friends into the woods located next to the school. During most of the day, rumors were swirling that a boy by the name of Zachary became heavily upset over his girlfriend talking to Shawn with her fateful attention. The ordeal grew into something of a spectacle, but Shawn was determined to settle the issue after detention by speaking to him.

This meeting was earlier set up by Linda Lambert, the girl who silently flirted with Shawn throughout the schoolyear. It was a typical game most young teens play by getting boys to fight over them and Linda was no exception here. She had her sights set on the new kid with the crazy blue eyes all the girls chose to ignore. His soft curly hair and a light brown lazy mustache covered his upper lip. He was the shy boy with eerie ways of confidence, frightening most and becoming alienated.

He dressed differently from everyone with his long dress shirts and pale jeans, to his dirty tennis shoes and bright white socks. Linda began her obsession teasing Shawn with her sadistic eyes luring him with her charm. Despite her love for the boyfriend she sided with for the entire school year, Shawn was unaware of the intentions Linda began to crave. Starving for attention, Shawn enticed his curiosity by opening the Pandoras Box Linda was offering. It was a chance for him to meet other students because he noticed the buxom beauty was very popular. The young teens shared several classes together and the fixture of her curves and beautiful hair allowed him to imagine a life beside her. Daydreams of delight and thoughtfulness raided his mind each time they sat in the same proximity of each other. The day Linda approached him for the very first time would set the motion for an unlikely chain of events. Several months lead to the moment that he has hoped for and with a soft gentle whisper, the plan was set in motion.

The setting began in Science class earlier that morning and right in front of her boyfriend Zach, Linda approached the boy that she had always envisioned as the outsider.

"Shawn, right?" Linda asked happily. *"I am Linda and I am just curious as to why you look at me all year and never talk to me?"*

The frail teen wanted to say a million words to cover his anxiety at that very moment, but he froze. Sweat forming on his forehead, he replied, *"How does someone talk to an angel?"*

Linda stood back in a confused stance and didn't understand how to reply to such a beautiful question. *"It's easy Shawn, you speak. Being shy around me isn't acceptable sir."*

The conversation between strangers revolved around the next fifteen minutes due to the teacher's exit for an emergency. Amongst several seconds of overlapping jealousy from her boyfriend, Linda was conjuring up an unforgiving plan. Unbeknownst to the forging evil inside the bones of this imperfect teenager, Linda was about to awaken something she had no preparation for.

"Shawn, I have had a crush on you for quite sometime and it has taken a lot of me to approach you like this. I apologize for my behavior all year, but how else am I supposed to get your attention?" Linda asked.

The young boy had no reaction or reply to what Linda was saying, but his confidence began building. He cracked a smile and as each word escaped her beautiful lips, he was graced with her pleasant smell of rose and sage. His eyes focused on the waves in her auburn hair to a point she could be furious with him and it wouldn't matter. The pretty girl sitting in front of him represented a feeling that delighted his heart and it was fate that began to unravel a deeply hidden darkness. Yesterday was a memory that easily became forgotten as the next few minutes allowed time to stand still. Shawn was standing on a lonely cloud and he had just learned that Linda was asking to be her boyfriend. The sweat on his brow became frozen in irony as he stumbled to understand his new-found confidence. For everything to take place, this creature in front of him had to expire the current relationship she was entertaining.

Linda asked Shawn if he was willing to meet Zachary in the woods by the river after detention, so that she could confess to everyone her loathing of him. Linda's plan was to expose her love for Shawn while releasing her true feelings to everyone. The scrawny thirteen-year-old from Texas who was born into a military family never endured a relationship before now and he was excited to hear of Linda's intention. Innocence clouded the mind of the young man, but he was not interested in understanding the comprehension behind the poison that Linda was feeding him. In his eyes, Linda was a shade over five-feet-tall, she had beautiful curves, wore make up and her red hair was ecstatic. She was a perfect ten in his heart and he was bound and determined to abide by her demands.

Upon asking him to speak to Zachary, there was no hesitation in agreeing to what she was wanting from him. Each thought forgave every second passing on the clock in detention. The entire hour in the cafeteria seemed miniscule against the fifteen minutes with Linda earlier in the day. His gigantic smile gave way to the loud ring of the school bell as each student formidably walked out of the rear entrance of detention. The brief meeting had hidden intentions and Shawn's determination could care less. The sudden notion that more than nine kids in attendance became apparent, when more showed up in the parking lot. The cool arctic chill in the air was a bit hard to take inside the lungs, but Shawn was not worried. Temperatures measuring below thirty degrees hid the fact of wearing no protection from the wind, but an untucked button-down shirt and a pair of jeans was a result of his own stupidity.

The chilly air turned his nose and cheeks to a bright redness painful to the touch. His eyes focused on Zachary waiting in the parking lot with his few friends. Zach stood one inch taller and his preppy shirt and turtleneck coincided with his perfect wavy hair. With his eyes fixated on the beautiful red headed teenager standing beside her man, Shawn went along and followed the small crowd into the field next to the School.

The distance from the parking lot to the woods was a mere few hundred yards and the walk became endless. The cold grass and the mixture of white snow made it very uncomfortable to supplant footsteps into the ground. Their toes freezing as the cold ice covering the path would find its way through their shoes with each step. As each foot turned into a yard, Shawn's mind was clueless as where he was destined to find himself. Thoughts of his next few days with Linda at his side clouded the true intentions of what was unfolding.

The once clear skies suddenly became darker and groups of black clouds approached without precipitation. The group of teens had ventured into the opening of the woods and within minutes, they all met up with a few others who had been waiting for their arrival. The forest opened itself up with missing trees and on the ground was a large campfire started earlier to warm up those who had been waiting. Shawn was startled and introduced himself to the boys who were conjoined near the campfire. Showing no signs of nervousness, it was always the intention to place Shawn at this very spot in front of the river. The irony was thick in the air and not one teenager knew the consequence of their actions coming in the next few minutes.

The woods next to South Weymouth Junior High School was now a playground for the approaching darkness, and the air became lighter. The fire's beaming light assisting the teens with their premature disposition, the temperature slowly rose. Hugs and hi-fives were on display between all the teens and most faces were recognizable to Shawn. He was introduced to many of the awaiting kids with his gracious unselfishness.

One of the teens went by the name of Gregory and he introduced himself as Zachary's brother. He was a larger boy in his mid teens and he brought a few of his friends to the meeting. He was a site to envision with his muscular arms and it was hard to comprehend any reason for attending, unless his brother needed his guise. In total, there were several girls and boys gathered around the fire and Shawn kept placing his eyes on Linda. This easily angered Zach and he took the opportunity to ask Shawn an important question, as all took notice.

"Hey asshole, are you here because you think you can steal my girlfriend?" Looking around at the eyes of everyone, Shawn stumbled with an answer that seemed scared. *"Why don't you ask Linda?"* he replied.

Linda was nowhere to be found and Shawn began to think he was not here for the correct reasons. Hundreds of scenarios were running into the mind of this young man and he made the quick choice to offer a deal. With a sudden confidence like a cat backed into a corner, Shawn began to speak.

 "Why don't we fight for her? Winner will keep her", Shawn bravely stated.

The silent advantages that Shawn had over this young man were now being selfishly supplanted deep into the forest. Shawn's mother always planted the seed into his mind throughout his childhood that no one could ever experience his wrath.

"Shawn, you have to be very careful not to let anyone know who you really are. Is that understood", his mother always told him.

The sudden statement towards Zach came from years of anger and beatings from his father who toughened Shawn up. His plastic heart was beginning to harden, and this frail teen had never been in an actual fight before. Thoughts of bravery strengthened his soul and he awaited a reply from his opponent.

Zachary's brother began clapping and yelling at the top of his lungs, *"Fight! Fight! Fight!"*.

When the twenty others began chanting behind him, the confrontation of these two young men became unavoidable. It was apparent both boys were eager to unleash their will and it took a right hook by Zachary to begin the fight in the woods.

The right hand clearly missed Shawn as he ducked his head and landed a left jab to Zach's face.

"*Oh,*" replied Zach. The punch opened-up a small cut above his eye and his face felt the swelling begin. Dazed and confused, the blow to his brow had placed himself in a position he had never been before. The bully at South Weymouth Junior High School was about to get a dose of his own medicine as the crowd watched on.

The stunned look by the circling classmates was a sign that they were all unaware of the capability of what this young man had to offer. Clearly a surprise by the young teen who landed the punch, a feeling of adrenaline gave warmth within his chilling bones. Exuberating patience, Shawn waited for another attack from the young man who had a lot of pinned up anger and it began working brilliantly. The skinny thirteen-year-old would let Zack wear himself out with miss after miss with his punches and it weakened his opponent drastically. A total of twelve punches had missed, and in his thoughts, loud chants of "Rocky, Rocky" were silently screaming in Shawn's mind. After several jabs and crosses thrown by Zach missed their target, the exhausted teen became exposed to the cold air and his knees began to wobble.

Shawn noticed this right away and with a combination of two consecutive left jabs and a hard cross from his right hand, Zachary found himself on the ground. Rocky Balboa had knocked down Ivan Drago in the infamous battle of East versus West and the chants became louder and louder. The cold ground gave away the purpose for why everyone was watching as Zack lay motionless. A sudden thunder in the background coming from the dark clouds hovering above, the symphony of gasps from the watching crowd mixed perfectly in Shawn's ears.

With Zack unable to rise from the ground, his brother Gregory decided to take matters into his own hands and ambushed

Shawn from behind with a furious blow to the back of his head with an elbow.

"Get the mother fucker", Gregory yelled.

With a strong push to the ground, Gregory began jumping on top of Shawn and throwing punch after punch and landing each time to the back of the young teen's head. With no defense and a deafening silence in the air, six others jumped in and began punching and kicking the teen while on the ground. The peer pressure of those who joined were in satisfaction to the leadership of what Greg had placed inside them.

With several kicks to the groin, the face and the stomach area, Shawn had no reason to fight back. With each strike against his badly damaged body, the pain would subside into feeling nothing at all. The teenagers responsible for blindsiding the young man were all friends of the boy who lost the fight. While Shawn was being pummeled by his friends, Zachary laid back with his blurry vision in pain.

Each strike from the embattled teens became more of a pinch to Shawn as his soul was unable to feel what his skin was succumbing to. Shawn's eyes staring into the darkness of the sky above him, several fists found themselves blinding his vision. Zachary brought himself to his knees as the crackling sound of punches to Shawn from his friends became frightening. The eerie sound of broken bones and bleeding skin gave way to the frightful strikes of the thunder above them all. In perfect harmony, each strike to Shawn's body produced a louder effect from the sky above and the focus began to lighten.

Barely able to stand, the coward walked over and began to chime in with his own few punches to Shawn's face while he lay on the ground.

"*Nobody beats me and gets away with it. Do you understand me?*" Zack yelled as he grabbed Shawn's torn shirt.

"*Pick him up?*" Zack asked the others.

Gregory and two others lifted Shawn from the ground by his lifeless shirt and held him in front of Zach. While Gregory placed him in a headlock, the other boys held his legs and his broken body and swollen face gazed upon him. Zach looked into Shawn's eyes very closely and said, "*Look at me you piece of shit. She is mine and don't you ever forget it. Talk to her and you die.*"

The punch thrown towards Shawn missed and landed across the brow of his brother Gregory, causing him to let Shawn go. Laughter of the teens watching angered both brothers and they both yelled, "*Shut up!*"

The total of sixty to seventy punches thrown in the direction of the teenager who had fallen to the ground gave weight towards the chilling air. His badly swollen face unrecognizable to the others, moans and whispers from the onlookers pierced his soul. With his legs wobbling with weakness, the remaining adrenaline was used to muster up the courage to focus on those who had beat him. With one eye swollen shut and the other barely able to see, he was staring at those responsible for what happened.

The faces were memorized with grace and with each name stated in his mind, this moment was important to the young teen. Mike Tesser, Gregory Alexander, Chris Vincent, Stephen

Adams, Zachary Alexander, Robbie Pennington, Robert Anders and Christopher Pyles ran through his mind over and over.

The look of surprise from the teens who had just savagely beat Shawn weren't easily hidden. The look of horror upon their faces distracted him as Gregory flew across the path with a loud anger and buried a six-inch knife into Shawn's back. The force of the knife would place the teen a few feet from his stance as his motionless soul fell to the ground. The back of Shawn's head had fallen on a large rock near the campfire as he lay next to the open flames. His frail and broken body erupted in black smoke as his clothes began catching fire. The horrific screams of an innocent boy were quietly within the minds of those who looked on in absolute horror. The smell of burning skin placed a chokehold on the surrounding forest with sounds of gurgling leaving Shawn's body. The dark eyes of a blind innocence propelled fear into the minds of the murderous intent by the teens.

Gregory and his friends immediately ran into the opposite direction of the Junior High School afraid that they just murdered the boy they jumped. Racing through the minds of the entire group of teens was the horror that could barely escape them all and each breath taken was in vain. The several teens responsible for killing Shawn were sticking together and the slight laughter in the air was responsible for the wickedness they were bringing upon themselves.

The crowd witnessing all that had happened quickly disbanded as the wicked silence remained in the cold air of the forest. The young man's badly beaten body lay calm in a dreary motion over the burning wood. The soothing light of the fire began to dim as the slithering darkness calmly rolled in. The quietness within the forest soon produced a smothering thick fog crawling from beneath the ground and covering the wounds of his body. Several sets of crystal blue eyes began to appear through the thickness of the dense smoke walking slowly over the teen. The several hundred trees surrounding the massacre of this beautiful human would now be embraced by open arms coveting their bark. The suffocating air distinguished the remaining fire as it dissipated into an eerie calm. Several

moments passed while the blue eyes upon the mist gathered in futility gazing upon the lifeless teen. A few seconds of darkness gave way to a shifting of the earth as the ground opened beneath Shawn's body. The loose Earth separating in different directions as small vines began to appear from the cracks. With each inch of his frame, Shawn was completely engulfed by the hunger of hell as he slowly began to disappear. The quicksand under the body of the young man had taken his soul and buried him deep beneath the coldness of the red river. The thick smoke that hovered above was drifting away from the burial of the massacred child. Left behind from the eerie calm were broken rocks and burnt branches surrounded by the sounds of the running river. The invisible noose hanging from the branch above Shawn's body relentlessly hung in peril. Wrapped in gold and black, the symbolistic grace of the murdered scenery called out the revenge of its dead. The presence of its violence was to tip the balance between confidence and torture in the young man.

Several hours later, one of the witnesses to the fight had called the police in response to what she had seen in the woods and it immediately became a crime scene. Equipped with a name of the victim and a missing body, the details of what the woods had left was a mystery to most. Surrounded by yellow tape and several officers, the only detail of a crime being committed was that of what others were describing. Nobody really knew the mystery student and the several months of schooling didn't provide enough information for anyone to be close enough to learn much about him. He was considered a beautiful stranger to most and nobody befriended him to learn much from where he lived.

In the several days after the incident, not a sighting of Shawn or a clue to where he was, stumped everyone involved. The teens responsible for brutally killing Shawn felt relieved that he possibly could have wandered away from their lives and the police questions asked of them were meaningless. The woman responsible for it all was on a path of destruction in her own mind because she felt responsible for distancing herself from the entire crowd. Since the moment of the fight in the woods weeks earlier, she was unable to sleep while nightmares of Shawn rang through her head. Each sleeping moment for the gorgeous teen was a minute of hell for she was uncomfortable with the terror she brought upon herself.

Coincidentally, all the cowards that were responsible for the fate of the young teen in the woods that day suffered from unimaginable nightmares of a revenge for several months after the incident. It was evil's way of kindly reminding them that they weren't forgotten. That somber day in 1987 that brought forth a stranger amongst the lives of so many would just disappear and bring a hopeless fate into the world that was unprepared. It was always remembered that death brings a new life into this world and this incident was no exception, or was it? The stranger the detectives failed to properly investigate was deemed a false story and the whispers would wither away.

The silence of the woods would remain quiet for weeks as those who knew the death of a stranger would soon be forgotten. The calming ground surrounding the area of his resting place would now begin to tremble on this balmy dark evening. The quietness of the woods surrendered to the violence beneath the ground as cracks along the dirt began to open. The sounds of silence

would give way to the deafening chills of the awaiting nature. The rays of the full moon brightened the darkness of the woods as an arm slowly peaked through the rubble.

The fingers covered in dirt sought to reach for the heavens escaping the lost sight below. A once lifeless soul was now seeking vengeance with his everlasting identity and his black stained eyes attempting to find their freedom. Gripping the ground with brute strength, it pulled itself amongst the roots of the ground. Struggling with all his might, the teen who once appeared lifeless was now well and alive. Breathing heavily as if he held his breath for an eternity, the confusion set in on the mind of young man who appeared from the depths of the darkest of hates. The drops of rain upon his skin to wash the regrets of his past had come to fruition. The second chance to make right for endless wrongs was now among the wicked souls of the night and the darkness of the river was upon him.

The cold Weymouth night was reborn into a catastrophic burial of regrets and misery and it was about to position a new evil forty miles away in a small town above Boston.

The town of Topsfield and the reputation of a remarkable past time was now upon the eyes of a beautiful blue-eyed stranger. A few months would pass since the State became frantic over the senseless prank over a murdered boy never to be found. Somehow and someway, the same teen found his way onto the grounds of a Masconomet Regional High School asking for admittance into eighth grade with his parents. The school year was less than a month from completion, but it was the irony that brought this stranger into the office many miles away from where he allegedly disappeared. Shawn was equipped with a new smile and a darkness in his eyes never seen before. Inside those dilated pupils was a new person and a small vision of those several strong arms gripping the trees in the forest where he once lay. Shawn was reborn and now taking on the task of transforming away from the Red River he once laid beside and left for dead. Coincidentally the soul of the young boy who faltered in every way possible was about to transform his new life into the lives of those students at Masconomet Regional High School.

Chapter 3
Into the Fire

It would be coincidental to ever imagine that a new home for Shawn was possible, but his family had moved to the town of Topsfield, Massachusetts in May of 1987. Shawn's father had been awarded a home by the US Military which had been applied for many months before while living on the Air Force base in the town of Weymouth, Ma. The application approval excited the entire family and a new life was starting in the area located thirty miles north of Boston. The upside of the move put Shawn into a new school and his mother's willingness to maintain his privacy would be a blessing.

Ever since his birth in 1973, Shawn had dubiously exhibited unnatural behaviors. At the tender age of two, he was diagnosed with a severe pneumonia that should have ended his young life. Doctors had attempted to prepare his mother for her sudden loss, but that was never to be. His family would move from town to town over the tenure of his Father's duty in the Coast Guard. Towns like Key West in Florida, Galveston, TX and Virginia would become havens for Shawn's mysterious happenings.

Shawn's mother always knew he was special and she kept his gifts hidden from the world and it all came to face when he turned 10 years old. Living on a military base in Key West, Shawn had come running into his home from the backyard screaming.

"Mommy, Mommy, there is a man standing in our back yard", Shawn screamed.

Catching the attention of his mother, they both walked outside of the back screen on their patio and the site frightened her. A tall man dressed in a long dark peacoat standing a few feet above her son was staring at them. His greying beard covered most of his face and the dark pupils in his brown eyes began turning red.

"Let me in your house now", the stranger replied.

The dark stranger was holding a pitch fork and pointing it at the mother and her son demanding to be let in to their home.

"Please don't hurt us, please. What do you want?" Shawn's mother asked.

"Let me into your home or I will kill you", demanded the stranger.

The pain in her eyes kept her frozen and this angered the man standing in front of her. He began to lunge towards the young child with his pitch fork and with a swift push from his right arm, Shawn shielded himself away from his mother. Falling to the ground, her eyes caught the glimpse of her son placing his left arm in the air towards the evil man. The blinding light separating the child from the weapon held by the man would knock the stranger to the ground.

The weapon once held by the man found itself now buried deep inside the ground, unreachable of the stranger's grasp. The young child standing within a few feet of the man responsible for threatening his mother, stared down at him with his awakening pupils. Reaching for his throat, the stranger felt a strong grasp of invisibility choking the life out of him. Shawn's mother couldn't believe what she was seeing, but the last gasp of air released itself away from the lips of the bearded perpetrator. Lifeless and cold, the still corpse her son had become responsible for should have frightened her. It hadn't and the immediate need to covet her child was more important at that time.

Her son turned around and looked at his mother, *"Mommy, are you ok?"*

Without a murmur of anger, she grabbed her son and ran inside the home to call the police. She had swiftly stated that a dead man was found in her backyard and the secret would remain forever in her heart. She had witnessed her son kill the man responsible for threatening her life and she would protect her son for years to come.

The strange mystery in Weymouth was left behind and the unexpected community of Topsfield was a fresh start.
The location of 15 Nike Village was located on top of Route 1 surpassing the Danvers -Topsfield city limits sign. The elevation of the location where Shawn's family was to call home was inviting and the fresh air became inviting to his new life. The new neighborhood of sixteen homes would be called The Nike Site and its meaning was never revealed, but that seamed meaningless. The opening on top of the large hill produced a road from the highway with a sign "Nike Village" happily inviting anyone who approached. The large brown Bus Stop with it's sheltered roof was of historic means and the road would entice

the family for several hundred feet. The entire community was placed on a hill overseeing much of the town of Topsfield. Its desolate location was surrounded by a large lake to its south and woods to the east and west. The tiny three-bedroom house was more than enough for this family of three and the home was located near the top of the neighborhood adjacent to the highway. The new playground was a dream for any teenager willing to discover a new world and Shawn wasted no time introducing himself to the surroundings of the area.

In the few days that Shawn would begin his new life at the Nike Site, he would choose to broaden his world by venturing into every direction that was possible. To the south of the neighborhood stood several trees and an impossible decline that fell several feet. All the standing plants seemed to lean away from the ground parallel with the trees beside them and the path taken for hours would lead to a large lake. The lake was so large that it could be seen for miles and in the distance, Shawn could see homes on the other side. The grass deepened further with each step taken, so it was decided that he walk back and climb his way through the forest. The journey back reminded him of that fateful day in the woods in Weymouth. Faint moments of each punch and kick to his body strengthened his resolve to get out of the area he found himself in. The eyes of this stranger would turn blue to red in an instant and it was his heart that calmed him down.

The strength of a hundred men ran through his body while he pulled himself through the forest faster and faster. Shawn began to find a resolve inside of himself that he felt a few times before. What had taken hours to find the lake earlier took less than half of the time to find the road where he first began. Armed with a hidden strength, Shawn began to run around the neighborhood with abandon. The Nike Village was consumed of sixteen homes that were encircled upon a large hill facing the skies. Homes in the neighborhood began upon the entrance from Route 1 after driving three hundred feet to reach them. The highway was one of the longest in the United States running from Maine to Florida and the Nike Site was smack in the middle. Upon entering the neighborhood, trees were on the right and the houses were on the left of the road. The houses would wrap themselves around a large circle and the entire north side of the neighborhood was settle on a large incline. The steep road began from the bottom of house number ten and other homes would follow up the hill to the right. Shawn's new place was located on the corner overlooking the others. It was a perfect spot to see most of the activities of the day as his new neighbors weren't shy. The hill his home sat upon began at the top of the road and a simple bike ride would resolve itself like a roller coaster with the height of the road ending as a several second drop to the bottom. The three-hundred-foot drop was an excitement for most and a complex climb for others. During Shawn's venture out of the woods to suddenly start running began at the bottom of the large hill. Looking upwards at his new house at the top, he began running faster and faster. The once frail body of this teenager who once could never run anywhere without falling over discovered a new power within himself. Without exhaustion, Shawn would run for the next thirty minutes and surpass the long upwards venture several times. The Saturday morning that began with a journey to the lake would now find itself in front of a large gate that separated the neighborhood from another area that was unrecognizable.

During the few-mile sprint Shawn endured, he had noticed the front of the gate at the back side of the neighborhood. His curiosity brought him to where he stood with his dumbfounded curiosity. Both gates together were wide enough for two cars to pass side by side and were held closely by a small pad lock. Through the gate was a road headed into a direction away from where he was standing, but on each side of that same road lie a few buildings. Unsure of its purpose, it was the posted sign that put the teenager in his place. The keep out sign was large enough for everyone to see and it temporarily silenced any curiosity to climb through for the moment. The abandoned buildings would have to wait for his visit another time and he sprinted away with the thoughts of visiting other parts of the neighborhood. Upon running halfway up the large hill below his home, a small entrance would open to the right of the road. Leading downwards on a concrete path large enough for himself to walk through, he found himself in front of a small water pump station. It appeared that this gated enclosure was responsible for pumping the neighborhoods sewage and water. Surrounded by several woods and a large hill, Shawn began climbing westward up the large hill and in a few moments time, he found himself behind his own backyard. Looking behind him as he stood on top of the massive hill behind his house, the steep decline was a mere few hundred feet from where the pumping station was located. Thoughts of winter time in the upcoming several months would delight him because of the ability to sled down this hill in the snow.

Upon the top of the road in front of his house, four homes would subside along with an enclosure. It had prevented anyone from driving onto the cornfield located beyond the road. Behind the blockade was a large field of corn stalks that invited the teenager to rummage and discover. Route 1 had found itself running north and south throughout Topsfield and most of the cornfields amongst it on each side.

The Nike Site was located on top of the world surrounded by a lake, an apparent abandoned base and corn fields. The life of this teenager was about to have its limits tested for the next few years with this mysteriousness and newly found power. Shawn had come to realize that he was in a place that allowed his vision to become brighter and he wasn't inquiring how. His new strength and durability was inviting to himself and within his new neighborhood. This new playground became tested over the first weekend and it was only a short amount of time before he would realize that his first day at his new Junior High School was about to begin.

Chapter 4
Masconomet

Sounds of Van Halen blaring through the teenager's cheap headphones had given new life to a brand-new Monday. Today is the day that Shawn's mother would bring him to his new school. Six in the morning was the normality of his routine and staring inside of the closet full of minimal clothes was beside itself. Freshly showered skin with droplets of water falling to the cold floor, his bright blue eyes were focused on his new apparel while words of the song in his ears whispered softly through his lips. Equipped with a bright yellow short sleeve shirt, pair of Jeans, new tennis shoes and a new attitude, Shawn was on his way to his adventure called Junior High. The location of the school was on the other side of Topsfield placed on the street of Endicott Road in Boxford. The short trip that lasted a mere fifteen minutes began the adventure jump-starting his once keen heart. The town of Topsfield was a small community with post card style homes and buildings for all to see.

The car ride towards school that morning produced a small glimpse of the town that Shawn would call home for the next few years. Route 1 was a historic highway that elevated itself over several hills, feeling more like a roller coaster in his family's Ford Truck. The miles of traveling several hundred feet below and above the skyline of Topsfield through cornfields and trees eventually opened-up a small road of escape. Elevating his excited heart on the road to his new escapade would only suffice for a moment while his eyes began to focus on his new reality. House upon house and tree after tree soothing the nervous calm deep within his veins, his dilated pupils canvasing the population Topsfield had to offer. The innocent community appeared to be like any other and it had no idea what evil was passing through it. By chance, Shawn was going to attempt to fit inside of its calm borders without incident and visions of Weymouth slightly began to dissipate. Staring into his reflection upon the window transparent to the beautiful landscape, were images of an innocence he deserved. Unable to reconcile a normal child hood, his mother reached over and calmly stroked the side of his face.

"We are going to be happy here son, I promise," his mother gently stated.

Hearing her words soothed the nerves of the gentle beast within, but his focus remained on his new surroundings. Witnessing the universal happenings upon this path to his new school would conjure up visions of a beautiful life for the next few years. Staring into the glass upon the solace of his reflection, Shawn would see moments of his childhood flash within moments. Thoughts of seeing himself on a small raft floating upon the water of the Gulf of Mexico in Key West gazing upon the setting sun. The scene shadowing the visions of beautiful homes and winding streets of Topsfield, the lonely sun surrenders peacefully to the setting of the night. Upon the ocean wades the calm of his craft and the beats of his lonely heart facing the appearance of a bright moon. Despite this same memory fighting within his soul over and over, it was the only way to bring a peaceful solace to his heart. Irony has no meaning with his vision, but the true purpose for its peace would remain unexplained. At any point in time for the past several years that Shawn would become out of control, it was this vision that rested inside of his veins. His calm was at ease and his destiny would become slightly focused with a simple thought of that beautiful night on the ocean.

41

His vision would disappear upon the reflection of the window with a hard turn to the left, pushing him against the truck door panel. His mother's driving imperfect and unrelaxing, his destination has reached its final foot. The school of Masconomet was upon him and the round-about circle located in front of the school enclosed the flag post. The wind blowing slightly at a few miles an hour produced a crisp morning breeze with smells of fresh cut grass and sounds of nature clear in the distance. Shawn's mother had noted that she was at the wrong school according to her hand-written notes, so the stop became very brief. The misconception of her words allowed the ride in the truck to continue onwards to the other side of the massive school. Endicott Road had focused mostly on the face of the High School while a side road had hidden purposes to reveal more of what the school was hiding.

The Junior High was located on the far opposite side of the High School near the backstop of what appeared to look like a baseball field. Chiseled terribly upon the field of a horrific dream, Shawn and his mother would surpass miles of consequence to arrive to a place that seemed completely lost. With the jumbled mess to his right, the Junior High School appeared on the left and it was much smaller than the High School had offered. Parking the large truck into the parking lot next to the entrance, Shawn and his mother walked side by side upon exiting the vehicle. Step by step towards the school entrance, voices of the wind crawling inside of his head as if there was a resistance to his presence to save the faculty and students from himself. The previous school in Weymouth was a much smaller school in comparison and upon entering the double doors, the large openings to the hallway could be seen like a tunnel for what seemed like a mile long. From the sun filled sky into a darkness unadjusted to their eyes, the hallways appeared dreary and quiet while classes had already begun.

The destination was the office for the woman and her son as they would introduce themselves as the family who had just moved to the area a couple days earlier. The registration process was a mere few seconds, but the office brought a dreary atmosphere for the young teen. Pictures in the office reminiscent of years past, the tradition of sports at this new Jr. High School was on mark. Shawn had dabbled a bit in a few sports throughout the years, but it was baseball and basketball that were secretly his passion.

The teen and his bright yellow shirt had spent thirty minutes with the guidance counselor and the intuition of the young lady behind her desk was as noticeable as Shawn's obnoxious apparel.

"The presence of a new student at our school this late in the year is very rare, but since you are already prepared for High School, I recommend placing you in our honor's program", implied the counselor.

"I would like my son to be normal for a change if that is ok?" Shawn's mother asked. *"I prefer to place him with the regular kids in this school because my husband and I try to stay away from the particulars"*.

"What does that even mean Ma'am?" the Guidance Counselor asked.

Replying abruptly, *"It's our decision regardless here. We just want our son to fit in and your honor's program would complicate things for him. My son is specially-gifted and it is preferred we simplify things, understand? The simpler the better*

in our lives and this has been quite a road for our family",
Shawn's mom stated.

"Yes Ma'am, and we will completely abide with an easier schedule for young Shawn here", the Counselor replied.

The hour-long negotiation to place Shawn into the Jr. High School had finally subsided and despite only having a week remaining until the end of the school year, it was a necessary evil. Over the last ten years, Shawn had been placed into a few different schools, so the process was never an issue. The nerves of steel by this teen exemplified how special he is, and it was coming to fruition that this stay may become more important. Unaware of what was coming, the Jr. High and High School students of Masconomet Regional were about to be introduced to an abnormality within their community and it began with the opening of the main office doors and into the darkness of the awaiting hallways. The separation of Shawn and his mother had become natural and the young teen was again on his own. Feeling buried alive in the shadows of the lockers amongst the halls, the short walk to Shawn's first homeroom class rapidly approached. Since class had already began, the interruption of roll call silenced the room of twenty students. Traditionally in most schools, homeroom was the first class in the morning, but Masconomet was a different beast all together. Shawn had walked into the second class of the day and as he was introduced to everyone by the Guidance Counselor. The Counselor was abrupt in stating that he was a new student from another area, bringing silence of everyone. Prompted to find the nearest empty seat by the teacher, Shawn suddenly caught the attention of the eyes of a very beautiful brunette sitting next to him.

Students names being called out in the background during roll call became clouded with a soft whisper. *"I am Sheryl and it is very nice to meet"*. Gazing over at the girl who had spoken the beautiful words from her lips, he replied, *"I am Shawn."*

"Where are you from and where did you get that awful looking shirt?", Sheryl asked with a small laughter.

"Hey, don't knock the yellow here. You can see me coming a mile away and I don't mind the attention. I am from far away, but let's keep that between us, what do you say?" he smartly asked.

Sheryl scratching her head, she gasped for a second and replied, *"Ok, sounds good to me. You have the bluest eyes I have ever seen. I think you are going to be a big hit with some of the girls here at our school. Do you have a girlfriend?"*

Feelings of Linda and her deceitful words reminiscing in his head, Shawn backed off from the question and changed the subject quickly. *"Thanks for the comments. Sheryl, right? That is your name? What time does Homeroom end?"*

Before an answer could ever roll off her lips, the school bell rang. *"Now"*, she replied quickly. Equipped with the class schedule given to him from the Guidance Counselor, his next class would entail Algebra.

"Sheryl, where is Mister Oliver's classroom? It's my next class and I have no idea where it is", Shawn hinted.

"Seriously? That is my next class as well. Here, let me see your schedule?" Sheryl asked. Looking over each class listed on his itinerary, the shock on her face was priceless.

"Shawn, you are in every class that I am. Looks like you and I are going to be close friends," Sheryl gladly stated. Feeling relieved, Shawn would spend the next few classes tailing around the pretty eighth grader with a keen friendship on the horizon.

Later that morning, a few hours already spent on his first day at Masco Junior High School, Shawn had learned quite a bit about the students. Sheryl was filling him in on the different types of students and those to avoid if all possible. Math class would be followed by Science and Sexual Education. The twelve o'clock bell would ring for all the students to enjoy the first lunch period and Sheryl escorted Shawn to the Cafeteria. The walk to the lunch room was a bit segregated from the Junior High, due-to the fact that it was shared with the High School. On the way to lunch, Shawn and Sheryl would converse over the type of students to make friends with and those to literally avoid at all costs.

Entering the double doors to the cafeteria, Sheryl stopped and began explaining to Shawn all the different students that found themselves grouped together at each large table. The cafeteria was quite large and with a small guess, it appeared that twenty to twenty-five circular tables were surrounded with six to eight chairs. The massive area was slowly filling up with students and Shawn's concentration stayed with Sheryl and her descriptive details.

"The first table you see to the right here are the non-socialites in our world. They are the gifted students who rather not talk to anyone but themselves. To be honest, they fucking-creep me out. Next to them at this table are the ABC kids. That stands for A Better Chance and as you can see, most of them are black.

Between you and I, they are the only black kids in our school and they aren't even from here. I guess their parents paid others to take care of them, I don't know", Sheryl curiously stated.

"Moving forward my new bestie. Do you see the next few tables here on the left?" Sheryl asked.
Shawn nodding his head in the up and down position as to agree with her question.

"Well, do you see that they all have something in common?" Just agree with me here because they are the nerds of our class. These students are packed in bunches here at school and they are easy to befriend. These are the kids you want to learn a lot from because they will get you out of homework jams in a jiffy."

"You use them to get your homework done?", Shawn asked.

"Well, not exactly, but moving forward. The next three tables after my nerds are the jocks. Normally you will see these guys wearing their football jerseys or just enamoring themselves with rowdiness. Shawn, this is the table you don't want to sit at. These guys are commonly always in trouble or they look for reasons to bully others inferior to them, if you ask me, I think these guys look for reasons to feel slap other's asses and feel dominant?" Sheryl stated.

Literally after explaining to Shawn who the Jocks were, they both witnessed a teen throwing a few grapes over at the kids behind their table. The nerd table was a common barrage of insults and food, but the sight was sad. In his own way, Shawn was thinking back to the severe beating he had succumbed to and it slightly angered him. His blank stare into the wickedness behind the bullying was noticeable.

"Shawn, ignore them please. No need to involve yourself with these clowns because they will get theirs someday. In the middle over here to my right, you will find yourself in an ocean of females galore. Sometime last year, the ladies felt it was necessary to become the focal point of the student body and chose to sit square in the middle. If you ask me, I think its brilliant because we all want to be glorified by every swinging dick on the planet", joked Sheryl.

While his eyes were canvasing over all the tables of females, Shawn had noticed a beautiful blonde and her amazing smile. Curious, Shawn had asked Sheryl a very vague question pertaining to the perfect brilliance he was staring at.

"Who is the gorgeous little blonde with the perfect hair over there?" Shawn asked.

"Oh boy. Shawn, that's Melanie Harris. She is untouchable by-all-means and she is every boys dream", Sheryl replied.

Sheryl turned around and placed her finger into Shawn's chest. *"Girls like her are going to hurt you here Shawn. It's best just to look and move on man,"* she aggressively stated.

The words pierced his kindness, but the eyes of this new stranger looking at this gorgeous girl reminded him of a movie trailer he has just saw. The movie was called "Can't Buy Me Love" and he attempted to recall her name in the trailer, but it wasn't coming to his lips. Melanie was a cutie in his mind and she was as beautiful as an actress, but he began to continue to follow Sheryl through the cafeteria. Just as each step away from Melanie occurred, the name came to him. The words gauging themselves from the lips by the nerd in that same trailer produced two words, *"Cindy Mancini".* That was her to a tee and she was just as ravishing and as Shawn began to daydream about the blonde, the same finger pointed at him before was now pulling him out of his own daydream.

"Hello handsome, remember me," asked Sheryl.

Pulling Shawn back to the direction they were intending on walking, she introduced more of the student body with grace.

"This sea of females here can get anyone lost, so follow me and remain calm for the love of god dude. Keep your tongue in your mouth and focus on my ass or something, he he", Sheryl jokingly stated.

Sheryl walking gracefully beyond the middle of the cafeteria, Shawn began to see what appeared to be several teens with long hair and Metallica T-shirts. The darkness of the table in the south west corner of the cafeteria was like a hidden tree with efforts to hide from everyone. To his amazement, Sheryl walked up to the table and began hugging everyone. His eyes focused strongly on the smile and kisses she gave everyone, while succumbing to the awkwardness.

Shawn's brain was scrambled because he was a prodigy of the late seventies and early eighties music his parents had introduced him to. The names on the shirts made no sense and he was unaware of the type of people he was about to converse with.

"Everyone, this is my new friend Shawn and he is from... let me think for a second. Hey, wait. Where are you from man?" Sheryl asked.

"I never said where I was from. Let's just say I am from the other side of the continent", Shawn jokingly replied.

"Well, that's about right coming from a newbie. Pleasure to meet you, I am Jason. This here is my friend Craig and this handsome man is Bill", Jason replied.

The sarcasm was thick in the air because Shawn noticed Bill was not a nice-looking person. He was tall, scrawny and large craters of acne covered his entire face. *"I wonder if I stand too close to this guy will I catch something",* Shawn thought to himself.

"Nice to meet you all", Shawn softly replied.

Staring at all the teens and their faces sitting at the table, the reminder that he wasn't allowing anyone to become close to him didn't scare easily into his mind. He knew that he was going to have to fit in and that was the phenomenal presence he carried towards people. All through his entire life, Shawn fit in everywhere with his wit, charm and great sense of humor. When his parents had friends or family over, it was Shawn they all sought out for entertainment with his quips and jokes. It was tne realization that he was having to take his time to mesh with all the students because his chameleon like ways would fit well anywhere. With brilliance in mind, Shawn excused himself from the table to enter the cafeteria kitchen. Not too far from where he was standing, he would invite his craving for food into the line that was substantially full.

The food choices in line were spaghetti for the day and since it was his favorite meal, the first day at Junior High was shaping into a decent day. While waiting with each teenager being served one at a time, Shawn began to strike up a conversation with a fellow blonde-haired female classmate standing in front of him.

"Is the food good here?" Shawn asked.

The young lady standing in front of him turned around and her blonde hair brazed upon his face and the smell of flowers rang through his nose like he had just walked into a field of dreams.

"Not at all. Let's pretend I said yes so you don't run off. You are Shawn the new guy, right? How are you. I'm Meagan and this is my friend Valerie."

Reaching with her hand, she extended a hello by introducing herself with a handshake as did her friend Valerie.

"Nice to meet you both. Is every girl here look as great as you guys? Please don't take what I am saying wrong, but that Melanie chick over there and all the others look like models", Shawn replied.

Quietly turning red from what he was telling her, she quickly replied, *"Nah, we all grow on trees out here"*. Her laughter was quite pleasant to his ears and it was the friendship that Shawn experienced all morning that allowed him to enjoy his new school. The few minutes of standing in line and gathering his lunch, Shawn decided to gather himself and find a table in the south east part of the cafeteria. Each table passing with his tray in hand, girls to the left and guys to the right all smiled at the new stranger. Masconomet was a new start for Shawn and his fascinating skill of being like a chameleon worked brilliantly. He was tempted to fit in and becoming one of the student body was important and this was the promise he made to his mother. The will to fit in right away was not a smart move for his patience would remain cautious from his past. It was at that very moment he was lingering the decision to choose his own space over invading others. Relaxing with his tray of spaghetti, bread and milk, Shawn would begin to focus on his surroundings and canvasing those around him.

It was more than the table of hot chicks, nerds, jocks and metal heads that intrigued Shawn. This was the perfect situation for what was coming in the several months ahead. This entire School was about to indulge itself into the mind of a fourteen-year old capable of something he was unwilling to discover. Regardless of the classes left remaining in the day, it would resolve itself for the rest of the week as everyone began to countdown each hour until Summer officially took off. The summer of 1987 began with a silent discovery found by a canny teen who befriended the wilderness surrounding him at the Nike Village. It was that curiosity that began to captivate the true meaning for Shawn's existence into this selfish world and the evil that awaited his defined fate.

Chapter 5
Euphoric Discovery

The Summer was upon the tri-town area of Topsfield, Middleton and Boxford and the Saturday morning began like every day before it. During that previous evening, Shawn's bedroom was front and center with curious noises from the woods behind his home throughout the night. The bedroom he chose upon moving in would face closest to the trees and the uninvited mystery from mother nature brought the young man to his destiny. What seemed like a long night of whispers ended up becoming a nightmare with a brilliant disguise. Shawn took notice, but since he had been living his entire life near the ocean or the woods, he became used to the sounds. Unaware of the evil that had kept an eye over him since he was a baby, fearless was built into the magic surrounding Shawn and his universe.

The Nike Village where Shawn now resided sat upon a large hill over looking the towns of Danvers and Topsfield on each side. The sixteen-home community became brightened each morning from the crisp setting sun and its fresh cool breeze. The wind rapidly changing directions at several miles per hour would embrace each home with a symphony of music that was calming in the 15th home in the neighborhood. Shawn awoke with gracefulness and a new confidence that the Summer was going to be his time to shine. In the week at school at Masco, he was made aware from others that baseball tryouts for the local Topsfield team was around the corner. Shawn was never that good at baseball, but he was considered a "good" player and that was just enough to entice the youth to enjoy playing with others. To the scrawny teenager, baseball was a way to bring all the aggressions from his surrounding world and defeat them with the swing of a bat or the crisp of the glove from his pitches. Baseball was in Shawn's life to stay and he was not involved in any sports, but his Father aggressively pursued what he could to detour Shawn with his special gifts.

Shawn's father was a military man in the branch of the Coast Guard and he brought forth an uneasy life for the teen. Moving from Coast to Coast would be a regular occurrence in the household and it developed a resistance in Shawn's life unable to keep any friends. It all began in Miami, Florida with the birth of Shawn in 1973 while his father and mother were preparing for a life in the military. With tours in Miami, West Virginia, California and Key West, Shawn slowly grew up without his father being around while his mother would raise him. A lonely child, Shawn was eagerly protected by his parents while developing the ability to being special beyond any comprehension. With each grade passing for Shawn, his Father was spending more time with his career on the Oceans the World had to offer while his Mother was left behind to care for her son. Resentment and tensions would build, but it was the silent World of Shawn that kept his mother's sanity from faltering. Left alone to care for him throughout his entire child hood, the bond between them was built strong like unbreakable chains and she felt safe while he was with her. That dreadful day in Key West when the stranger in her backyard attempted to silence her family, Shawn withdrew his silence and allowed his mother to witness what he was capable of. That day etched in his mind forever brought forth the ability to learn how to control his emotions. Each day since he was presented that challenge, Shawn would covet his new-found gift inside his heart and the next several years in Texas and Massachusetts would develop a much stronger bond.

What seemed like a long night turned into a much calmer morning and while his mother was sleeping, Shawn took it upon himself to venture back into the offerings of the Nike Village. The previous evening's shower gave way to the invitation into a bright t-shirt and black shorts as Shawn arose from bed and out the front door with his old worn sneakers. Each step progressing away from the fact that his father was cheap and spent barely any money on his son's garments. The million-dollar smile on the scrawny teens face changed his attitude and nothing was going to stop him from venturing into the wilderness.

The Saturday June morning was a subtle seventy-five degrees and the cool air was inviting from the North. The time was six thirty and the darkness was quickly succumbing to the beautiful sunset and Shawn found himself on top of the concrete road overlooking the neighborhood. Unsure of where to begin, Shawn looked to his left and his direction of sense brought a smell of corn and leaves. The scent of mother nature was always a welcomed proportion in Shawn's life and it was his for the taking. The quick decision to begin walking to his right brought forth a path leading to the road that welcomed itself from Route 1. The road piercing through the outskirts of the south side of the neighborhood, the 4th house was its first location on the left. With houses numbered from four through seven, the road quickly turned left. The brisk walk towards his fate allowed him to remain straight on the path towards a large gate. The fence had seen his blue eyes once before, but there was nothing that could impede the teenager's curiosity. The gate separating a different world from his new neighborhood, the small lock and chain holding the two large fences silently called him forward. The chance to open the invitation that was calling his name would quickly subside behind his curiosity. Slightly struggling to squirm his way between the narrow opening, Shawn's effortless pressure squeezed onto the abandoned side of the double gate.

Unaware of the surroundings he was facing, Shawn turned away from the neighborhood and began canvasing his new environment. To his immediate right, an old guard shack that looked like an oversized outhouse from the 1900's. Walking over to its presence, Shawn peaked inside the broken window of the shack, which revealed nothing inside. Peaceful and desolate, the faded white paint upon the guard shack stood about seven feet tall and it appeared to be measured at five feet by five feet. He began thinking that he may be in the same place a guard had once greeted cars some time ago. The weeds were thick and the small cracks in the road gave way to small ant hills. Turning away from the small enclosure and facing the east direction was another small building not too far away. Measured about four times the size of the guard shack, the concrete building looked dreary. Separating the tall weeds with his hands, Shawn's few second walk towards the larger structure was now front and center. The abandoned concrete building was painted in a military green with shades of white and the entrance was missing a door. The structure assembled with large cinderblocks was chiseled to perfection without any cracks visible to Shawn's eye. The position of the building behind the guard shock gave zero meaning to its existence, but Shawn's curiosity grew with each step inside of the entrance. Dark and balmy, the eerie feeling of cold resided over his skin while small noises of creaking from the wind blowing up against the building echoed. Strong with its stance, the building was constructed to keep something in and Shawn was unable to process its true existence due to the room becoming so desolate. Without a true understanding, Shawn escaped the lonely grasp of the structure and headed for the light from the entrance.

"I will have to come back with a flashlight in order to see anything in there", Shawn said to himself.

Standing at the entrance as the sun's beaming rays brightened his previously darkened eyes, Shawn garnered his sight. Looking straight ahead revealed another building within walking distance. The broken concrete road separated that building from another set of structures across the street. Curiosity gave way to purpose as it appeared Shawn may be on a former military base or a housing project. Throughout his entire life, Shawn had found himself living on military bases due to his Father's career and he noticed a similarity. Unable to prove it at that very moment, Shawn began walking over to the building directly in front of the entrance he was standing at.

"What happened here? Why is this all abandoned?" Shawn asked himself over and over.

His mind scrambling with ideas for his new adventure, Shawn's resolve brought him to the building his intentions were set for. The building was constructed with several windows and it appeared to be a smaller barracks. The structure was eerily similar-to the smaller building he was in, but the wood frames of the windows were cracked beyond recognition. The building resembled a smaller hotel that Shawn found himself night after night during his life when his parents would move from town to town. Standing on the broken road facing the building, there were four closed doors and all windows broken as if someone had violated them for no purpose at all. The chipped paint falling profusely off the face of the doors presented a feeling of loneliness and Shawn's few steps forward landed him at the first entrance. The sidewalk leading in front of the doors were covered with long weeds and grass and the neglect of mother nature was attempting to cover the once beautiful community. Reaching to grab the rusty knob, the sudden quick turn opened the door swiftly while a loud creaking sound from it's hinges scared the silence the room once held.

Stepping inside to invite his will throughout the room, the presence of vandalism and paint covered the walls. Large holes in the drywall presented a complication for the once beautiful structure succumbing to a violence of stupidity. Sifting through the room, Shawn found a small desk and chair next to a bed up against the wall. Trying to understand what the room was offering, he recovered a date listed on a piece of paper lying next to the broken chair.

Reaching down to pick up the white piece of paper that suffered from age, it was a small remanence of a life left behind. Faded with its words on the page, Shawn was only able to make out the date on the top of the paper. The date of March 5th, 1974 typed onto the paper, it appeared to have a fading Army logo embracing the top. Each word fading, it resembled a letter of urgency to someone at the barracks. Unable to determine its meaning, Shawn placed the letter in his shorts pocket and continued sifting through the room. The morning sunlight peeking through the broken windows allowed Shawn to see everything the room had to offer. The room had been ransacked beyond recognition with holes and graffiti upon the walls. The eerie silence heard through the walls piqued the interest of the teenager as he would spend the next several minutes going from room to room.

No evidence existed that someone was staying in the abandoned building that Shawn was sifting through, but the amount of carnage was unreal. The rampage through each room created peril and the suffocation allowed him to feel sorry for the previous tenants. Carefully walking through broken tables, drywall and chairs, Shawn noticed a small insignia painted on the wall in the room farthest east. It was the last room he had rummaged through and it was a mark of fresh paint. Looking closer, he ran his finger up against the marking on the wall and it smeared instantly. The smell was of copper and he than realized it was blood.

"What the hell is blood doing here and how did it get on this wall?", Shawn stated to himself.

The symbol on the wall was of a brightened origin with mystique behind its drawing. Precise and perfect, it stumbled Shawn and his virgin mind. Freshly placed on the wall, the blood slowly dripping resembling a warning for all to vacate the area.

Scratching his head, he tried to understand the meaning behind the symbol staring back at him, but he chose to snap a photo with his mom's disposable camera he placed inside of his pocket. Unable to comprehend the moment, he devised a plan to canvass the rest of the area and study his findings later.

Entangled into the abyss of the Nike Village, Shawn ventured out of the broken four-roomed building and looked across the road at another building. It was a much longer and bigger building and Shawn couldn't walk fast enough to get into it's enclosure. The windows of the building facing the road were covered in weeds, so Shawn walked back towards the gate he first entered through. Now at the west side of the structure, he slowly parted the brush and weeds covering the broken door. Chipped white paint falling profusely to the ground, Shawn pushed it open while the loud creaking sound echoed down the dark hallway. Misty and full of cobwebs, the haunted house-like setting raced the heartbeat of the curious teen. Stepping one foot inside with a deep breath, he lurched forward without hesitation. Each step taken inside of the structure beyond the broken door, a clearer path would result in his eyes focusing on four doors to his left and three to his right. Slowly walking to the first door within his grasp, it was easy to see that the vandalized drywall had succumbed to the floor. Able to see clearly through the first room without reaching the door, remanence of a lifetime before were present. Broken bed frame pieces, a collapsed desk and chair were pinned up against the wall covering the broken window. Wet, dark and cold, the room gave way to whispers of the dark amongst the smell of mold. Thick cobwebs covering most of the corners of the walls, the slim light peaking through the top of the window allowed Shawn to see the macabre of hatred plastered on the walls. Shades of dried up paint on the broken drywall pieces scattered on the floor from being kicked and beaten in. The room appeared to be a vandalized war room of stupid kids who had nothing better to do than destroy history and this began to anger Shawn.

Walking into the next room through the broken walls, Shawn noticed that the rooms were the same in size. Ten feet by ten feet and it reminded him of when his father had brought him to his living quarters on base. It was easy to assume that he was standing inside of the living quarters of a base that once stood tall. Were the men and women here previously killed or transferred in a hurry because it appeared to the teen that everyone left in a hurry. Combing each room for clues, the relentlessness of Shawn's curiosity resulted in nothing. No paperwork in site for Shawn to view other than the destroyed battleground of purposeful hatred amongst the structure. In total, eight rooms were inspected resulting in broken dreams and endless nights for the previous vandals and no evidence left behind of its history. Possibly taken by others, his angst led him to the far east side of the hallway towards the exit sign. Hanging by a moment, the sign on the ceiling was still in tact and Shawn pushed the heavy door open.

Equally loud with a creaking sound from the hinges, Shawn used all his might to force the door through the heavy weeds and large brush. Falling forward into the daylight, Shawn entered back into society from the darkness and he proceeded to inspect the building from its exterior. Thinking to himself that he just walked himself out of a creepy Billy Idol music video, Shawn further evaluated what he attempted to believe was a military base evacuated under extreme consequences. The confusing part only began further when he couldn't comprehend why the living quarters were located near the front of the gate.

Facing a determined purpose, nothing seemed unordinary throughout the outside of the building examining window by window. The callousness of the idiots responsible for the demise of its structure kept everything inside. Possibly afraid that the sixteen families living on the outside of the gate would hear, the silence of the destruction from within was the only solution to resolve their hatred. Moving forward by walking down the concrete path in an easterly direction away from the buildings, the scenery seemed a lot more pleasant. No structures in sight, the thick bushes and trees attempted to cover over the path. Wide enough to pass through, Shawn walked several hundred feet deeper into the wilderness of the Nike Village. The concrete path he was following began to open-up another road to his left while also continuing straight with nothing in site but trees. Standing still at this very moment, the young teen wanted to attempt fate and canvas the entire area as quickly as possible. Unaware of the size of the Nike Village, Shawn made a quick decision to turn left and head into the small narrow road. The path riddled with broken branches, weeds and small rocks, the quick journey off the road brought Shawn to a structure to his right. The massive building had three openings and stood about fifteen feet in height. The smaller openings were doors that used to stand attached to the building but appeared to be missing. The larger opening was also missing a door, but large enough for a car to drive through. The site was amazing to his eyes and he couldn't walk fast enough to see what was inside.

Coming closer to the large opening, Shawn saw yellow and black striped paint on the outside indicating protection beams from hitting the structure. It was clear to see this was a housing for larger vehicles because the moment he appeared closer, a large tire about the size of a small Volkswagen sat on the concrete floor. The building opening was transparent because both sides had large openings equally in size for vehicles to drive through. It was safe to assume the building was a garage for repairs to the vehicles on this base. Inside, Shawn noticed a large desk, windows with bars and a separate room to the left of the larger room. The smaller room was a bathroom and a separate room had no purpose with its emptiness. The broken history inside of the structure lie silent and canvassing the area took a mere few minutes with nothing to see of importance. Walking further through the structure and beyond its lifelessness, Shawn proceeded on the road. The pathway led several feet away from the large building and back onto the original creating a cul de sac. The motion felt as if Shawn walked in a small circle away from the larger road and back onto his destiny. The sky as blue as his eyes, the morning proceeded to turn into afternoon and the temperature of the air slowly rose to a balmy eighty degrees. Feeling the heat on his already darkening skin, he proceeded in an easterly direction walking through broken trees and grass covering the path.

The several minute-venture that felt like he had been traveling across the world suddenly opened to the delight of his temptations. The path took a sudden turn to his right and appearing through broken trees and a dying nature, a field of concrete began to peak through the ground ahead of him. Seeming more like a field of graves, his eyes wouldn't fool him to what he was seeing. Wiping his sweaty brow, Shawn took a deep breath and began walking closer to the concrete that spread like wildfire upon the ground. Seeming like large squares covering the Earth, the portals seems to him like they were hiding something from beneath. The reminder in his mind allowed him to realize that the paper he saw in the first building brought his wisdom to 1974. It was merely over a decade ago, but the remanence of trees and nature growing over what was lying in the ground made perfect sense.

Armed with more curiosity, Shawn decided to keep looking throughout the grounds in front of him. It was the mystery of what was beneath the ground that kept his heart pumping blood throughout his veins. Eager to find what his mind was hoping to seek, Shawn found himself walking over several hours of large squares of freshly poured concrete hiding an apparent secret below him. Standing in the middle of the escapade he stood upon, Shawn remained still while cooling off from the heavy wind. The sunlight beaming a refreshing outlook on his body, a voice in the distance was heard calling his name.

"Shawn, over here. Shawn over here."

The voice pierced his soul like a knife through the heart and it frightened him beyond any justification.

"Who are you? What do you want?", Shawn asked.

The voice failed to respond, but Shawn headed over to a large area where he thought the voice came from. Facing the north part of the area, a small path opened itself through the trees surrounding the concrete on the ground. The sudden adrenaline in his veins pushed him through the path and onto a smaller trail. Walking as slow as he could, Shawn walked step by step until he noticed what appeared to be a concrete enclosure with two doors on it. Looking closer, he noticed there wasn't a lock or anything holding the doors together. Reaching down to grab the handle on the door to the right, Shawn pulled swiftly to open the enclosure. The loud noise of the doors gave way to a swift pull and it opened with succession. Reaching to grab the left door, Shawn heard a slight noise inside of the darkness beyond the ground that he couldn't quite make out. The calming wind in his ears slightly covered anything he could hear, so he proceeded to open the other door covering the entrance into the ground. The creepy sounds of the door opening as he pulled hard gave way to the steps hidden beyond the doors. The loud slamming of the door hitting the ground caused Shawn to step back in surprise as his eyes focused on the hidden opening in the ground.

Gathering himself, Shawn saw that several steps were reaching themselves below the earth in an eerie darkness. Handrails on each side of the walls surrounding the steps, he attempted to see closer, but the sky above him was unable to reach further below the ground for him to see clearly.

Willing to walk closer to the opening, he would place his foot upon the steps leading beyond the open doors. Leaning forward to see the earth below, the teen caught a glimpse of what appeared to be water filling up the entrapment below. Unaware of its hidden purpose, Shawn slowly stood further away from the opening to collect his thoughts. His scared mind wanting to walk back to his new home, the sudden rush of heat expanded through his body. The sudden force tightened its grip and pulled him closer to the doors in the ground.

"Shawn, I have been expecting you. Come to me."

The force gripping his body like a glove holding a baseball, Shawn's lifeless body felt limp and susceptible to the demands of the whispers beneath the ground. Opening his eyes, Shawn looked again down below the ground and the water that once stood at the end of the stairs was rapidly subsiding. The release of the grip around him allowed his breath to free itself from his lungs much easier. His eyes focused on the stairs below, he slowly took one step a time while holding the guard rail on each side of him. The light of day soon darkened with each foot below the ground and within seconds, Shawn stood at the end of the stairs. With a sudden quietness in the embankment, a loud noise behind him shattered his hearing. Looking back suddenly, the doors above abruptly closed as any essence of light was now pitch black. The abrupt feeling of cold crept upon his body as if thousands of small fingers were caressing his skin. His heart began beating faster and faster and his stillness gave way to a glowing light in the distance ahead of him. The beautiful glow gave way to a pleasant deep voice that rang into Shawn's ear.

"Come my child, I have been expecting you."

The feeling of fear suddenly disappeared, and the darkness Shawn once found himself in gave way to a candlelit walkway. Not caring how the candles suddenly appeared, he walked forward with the guidance of the light on each side of him.

Hair rising on his arms, the coolness of the air turned warm with each step towards the glowing light. The once frightened boy had felt like he was in a place he had always found himself in. The noise of something walking beside him in the dark piqued his curiosity as he began to look down. The candlelit walk way would only allow him to see what lies above his waste, causing him to remain curious about his venture forward. While walking, a set of bright blue eyes gazed upon him in the eerie darkness next to Shawn as if they were walking together. Taking a deep gulp into this throat, Shawn swallowed the remaining saliva inside of himself that prevented his dry mouth from screaming at the top of his lungs. The beast walking beside him was guiding Shawn to the destination calling his name and he felt at ease. Unaware if he was being led to a grisly death, each step with his new companion would enlighten his heart to steadfast a true purpose for his presence. The brightened calm of the glow now in front of him, Shawn came to a door that opened itself as he arrived. The sound of the rusty hinges created the eerie feeling of death that rattled his brittle young bones as he awaited. Looking down at the eyes of the beast staring back at him, the shades of its body began to appear as it walked forward into the opening. The tail upon it brushed up against Shawn's leg as it released a small snarl from its lips like a purring cat. Shawn followed the creature and as soon as a few feet were made forward, the voice echoed deeply.

Chapter 6
Vincent

"Mister Shawn Lee, the man of the hour. What a pleasant surprise to make your acquaintance", the voice loudly stated.

The nervousness didn't quite immediately subside upon hearing the voice, but it shattered his ears as if the echo was blaring loudly behind him. Patiently waiting for another word to speak, Shawn granted himself the enduring task of allowing their confrontation to begin. Before he could open his mouth, the daunting voice spoke again.

"How rude of me sir. My name is Vincent and you already met Sebastian as I take it. Don't be afraid my young friend, he is quite the friendly beast", Vincent stated.

Confusion briefly indulging his nightmare, Shawn began to slowly unlock the puzzle that had been pinned in his mind for years. Within the first few moments of thought, Shawn was now ready to relay what his mouth wanted to say.

"Who are you? Why can't I see you? What is this place?" Shawn bravely asked.

"Whoa!!! Slow down a little for me and let's focus on your questions one at a time. No need to twist your panties in a bunch, jeez. Shawn, I apologize for meeting you so quickly, but we weren't supposed to meet like this so soon. I have many plans for you my friend and ever since you were born, I knew you would be something special. If you truly want me to answer your questions, I need something from you", stated Vincent.

"What would you possibly need from me?" Shawn asked.

"I need your focus right now. Look ahead and I want you to watch the wall in front of you to your right", Vincent mentioned.

The exact moment that Vincent asked Shawn to look to his right, the wall began to brighten with a distorted picture. Shawn focusing on the reality of what was now on display, he began to see a large projection upon the wall of the room. Like a movie, they began watching the fight he had with Zach back in Weymouth. The few minutes of Zach being pummeled by Shawn grew unreal expectations of what the presumed attack on himself had brought.

"Look closer Shawn and see the real picture here", Vincent replied.

Shawn's attention wanted to see the man of the voice that was talking to him, but instead he began to see a plan unfolding before his very eyes. The footage of the fight was played back over and over for a period of a few minutes and it began to focus on the brother of Zachary. During the fight, he was seen talking to others and somehow, Greg's voice was now on display in Shawn's ears.

"Regardless of what happens to my little brother, we pummel this little prick beneath the Earth where he belongs. When I jump on him, you guys help and don't stop until he can't move," Gregory stated.

Shawn heard the conversation that he never knew existed before he was jumped by the boys in the woods. *"Why are you showing me this? What happened to me?",* Shawn asked.

Silence followed his question as he watched in terror. His own demise unfolding before his weary eyes, Shawn stood breathless. The surmountable minutes that he suffered during the beating, gave way to sudden darkness in the room. The temperature rising higher within seconds, the room began to slowly lighten up and the shadowy figure appeared before Shawn's eyes. The silhouette of the man with the deep voice was now standing before him.

Appearing over six-foot tall, the stranger wearing a striped three-piece suit and velvet tie, stunned Shawn with his impressive demeanor. To him, he appeared to be more of an owner of a bank than a spirit harassing him. His shoes looked like mirrors and his million-dollar look gave way to his immaculate charm.

"Look closely my young friend and your questions will turn into answers", Vincent replied.

The room began to darken and for a mere second, Shawn imagined that Vincent showed himself to prove he was real. The brief second turned into a few more and Shawn's focus became fixated at the wall while his lifeless body lay on top of the fire. His eyes concentrating on the trees and the glowing fog from beneath him, he suddenly noticed a beautiful set of blue eyes appearing from the unclear air. The remanence of a wolf appeared out of thin air and Shawn became startled where he stood. At the very moment the vision was displayed on the wall for Shawn to see, the feeling of a wetness swiped against his right hand at his side. Looking down beside him, the same beautiful blue-eyed beast was now at his side comforting him with his nose. The feeling of ease ran through Shawn's body as if the two were always meant to stand side by side.

"Don't be afraid Shawn, he is here to comfort you. He has always been there to protect you," Vincent stated.

With his hand slowly petting the fur on top of the head of the wolf, his calm eyes looked back up at the wall. The eerie scene in the woods captured the moment when the wolf had grabbed Shawn's lifeless body with his teeth and began dragging him away from the extinguished fire. The whimpering sound coming from the beast as he pulled his friend a few feet away from the camp fire felt gut wrenching. His heart beating rapidly as he watched the beast stare at him in anguish nearly broke his heart, but suddenly dissipated as the once evacuated fog returned with a vengeance. Shawn knew he was not staring at a re-enactment of his life but was curiously beginning to understand the reasoning for his life and its purpose. The fog slowly rising above the ground at his feet, it began reaching further towards his upper torso and head. Within seconds, Shawn's covered body became swallowed beneath the ground while Sebastian howled in anger. The fog covering the burial of the teen slowly faded away in the darkness. The soft ground seen on the wall focused itself on the nature surrounding the resting place of the murdered teenager. In a shock, Shawn fell to one knee as he clinched his chest.

"Where did my body go, where did Sebastian go? What the hell is going on here Vincent? Tell me please?" Shawn nervously asked.

"Shawn, haven't you always wondered why you never been injured or why you are able to have this special strength your entire life?" Vincent questioned.

"C'mon, think about it here for a second." Vincent stated with a wicked laugh.

Filled with a thick confusion in his mind, Shawn stepped back and began thinking about the times he had near misses with bad luck, injuries and the ability to protect himself from harm.

"Hold on here. Are you telling me that I was given this ability by yourself?" Shawn asked.

"Now there's a question I don't get every day. What do you think the answer could be if we had never met Shawn?" Vincent asked.

Noticing that his sarcasm could be a sudden threat to his existence, Shawn stood his ground and realized that the person in front of him was an angel from heaven or just a figment of his imagination.

"Are you an angel or something?" Shawn asked carefully.

The hesitation from Vincent was all Shawn needed to realize that maybe he was correct in his assumption, but Vincent didn't need words. The grumblings of the ground and the shaking of the walls gave way to his evil laugh heard throughout the room they were standing in and Vincent's eyes begin to glow a slight red.

"Call me whatever you like, but what I am is nothing compared to what I could be. Son, what defines our very existence on this beautiful planet only can be explained in a matter of seconds on the clock that ticks far and away beyond our wildest imagination. Think of me as the cloud that hovers above those seeking sunlight from a storm of regret and hollowness. Think of me as a dejection from the Heavens above, but just don't compare me to the all mighty", Vincent stated with purpose.

Vincent began pacing back and forth while holding his lit cigar in is hand. The look of seriousness grazed his veins and the once innocent look became eager as his words were staining the walls with glorified purpose.

"I am no less the temptation that seeks the greed feeding the wolves of loneliness and despair. Maybe our destiny lies within our eyes of regret, but I am nothing without the hurt of vengeance and ruthlessness and that my friend, is where I lie waiting. I am the abyss beneath your questions of solitude and righteousness and you exist on this Earth because I have allowed it", Vincent boldly stated.

"Well, a simple definition would have sufficed, but ok." Shawn jokingly replied.

The laugh suddenly brushing away from the perplexity of his words, Vincent patted Shawn on his shoulder and stated, *"That's what I have always loved about you. You make me laugh."*

"Shawn my young disciple, you are very special to me and what I am wanting to accomplish in this world. You aren't ready yet, but I want you to feel as if you express yourself these next couple of years. When the time is right son, you will serve my purpose and define your true existence to me. In the meantime, go make as many friends as you can. Become active in your new surroundings and stay busy. Don't forget that I will always be close", Vincent stated.

Vincent reached out his extended hand to shake Shawn's and the electricity from the touching of their palms reached inside his young heart. The transference of the energy from Vincent would lie deeper into Shawn for a purpose he would soon begin to discover.

"Sebastian, take care of my son for me", Vincent asked.

"As for you Shawn, don't feel that you need to give Sebastian the attention he needs. He is your protector and he will at all costs make sure you are safe. It is you Shawn that others will fear, so be gone my child and await my calling. I will see you again," Vincent stated as his silhouette faded in the air.

"Oh, and one last thing sir. Please don't die anymore. You are detouring my plans here", Vincent laughed in the far distance.

The look of purpose beaming through the eyes of the young teen as he turned around and began walking out of the dark room. Down the hallway, he saw the light that peaked above the ceiling where the double doors had opened themselves. Walking slowly towards the exit, the thoughts of Vincent were running through his mind with wonders of what he was. Sebastian walking beside him, the two would exit from beneath the Earth and into the New England crisp air. Taking one step at a time with one hand on the guard rail, Shawn reached the top of the stairs, but something was missing. The beast that claimed his spot at his side had vanished and Shawn was again on his own.

The beautiful wolf walked back to the room where Vincent's voice had waited for him and he approached with caution. *"Sebastian, its time. This young fool has messed our scheduling up and we will have to pursue this much quicker than anticipated. You know what to do"*, Vincent's voice murmured.

Staring into the beauty of the bluish sky that surrounded his coincidence, Shawn could only begin to image everything that just happened. *"Take a deep breath Shawn, this is all just a dream"*, Shawn said to himself. Walking away from the doors that brought him deep within his beleaguered perception, he turned around and the entrance suddenly closed. His mind scrambling for reasons as to why he was the person chosen for what appeared to be a seismic reality. The steps taken back to the gate of the base he discovered hours earlier were frames of earlier childhood memories.

Thinking back as early as a small child, Shawn could fondly remember all the luck that persuaded his mind to believe everything that transpired. Chalking his entire short-lived childhood as the means to an end wouldn't suffice as his venture back through the village felt like an eternity. Each gifted memory playing over and over like a bad movie running through his mind at a rapid pace. His feet guiding himself through the path by intuition while his mind betrayed his sight with thoughts of his superiority. It was always thought to himself that other kids were inferior to him when it came to everything he became competitive with. Back in Key West at the tender age of seven, Shawn first held a baseball and with each pitch towards the plate, the ease of the fastball became fluent with purpose. Effortless with his timing, Shawn was always faster and stronger than the kids that surrounded him. Memories of his Father nearly breaking his hand as the fastballs thrown to him by his son would become faster and faster in the family's backyard.

The transformation from his childhood to his teen years were like night and day as his strength became noticeable. During a seventh-grade Junior High basketball game in Hitchcock, Texas, several hundred witnesses attending the game would watch a scrawny white teenager steal the basketball and travel the length of the court and end the game with a slam dunk. The glorious surprise on the faces of the crowd and his team mates that day remained etched in Shawn's mind because he was considered special. With no team experience other than shooting hoops towards a six-foot-high goal post in his backyard, Shawn would make a team considered one of the best in the Houston area. Memories of the tryouts months before were fresh in his mind. Shawn remembered from elementary school his first ever crush as a twelve-year old boy. The reminiscing moments of being a child entering your teenage years can never be forgettable and this was always rendered an exception in Shawn's eyes.

Considered admirably popular by his classmates, Shawn caught the attention of a gorgeous teenager by the name of Wyndie Schroeder. Throughout his ventures in his childhood, his brief tenured homes in Key West and Boston never allowed him to have feelings for any female. Puberty escaped his body most of the time before he reached the town of Galveston, Texas in 1985. The military-moving family considered Hitchcock as the home for the Lee family, but his Father became lucky with a rental in the town of Lamarque. Located a couple of towns over from Hitchcock, the property was more valuable and for the first time in his life, Shawn lived in a house with a large yard. The keen memories became forgetful with the day that Shawn's life should have ended. Less than ten months into his new home, Shawn did what most kids could do for their parents and surprise them with cleaning the entire home. The sudden memory shifted to his parent's bedroom and the engulfed flames covering their bed would reach as far as the ceiling above him. The family cat was trapped under the bed and the screaming entered Shawn's ears like a piercing knife and without hesitation, he entered the flames. Hot to the touch, Shawn ignored the burning of his skin to save his friend under the misery that hell was surrounding the room with. The terrified meowing through the thick black smoke helped the teen reach for its neck and quickly embraced it with open arms. The surprise of the fading feline soon began purring up against Shawn's neck as the miracle holding him would guide them to the outside of the burning home. Unaware of the reasons for the home fire, the miracle on that day would burden Shawn with a purpose he was not understanding. The thick smoke would soon give way to Shawn's footsteps as several onlookers and neighbors looked in awe as he stepped away from the burning front door.

"Son how were you able to save that cat?" asked the Firefighter. The air escaping from his lungs with quickness, Shawn was unable to render a response, but his mind was racing through questions to himself. Over and over he asked his soul what

happened that day in the fire, but Vincent may be the only person responsible to offer the answer. Inching closer and closer to the gate of the Nike Village, Wyndie Schroeder was front-and-center in his mind and she was a coincidence that kept Shawn focused.

Surrounded by all the events that led to his arrival in Hitchcock, it was his first day as a sixth-grade student that invited puberty into his life. Shawn took notice of this amazing female student who was impressive in her charm and tight Jeans. Uncapable of understanding the feelings that ran through his blood, her invisible touch to his heart made him realize that his new school was a blessing. The memories of the girl that captivated his moments for living became a stepping stone to impressing her with flashes of brilliance and Braun. From poems and letters penned by a secret admirer, Shawn's childish approach was inviting to her life and for the entire year, he never told the beautiful teen that she was the reason for his sudden maturity. Moving forward to the day at the Basketball game and the glorious dunk to end the misery escaping his heart, Shawn confessed. Wyndie had been the princess that stole his heart and it took a century of waiting to impress her eyes with an impossibility that is still unexplained years later.

The young heart of the teen built a barrier that allowed the grace of a young female to penetrate the collapsing walls within his soul. Her words kind to his ears as she let him down easy with her vibrance as her parents' stipulations to discontinue dating until High School had surpassed. It was a blessing to know that she had finally been given the opportunity to understand Shawn's willingness to open his heart. The impressions of his life were a mere gift from the gods, but his maturity to confront the shyness of his heart could only be made on his own validity. Standing tall, Shawn took his new outlook on life and moved forward to the city of Weymouth, Massachusetts and its mortifications of hell on earth. His hands reaching out to squeeze through the gate entering his neighborhood, the memories of a life left behind soon fading and his reality was above him. The same sky that woke up the town was now turning to grey as afternoon began to chase the sun into the clouds of regret. Shawn sat on his bed with his Mother's meatloaf settling in his stomach, hands in his head as nightfall began. The minutes of the day were rapidly chasing the hours like a horse race and before Shawn knew it, he was in awe embattling within himself to comprehend the events of earlier.

What had he gotten himself into and who was he really? The riddling questions filtered his curiosity for his entire life was described too fast to comprehend. Combing each year in his head for clues as to describe the events of who he could be would last through the remainder of the evening. Shawn's curiosity within himself came to an abrupt halt hearing a low-pitched howling sound from outside his bedroom window. Standing up to notice the essence of the moon shadowing his backyard above the trees, his sense of sight focused on a movement amongst the bushes. The moment was drawing a line between himself and the reality that stood between his fate and the still of the night. The blue eyes of this teenager were attempting to peak through the cloudy window and a sudden voice over himself spoke to him.
"Shawn, come with me", the deep soothing voice stated.
The words appeared from deep within his sense of hearing as it threw him off balance. Holding his breath to listen closely, the voice appeared again.

"Shawn, come outside", the deep voice stated.

The small hairs began rising on his neck and the goosebumps attempted their best to escape from his skin. Shawn reached up to his ears and placed each finger inside to release any doubt from what he was hearing. Placing his hands back on the sill of the window, the light of the moon soon eclipsed into a blackness beyond the starry night. Attempting to focus on the movements in his backyard, the sudden lights that were easily seen began fading to grey and something in the distance began to appear from across his yard.

Chapter 7
Feed the Wolf

Unable to recognize the apparitions through the window, Shawn escaped quietly through the back door of his home into the yard behind his room. The house was a mere thousand square feet of solace for his family to live in, so the planned route to escape was quick and abrupt. The door leading to the carport from his small kitchen stood between Shawn and his fate as he continuously heard his name called throughout the darkness. Arriving into his backyard, he remained unphased by the creepy shadows under the bright full moon. Taking advantage of the stars light from above, Shawn began adjusting his focus through patient eyes. With little separation between the home's small back yard and the thick forest, sounds of crackling enlightened the symphonic sounds through Shawn's fearless heart. The smell of fresh cut grass and the evening dew encrusted his sense of smell as his sight began focusing on the several eyes gleaming through the thick brush slowly one by one. Shawn's backyard was measured only less than twenty-five feet from the inviting trees hovering on the steep cliffside of the hill. The tiny landscape behind his home spread itself to the edge of a steepness that embraced the strength of the forest staring back at the shadows of regret. The rays of the moon covered by the hidden darkness of the trees, Shawn noticed the continuous beams of blue dots staring at him. Several sets of creepy pupils surrounded in the color of a clear sky became fixated on the young teen.

The chilling air raising the small hairs upon Shawn's neck, a smoldering fog began to set from under his feet. The coolness of the breeze facing his back, a sudden shift of weightlessness

took over his body. Light as a feather and unable to escape the feeling of walking on the beautiful moon above, an incredible strength began racing through his veins. His stomach feeling quickly nauseous giving way to his burning skin near the tips of his fingers. The audience of curious eyes transparent through their energy began the transformation with eagerness. Silence throughout the neighborhood attempted to cover the growling of the beasts upon the night staring back at their prey. Shawn's eyes attempting to focus themselves through the sudden blurry stars above him as he fell to both knees in the grass amongst the thick fog. The dew upon the grass showering his skin to shield the heat within his body while his hands lay numb. Silence surrounded the temporary resting place as the pressure of his skin began to push against his bones. The feeling of growing a few inches in a painful spurt inside of his small frame created an energy that ignited his once lonely molecules. Losing each breath within his lungs, his mouth opening to invite the welcomed air inside of his body. Nature's eyes began witnessing the clouds of fog engulfing the body of the frail teen. The sounds of growling and screams from the creatures of the night began to spread silently throughout the neighborhood. His veins of fire quickly placing his once calm heart into a defensive castle of emotion, Shawn's eyes would capture a bright light between his hands in the grass.

Staring into the ground below him, he would envision the reluctance of his past in mere minutes. Unclear to understand its meaning, Shawn would feel a sense of overwhelming strength within his mind. Visions of victory in his heart would stare back at him to consult his life with determination and will. Becoming clear began the purpose of realizing that his premonitions were all coming true from his years of dreary dreams. The enlightened visions through his blue eyes propelling Shawn to willfully understand that his life had great meaning. The thousands of questions the teen had for his unexplained strength began to answer themselves within his cloudy visions below him. Each fallen answer sending wavelengths of a white lightning amongst the clouds hovering above the small neighborhood. The unanswered resolve dissolved beneath him and his mind began washing every doubt ever claimed deep in his soul. The purpose unclear, it was the new beginning that these creatures lead Shawn to transform into. The rapture controlling each movement of his defenses, Shawn began to slowly creep to one knee while his strong knuckles bury themselves into the grass. His abrupt force through an effortless plight raised his body landing him in an upright position upon his bare feet. Standing in a surreal moment of shifting proportions, Shawn turned around to see his reflection in his bedroom window. His eyes as blue as the afternoon sky, the confusion of his being would suppress all feelings of regret and his collection of thoughts would slowly organize in time.

Looking back into the eyes of those who placed him where he stood, they all began to slowly subside into the fading darkness.

 As each set of eyes disappeared, one exclusively remained at the edge of the forest. Shawn's eyes focusing on the curiosity looking inside of him, the appearance of the white wolf stepped from outside of the smoke. The creature's gorgeous white fur glistened in the moonlight and his strong posture held tight in front of the teen.

"I am trying to understand all of this. Are you hear to teach me?", Shawn softly asked.

The deep voice that earlier called out to him began speaking inside of his mind once again.

"Patience Shawn, patience. Your time here will bring meaning and he will visit yet again."

"What does that even mean? Are you messing with me?", the teen asked.

The wolf quietly walked up to Shawn and placed his head against his leg. Rubbing up against his skin, Shawn felt the beating of it's heart as if they were conjoined. The feeling of the strength deep inside of his body being ripped apart, the weakness of his defenses brought Shawn to the ground quickly on his back. Lifting his weary head away from the grass, the snarling of the wolf stared back into his eyes as they became face to face. The evil within the painful eyes of this beast placed Shawn back into his own world. It was a quick message inside of the teen that he was to never doubt his existence.

"Ok, I get it. I am sorry", Shawn responded.

The anger seen inside of the dilated pupils of the white wolf was enough to make Shawn understand his place. Backing off and stepping away from the teen, the wolf quickly subsided back into the forest. The bluish set of eyes staring back at Shawn would brighten to a point of blindness and a feeling of unconsciousness overwhelmed him. Laying his tired head back in the grass, Shawn would soon wake up and find himself in his own bed.

Quickly raising his upper frame away from the softened pillow, Shawn sat up in disbelief and began placing his hands on his face. Rising fast on his feet, the five-foot mirror in his room glared back at him a reflection that made him smile with confusion. The presence of his once blue eyes in the mirror now gone, he began to look below at his feet and noticed the difference. Somehow, it appeared that Shawn spurted a few inches of height overnight. The look of shock presented itself as he felt that his dreams again were getting the best of him. Glaring back at his body, Shawn noticed the form of a chiseled muscle within his skin. The once skinny kid who was easily blown over by a calm wind was now taking shape of a young adult.

"What the hell is going on?" Shawn asked himself.

The new appearance of his body was appealing, and he started to pinch himself as he began looking out at the window of his bedroom focusing towards the backyard. Staring at a spot in the grass in the middle of the yard, an appearance of a black imprint piqued his interest. Shawn was unable to get out of the house fast enough to place one knee in the ground to examine what he had seen from the window. Placing his fingers on portions of the burnt grass, Shawn felt the stillness of the heat rising from the ground and it perplexed him.

"Last night really did happen, oh crap", Shawn told himself.

Intoxicated with regret and misinformed doubt, Shawn still had no idea what was in store for him and the feeling of curiosity ran through his mind. The only way he was going to understand everything was to grip his determination and venture back to the playground that began it all. Walking back inside of his home while his parents slept, Shawn quickly covered himself with a t-shirt, shorts and shoes. The shirt felt small while placing it over his body because it barely covered his flat stomach. Not caring a bit, he started to place his shorts through his legs and noticed that his feet appeared to be much bigger. Without hesitation, he began to conclude that there was a possibility that other parts of his body may have grown, so he took a quick peak under his boxers. For a brief second, his eyes became dilated at what he was looking at and equipped himself with a new smile from ear to ear. Shawn placed his now small shoes on his large feet and began limping out of the house uncomfortably. On his way onto the street in front of his home, he armed himself with a canned coke and peanut butter sandwich. Changing pace once his feet became familiar with the lack of space inside of his shoes, the curious teenager began walking faster down the hill towards the bottom of the neighborhood. The sunset brightened the path of righteousness towards the fate that he had been seeking and on his short journey, he noticed two kids and a teenager at the bottom of the hill.

Chapter 8
Silent Running

The feeling inside of his gut wanted to bypass the kids he just came across, but his heart respected otherwise.

"Hey, did you just move in here?" asked the smaller kid.

"Hi there, I am Shawn and yes my family just moved in at the top of the hill there", Shawn replied.

"I am Joey, this is my brother David and my other brother John. We live right here at this house", the smaller child replied.

"Dude is there something wrong with your shirt?" John asked.

"It seems there is apparently. My parents are in the process of getting me clothes for the Summer", Shawn smartly responded.

"I know what you mean. These damn pants are hugging my nuts too close to my legs", John stated with a concerned look in his face.

"Yeah, they look a bit uncomfortable if you ask me. So, what are you boys up to today? How long have to lived here in this neighborhood?" Shawn asked.

"We are just waking up", Joey responded.
"I am trying to get these idiots to play baseball", David funnily responded.

"Screw these punks, I am just getting out of the house because our parents are making weird noises in the bedroom, if you know what I mean", John mentioned.

"Yeah, its super annoying", Joey responded.

"Have any of you boys been to the abandoned buildings behind your house?" Shawn asked.

"You are talking about over there", Joey stated as he pointed to the direction behind the neighborhood.

"Of-course that's what he means you idiot. Yes. That's my answer to your question. I have been back there a couple of times and had some fun tearing up a lot of the walls in the buildings", John mentioned.

"I noticed yesterday, good job by the way. Did you notice anything weird when you were back there?" Shawn asked.

"Not really and I was back there a few days ago. Why are you asking anyway?" John asked.

"It's much easier to show you if you guys are up for a walk", Shawn gracefully requested.

The two younger brothers agreed happily through their older brother John and all four boys were on their way to the front gate. The appearance of the boys never concerned Shawn because it was a blessing to find someone to talk to amongst everything the teen faced the last week. The older teen John was a bit of a greaser in his mind. His tight pants and tight shirt reminded him of a cast member on the movie Grease. He wore ridiculously funny looking high-top sneakers with the shoe laces unraveled. His posture was a bit uncomfortable and he just seemed to walk as if something was up his ass, but Shawn slightly giggled to himself over it.

The appearance of John's younger brothers became a delight to Shawn because they seemed like average kids. Little David was the middle-aged child and he seemed to be around eleven and twelve years old. Little Joey was the adorable young kid and with the baby face of a nine or ten-year old, it wasn't an option for Shawn to ask their ages. His new friends were about to be become witnesses to a phenomenon that Shawn was gracefully preparing them for.

Since the kids literally lived near the front gate of the abandoned base, the walk took a mere few minutes to arrive. With ease, each of the boys squeezed through the gate and began following Shawn. David and Joey had astonishing looks on their face because they were never allowed to venture into the base as John explained life in the Buffer household. Acting like children in a candy store, each youth began combing through the buildings one by one.

"Your brothers don't get out much, do they?" Shawn asked John.

Standing next to each other, John replied, *"Depends on the mood of our parents. They can be real sticklers on what we all do. We always get up early while they sleep to basically get away and do what we want."*

"Sorry to hear that John. How long do you plan on staying here in the neighborhood?" Shawn asked.

"We just moved here a couple of months ago. My dad is in the Army and it appears we are here for three or four years. What about you?" John replied.

"Who knows with my dad and his career. Looks like I am hear for the next several years. Since we both are here a while, looks like we should make the most it. Let's have some fun today and I want to show you guys something", Shawn stated.

The walk throughout the Nike Site was like a playground for the young brothers David and Joey. Running through each building to venture into the mystery of the place they never visited before, Shawn and John stood back in glorified humor. Shouting of victory could be heard amongst the dead of the village, yet the silence of their hearts remained in vain. Shawn's beating legacy was about to be born and he was looking to amplify his cause with the small audience that followed him to the back of the Nike Site. Since the boys took their time with their playful discovery, the normal fifteen minutes of arrival time to the open stairway took four times that. The morning brisk and the cool ground softened the heat from beneath the pathway the boys walked upon. Enlightened by the leadership Shawn displayed, the boys followed him with confidence and they were unaware of where he was taking them. Like young boys do, the questions were rolling off their tongues, but Shawn was directly focused on the opening in the ground. The boy's voices in the background slowly swept away as Shawn's pace began to pick up. Within a few minutes, all four boys were standing aside themselves with the reflections of their faces staring back at them. The opening that once brought Shawn below the ground was now filled with water.

"This wasn't like this yesterday, what is going on?" Shawn stated loudly.

"What do you mean? These tunnels were flooded many years ago according to my father", John mentioned.

"Whoa, how do you know that? How does your father know that?" Shawn asked abruptly.

"My father told me that his job briefed him on the base before we moved in here. Dad sat me down and told me that this base was closed in the 1970's because of some presidential order to close the missile silos. I can only imagine what the families went through moving away from here, but we are the lucky ones", John stated.

"John, believe me when I say this dude. This stairway was clear yesterday and I walked out of it. You know what, never mind. Maybe it's all the stress from this move here. Sorry to bring you all out here, this was my fault clearly", Shawn stated in frustration.

Looking back at his younger brother David, Joey pointed to the side of his head and began circling his ears as if he thought Shawn was crazy. The boys began walking away from the entrance inside of the ground. Shawn remained for a brief few seconds and began to turn back around towards the direction of the stairwell. His eyes couldn't fool him, but the vision of Sebastian staring back at him slowly dissipated into the reflection of his own face in the water at the bottom of the stairwell.

Shawn whispered to himself, *"Ok Vincent, this is our secret and maybe I am not crazy, but ok. Do what you will with me."*

"Wait up guys", Shawn said the boys ahead of him.

Shawn caught up to the brothers and asked, *"So, what's on the agenda for the Summer around here?"*

"Now you are talking finally. David and I are going into Baseball next week. Do you play?" Joey asked.

"Yes sir. Since I was six years old and people tell me I am pretty good", Shawn replied.

"Well I am a pitcher and David's a bat boy because he sucks", Joey laughingly stated.

"Your mom", David replied quickly.

"John, your brothers are something else and damn they are funny", Shawn stated.

"Don't listen to these dumb asses. They talk out of their dirty pieholes and who cares," John angrily replied.

It was apparent that John was very protective of his parents and it was very common in military families. The little brothers were competitive, and Shawn decided that the two younger boys would be perfect to entice. Thanks to the mention from the younger brother, Shawn would ask his parents later that afternoon to venture into town and see if a Summer baseball league was forming in the town of Topsfield. It was the question to his mother that allowed Shawn to become a fixture in a town that was aching for excitement. Weeks would pass before Shawn was to show up with his Father to the first practice of the Topsfield baseball team and it would be a day for all to remember.

The scrawny fourteen-year old stepped upon the mound to throw a few pitches at the request of his coach. The audition to pitch for his new team would gracefully take center stage. With the eyes of only the catcher and coach looking upon him, Shawn stared down the strike zone with a boy possessed unfurling his wind up with a blaze of heat. The sound of a popping seemingly awoke all those around the diamond. The catcher instantly removed his glove and began shaking his hand like it was on fire.

"Coach, I can't catch another like that, my hand stings", replied the catcher.

With a brief thought and a huge smile on his face, the coach ran to his car to grab a sponge that he remembered being in his back seat. Returning from his vehicle, he handed his catcher the sponge and told him to place it on his palm inside of the glove. At his request, the catcher than relieved his pain-stricken hand inside of the glove with the sponge encased in his palm and slowly placed its target over home plate.

"Alright kid show me what you got", he nervously replied.

The eyes of the entire team and the parents attending were focused on the bolt of lightning coming from the arm of the new pitcher. Three pitches of high speed were all inclusive of a rocket unfurling itself into the atmosphere and it was magic. Shawn would settle down with a simulation of twenty pitches before the coach asked him to stop.

"Shawn, where did you come from son?" the Coach asked.

"My mother Coach", the young man funnily replied.

"Well, you have the quickest fastball I have ever seen, and I would be honored to have you pitch for this team son," the Coach stated.

Shawn's face glistened with a smile as his new team mates embraced themselves around him. He felt alive again and standing on the mound, he caught a glimpse of a shadow in the distance beyond the backstop. Catching focus through his eyes, it was a moment that Vincent was watching him carefully. The motion was set for the Summer as Shawn was now silently running throughout the craziness of his new baseball career. Sudden whispers that the golden arm of the new and upcoming freshman was entering his High School years as a favorite to dethrone the number one pitcher for the Varsity team.

As each day of Summer passed, Shawn slowly began racking up strikeouts and wins as his team of Topsfield is blew away the competition. Ahead of the victories was a gigantic showdown with the team from Middleton. The irony of the game will gracefully match the two best pitchers in the league against each other on their undefeated teams. The showdown would become legendary as the pitchers for each team would capture the attention of the surrounding areas. The gathering crowd would smother each inch of the bleachers in anticipation for this once in a lifetime moment between giants. It was Clemens versus Gooden all over again and the three days leading up to this game for the town of Middleton was pure chaos.

Rick Antonio was the number one pitcher for the Masconomet's High School Varsity team and he used his last year of eligibility in the league to attempt his third straight championship summer league trophy. The rumors of a new kid in the next town became such a buzz, he attempted to tune out the mess with his usual wrecking of other pitcher fastballs out of the ball park. Leading up to the game against Topsfield, Rick has amassed a batting average of over five hundred and tuned himself to a record of six wins and no losses as pitcher. The statistics were rivaled evenly with the young kid from Topsfield with a near perfect eight wins and no losses and an earned run average of less than one. The two teams headed on this collision course caught the attention of the local newspapers and High Schools within a thirty-mile radius. The matchup on a brisk Saturday morning would eventually begin with anticipation as the over six-foot pitcher from Middleton took the homefield advantage with ease as he approached the mound. The hype placed on the game of the year was now front and center and the first pitch amongst the thousands in attendance would witness this colossal showdown.

Chapter 9
Blind Nemesis

The town of Middleton anticipated a matchup of the century between two pitchers that were young and enticing to watch. Their beloved Rick had exuberated his dominance over the Summer league for years and it was the excitement that their second-place team defeat Topsfield and its renewed confidence. The cross-town rivals were at war and Rick's first pitch would land in the center of the place and the yelling of "strike" from the umpire gracefully swept through the ears of those watching in the stands. It would be a young second baseman by the name of Andy that would suffer silence on the second pitch from the Middleton pitcher. The fastball somehow got away from his telling grip as it's projection would aim itself at the body of the young man in the batter's box. The speed of the pitch too quick to make an adjustment, its landing spot would find its way across Andy's bat during his bunt and somehow projected the ball through his jaw. The broken noise silenced the crowd as they witnessed the young man hit the ground quickly. The Coach of the Topsfield team saw his son take a fastball across the face and the hysteria drew a fear through his mind. The several minutes that his son coveted the ground in pain, it was obvious that Topsfield's best hitter was now removed from the lineup with a pitch that angered his teammates. The smile of those on the Middleton side of the diamond were reluctantly hidden and they were unaware of the giant that they were about to wake up.

Andy was escorted by his parents to their vehicle as he would be brought to the local hospital by his mother. The Coach stayed at the game and the umpire swiftly mentioned that a batter had to take his place. The foul ball was the first strike for the approaching new batter and he would have to face the tall task of facing the hard throwing righty on the mound. With a look of confusion and concern for his son, a young man placed both his feet on the ground from the bench and placed him arm around his coach.

"Coach put me in. Give me a chance to get an at bat against this guy. I will not let you down, I swear", the young man asked.

The coach looked down at his pitcher and with graceful eyes, he agreed to his demand and allowed him to grab a bat.

"Shawn, do this for my son and get a hit", replied the coach.

Shawn walked over to the bag of bats and after holding two bats, the third one was to his liking. Swinging a few times with the bat in his hands, he looked over at his team mates and voiced his confidence.

"C'mon guys, we got this. Let me hear you guys scream, look at him, he is a man", Shawn loudly stated to his team.

Taking a step aside with the batter's box, Shawn slowly dug in and positioned his feet parallel with home plate. The stance was a bit unorthodox, but Shawn was onto something. With his teammates looking on, they began to take notice that he was crowding the plate. The second official pitch of the at- bat was thrown low and outside as Shawn never took his eyes away from Rick. Staring him down creating a transparency for his teammates to witness, the weakness began to unravel within the pitcher. The third and fourth pitches were again outside and low and the pitcher's concentration was vastly disrupted. Taking a moment to capture his breath, Rick again applied his focus and delivered his hardest fastball of his life. The windup was perfect like many times before and with the right foot pressing away from the rubber on the mound, his weight assisted his right arm with a fireball straight towards the plate. The eyes of the catcher began to close with anticipation of the baseball landing in his glove over the middle of the plate. That was never meant to be as the deafening sound of the aluminum bat would crack as loud as he had ever heard. The catcher opened his eyes to witness the baseball travel away from him in a hurried pace like he had never seen. Looking at the back of Shawn's number thirteen on his jersey running towards first, it was the baseball that took an endless amount of time to land. The five hundred or more feet of space the ball would travel silenced the once loud crowd and enthused an entire team from Topsfield. That morning in Middleton awoke a star in the making as the game would end in favor of Topsfield six to one. Shawn had pitched himself into a two-hit gem of a game with both hits against him coming from the bat of the pitcher who suffered defeat. The crowd was in awe over what they all had saw and it would begin the whispers that would reach as far as the city of Boston itself. The new boy in town was going to ravage the rest of the Cape Ann League come next fall and most believed the theories, except a few skeptical people.

Rick was beside himself of the tough loss he suffered and the thought of knowing he could be a possible team mate next year in High School sickened him. Avoiding the entire team of Topsfield at the end of the game while they all shook hands, he stared down the new nemesis that had positioned himself above the legacy he built on this very field. The days of Summer were starting ellusively and these two amazing pitchers would attempt their hardest to meet again at the championship towards the end of the next couple of months. The eerie feeling that Rick displayed inside of his heart that evening propelled him to believe that Shawn was different than the rest of his friends. Thoughts of this teenager coming out of nowhere to display the perfect mechanics of a baseball player were surreal and impossible. The anger was on display during the ride home with his Father and the boiling point of a young man could be felt for miles.

"Dad, where did this kid come from, huh? I have never been so humiliated in my entire life and for this punk to just waltz in my own town and sink me beneath the ground is just, I mean, it's just so damn wrong", Rick angrily stated.

"Son, you knew this day was going to finally come. Why are you so upset over some kid who had a good game? It's just a game Richard, calm down", his Father replied to him.

Rick's father was always the guy that leveled him to an even keel since he was growing so fast. The town of Middleton embraced Rick at an early age and the tall six-foot three teenager was wowing baseball scouts in the Major Leagues with his amazing arm. The Father who always believed his son was going to be special would always bring him back to earth with his own realism. Whether excelling in Karate, Hockey or Baseball, Rick was the epitome of most kids in the surrounding towns of Masconomet High School and he was a hero to all.

"Dad, what are you telling me here? Should I just embrace this embarrassment and look beyond tonight? I don't think I can because I just want to deliver a beating to that kid", Rick yelled in anger.

"Boy, you better loosen that tone. Are we clear!" Rick's father stated as he began looking down on his son.

"Yes sir", Rick silently murmured.

"Look at me son. We move above all this and you play him again and you beat his ass. Plain and simple. But, we need to develop a positive here Richard. If he plays with you next year in High School as all the parents are stating, don't you want to win a State Title?" He asked his son.

"More than anything Dad. More than anything I have ever wanted", Rick replied.

"Then embrace this young man and teach him. Be his mentor and work together and bring home what we all want. Is that workable?" He asked his son.

"Sleep on it and let's take it one day at a time", his father calmly stated.

"I will be fine Dad and it's the baseball that still hasn't landed that I am worried about", Rick said with loud laughter.

"That's my baby boy, come here and embrace your father", his dad boldly stated.

Rick and his father embraced that night in the car and the conversation would transform Rick into an understanding that his new nemesis would be his best ally. It was a difficult realization when just ten minutes earlier he wanted to beat the kid into the ground. Rick would settle down in his own heart and venture into an unforeseen friendship with the kid who was an unknown to most of the town.

The Summer of 1987 would see an endearing relationship grow amongst the parents of all the other teams throughout the league Shawn was playing in. Game by game, Shawn would wreak havoc and win every game he started on the mound while the crowds would begin to grow and grow. The quiet whispers were no longer silent as the talk of the three towns of Middleton, Boxford and Topsfield were of this young extraordinary talent and his vibrance. Shawn had joined a team that barely scraped themselves from the bottom of the division over the last couple of years, and to immediately become the best team was breath taking to most. Each game displayed a unique point of view from those who embellished his talents. The crowds watching Shawn's games began to garner the attention of the local Universities and Coaches. The attention given was beginning to pressure Shawn into a situation that he was unaccustomed to. It was the conversation with his own mother that relished him to slow down and back away from his new-found stardom. She made it clear to him that he was to attempt to live a normal life and to not draw so much attention to himself. It was a mere few sentences from his mother's mouth that allowed him to realize that his dreams to become a baseball player in the Major Leagues should wait. On a hot Summer Night in July of 1987, Shawn decided to withdraw himself from his baseball team and focus on trying out for the Freshman football team for Masconomet High School. That decision would shock the entire community and devastate his teammates. Without him, the team finished with a record of one win and four losses in route to a first round loss in the baseball playoffs. Without any reason for leaving, Shawn relegated himself to becoming a normal teenager as he would venture into normalcy.

While the Topsfield team struggled at the end of the season, Rick and his Middleton team would prosper and win the Championship. Despite his win, he always knew that the matchup with his cross-town nemesis that didn't happen ate a hole in his heart. Since the loss to Shawn and Topsfield, Rick would go on to win every game he played capturing the Most Valuable Player of the league. It was the accolades that disturbed Rick because it was basically all for not. Shawn was absent from the league and nothing would ever rectify his thoughts of what would have been if his arch rival remained in the league. The two wouldn't meet again for a long period of time and his friendship was placed on hold for over a year. The football program at Masconomet was now awaiting a new leader and it was the freshman named Shawn Lee that stepped onto the field without any knowledge of the game.

Chapter 10
Breaking the Silence

The entire rest of the Summer from July to August, Shawn would spend each moment waiting to hear from Vincent, but the silence of the Nike Site would blanket his anticipation. The neighborhood embraced the sweltering heat with fun-filled days of playing on the streets with an abundance of annoying kids. Each home equipped a family of no less than one child and while the parents were away at work, it was the mid-day fun that Shawn enjoyed the most. Leaving behind his newly found fame on the baseball diamond, he developed a liking for the silence that brandished his friendship with his three new friends. David, Joey, John and Shawn would become inseparable for the duration of the Summer and trouble was brewing. The young boys would venture further into the playground the Nike Site provided, and it opened a wilderness of hidden mystery. New trails amassed in each direction through the surrounding woods leading to a lake, a cornfield and the haunting of the abandoned military base. Each day that passed was a new adventure, from picking on the other kids in the neighborhood to enjoying the many hours of playing Nintendo. It was the solace that Shawn needed because he was unaware of the many nights of bliss that were slowly approaching. Shawn's parents signed him up to play football for the first time in his young life and it was his Father's wish to become the Quarterback that he always respected. Shawn's Father was a huge Dan Marino fan, and anyone affiliated with knowledge of the NFL knew who he was. The Miami Dolphins in 1983 surpassed all odds that year in the draft and they took a young and experienced Senior Quarterback from the University of Pittsburgh named Dan Marino. Fresh off a terrible senior year, the rumblings of other Quarterbacks taken that year angered the Pittsburgh prodigy and it fueled his desire to become the best Quarterback in the league. Shawn's Father saw the same intensity in his son when he began playing baseball at an early age, and in all the destinations his family lived in, the football programs were non-existent. It was until the day that Shawn began going to school at Masco as an eight-grader that his Father began seeing the possibilities. His son had a golden arm, the ability to throw a heavy fastball and his mechanics with this delivery were that of his idol, Dan Marino. That Summer, Shawn's dad would arrive home from work and have Shawn work on his throws in the front yard with an official sized college football. The first time that Shawn developed a liking for football was when his father had him watch the 1982 Super Bowl. The Miami Dolphins that year were favorites to win it all and they were matched against a formidable foe in the Washington Redskins.

It was that night that Shawn realized his Father's passion for sports because of the irony he felt inside his soul. Watching his dad's heart break in front of him that night during the loss to the Redskins, symbolized his passion for something and he became his hero. Not wanting to let him down, Shawn began to work on his mechanics before his Freshman year. Throwing the football with amazing accuracy and a tight spiral blew his Father away. Not having much experience, Shawn began to spend night and day studying the game films of the Miami Dolphins and their legendary QB. If his father was right, Shawn would step right onto the field and make an immediate impact for the freshman team at Masconomet.

The day emerged for Shawn to arrive for his first practice and familiar faces began to emerge. The same teenagers he once played with and against during the Summer baseball league were present. The brief time he spent in eighth grade with some of the current freshman weren't as familiar at Masco, but his desire to impress his new coach began immediately. In Junior High School, the same kids that took the field in attendance were those who just lost their Quarterback to another High School and all were in disarray. Upon Shawn's arrival that morning, the argument over who was going to step up and play the position allowed Shawn to drop his bright red colored gym bag in excitement.

"Hello boys, hand me the pigskin", Shawn spoke.

Pointing at one of the teenagers staring back at him, he spoke, *"Go out ten yards and run a button-hook."* Shawn waited for the receiver to begin his route and before he turned, the boy with the golden arm flung a fast ball in perfect motion with a tight spiral and landed heavily in between his awaiting arms. Surprised by the speed and accuracy, the sounds of the other players watching began to turn into excitement.

"Yeah, we got ourselves a Quarterback", were announced by all the players on the field and as the Coach arrived for practice a few minutes later, members of the team began to thrive on the new arm they just found. The day of practice began with running and developing the endurance of all the players and in the next few weeks, the team would shape into a solid unit for the freshman coach. In the many days of learning the plays developed by the High School Coach, Shawn began to take notice that he was running a freshman offense that was terrible. The idea to run the same offense in correlation with the Varsity team made a lot of sense since the next step would to be join the team ranked above them. The Varsity football team was in the-midst-of one of the worst droughts in Massachusetts history

and it didn't take long for Shawn to realize why. The coaching staff had been around for years and the plays written in the Masco playbook belonged to a running offense. The wishbone offense was developed with the college ranks of the Nebraska Cornhuskers and the Varsity coach intended on implementing the same mentality on his boys. Shawn began to take notice and after the first week of practice, he took it upon himself to walk into the Varsity Coaches office and invite him to a conversation that will never be forgotten.

"Coach, can we talk for a few minutes, its urgent", Shawn asked.

"Good morning young man, what the hell are you doing in my office? Don't you know that you are needed on the Freshman team this morning?" The Coach angrily asked.

"Coach, I like your enthusiasm here and I am listening, but will you listen for a second?" Shawn directly asked.

"You have two minutes", the coach replied.

"Coach, I am studying these plays and we don't have the correct offensive line to hold the blocks necessary to sustain any advantage. My team definitely needs an upgrade at those tackle positions and I am here asking if you will allow our team to implement a few passing options to help establish our running game", Shawn asked with confidence.

"Who the hell do you think you are to come in with your new game plan and supplant my ideas? I have worked hard to get

my boys to follow this running offense and god damn it's going to work. Are we clear?" The Coach asked.

"It's your offense Coach and I am saying from my perspective that it isn't going to work. All I am asking is that you let my team implant a few plays to the offense. Let me have this one thing and if it works, then I will never say a thing and you decide what's best. Our first game is in two weeks and I would like to prove to you that the system works", Shawn gracefully stated.

"Just this one-time Mister Lee and I swear if it doesn't work, I will have you running laps until your entire team pukes. Are we understood sir?" The Coach asked.

With the positive news from the Varsity Coach, Shawn and his Freshman coach would implant an entire new playbook aside from the old one and script an offense of beauty. Shawn had the idea that his arm should be used to set up the running game that the Masco offense was accustomed to. Coach Swain was preparing his new offense over several practices and his team was elated that their new Quarterback stood up to the grumpy Varsity Coach. Years of losing on both the freshman levels and Varsity teams became a habit that Shawn wanted better for his new school and the silence broken over his disappearance during the Summer came to fruition. The anger of his leaving the baseball team was now in the past and it all came down to the first day of school as a freshman. Would Shawn be welcomed in with open arms or will his desertion of the baseball team bring a lot of anger? That was still to be determined and equipped with new friends from the football team, a new outlook on his entering High School emerged. A sense of belonging was important to Shawn, but the relevance of his past would be something for him to endure.

Chapter 11
Mother's Pride

The night before Shawn's first day of school ended like most that Summer with an escapade through the woods behind his house, but tonight was different. The water station located down the hill from behind his home always had a locked gate surrounding its perimeter, but Shawn noticed it was unlocked. The gate door was slightly cracked and with nightfall about to approach, Shawn ventured past the secluded opening. The small building inside the gate attached itself to a large pump that was surrounded by large pipes. The sounds of rushing water could he heard as Shawn attempted to approach the entrance. He grabbed the handle of the swinging door and entered with caution. He noticed the echoes of the water surrounding his body as the sun gave way to the darkness inside of the small shed. Looking beneath him, he noticed a large mat barely covering a small door into the ground. With a little courage, he reached down for the small handle and without hesitation, the hatch opened with a large creaking sound. The hinges without oil causing the noise to awaken the silence from below, Shawn began to crawl into the small hole. The coolness of the air brushing against his cheeks, Shawn noticed a small stairwell beneath his feet. Aside from the hour he had remaining before he had to arrive home for supper, Shawn's fearless heart was determined to see what lied ahead.

The darkness of the tunnel that Shawn discovered, was now beginning to lighten up with lanterns on each side. It was a beckoning of his will to follow the path to whatever lie ahead. The smell of rock and Earth were upon his senses as he slowly approached each few feet ahead of him. Shawn was barely able to see more than ten feet ahead of him and with each passing of a lantern, another would lighten up. The eerie passage was something out of a Pitfall Atari game and it intrigued him more to follow through with its final-destination. Unable to keep track of time, the seconds turned into vital minutes as Shawn closely approached another door in front of him. The walk seemed like an eternity and now it was finally at heaven's door and Shawn opened it without hesitation.

Shawn's eyes instantly opened as he found himself on the other side of a door that intensified the beating of his heart. The floor was illuminated with soft blue lights and the three walls opposite of the door were dark and surrounded with red lighting. The flickering candles were dim upon each wall and while taking a deep breath to observe the room, the sudden slamming of the door behind him awoke his frightened soul. Pitch dark ruled the room and the tingling of his hairs upon his neck ran chills through his spine. Sounds of things crawling on the walls around him, Shawn stood patiently as the candles began to burn brighter and he was finally graced with Vincent's presence.

"*Shawn*", Vincent nodded.

"*Vincent*", Shawn replied.

"*It appears you are on your way to making a lot of friends my young disciple*", Vincent boldly stated.

"*Vincent, what is this place?*" Shawn asked.

"I lead you here to give you a small taste of what is to come, do you think you are ready?" Vincent asked.

"Hmm, I think so", Shawn politely replied.

"Ha! Ha! Calm down my young disciple. I was only kidding for God sake. It is a good thing you were able to find this place because it was made for you. The room you surround yourself in will be a place that will develop your powers beyond your own imagination", Vincent mentioned.

The walls of the room began turning like a circle while Vincent was talking and transformed into a small room of four walls that seems like large televisions. Within a blink of an eye, each wall was showing a different angle of the sky that glared above the Nike Village. Like inside the eyes of a soaring Eagle, Shawn was able to encircle himself with the vision of everything around him.

"Shawn, this is just the beginning and I want you to spend countless time here learning how to use your new weapon," Vincent told him.

"Weapon? What do you mean this is a weapon?" Shawn asked.

"Give this time and you will understand what I mean son. You are going to wreak havoc in this world and before you do, it is on you to develop yourself with the correct mind set to control you gifted power", Vincent stated.

Standing in front of Shawn in his tailored suit, Vincent's beard reminded the young man of the pain and anger that suddenly became transparent to him. Shawn's mind was wandering endlessly through its entire process of watching the sky surrounding him in the room and without a pause, Shawn brought Vincent to a sudden boiling point.

"You are Satan aren't you. Tell me the truth Vincent. How in the world can all of this happen without the evil plan you are planting inside of my brain? I just have one question damn it. Why me?" Shawn asked bravely.

"My young boy, your path was easily chosen by your mother. Some choices will define an eternity without explanation and I don't deem this necessary to explain. You must know that you are the key to our survival in this world and regardless of where you remain, lets be clear that you are to serve my purpose", Vincent explained mightily.

Taking a deep breath of relief, Shawn was now suddenly understanding his purpose and realized that his mother was the direct result for why Vincent entered his life. Exuberating patience, Shawn directed his next few questions at his reasons for his new alliance with the devil.

"What are you asking of me Vincent?" Shawn asked.

"In due time Shawn. For now, I need you to prepare for your first day tomorrow in school. The time will come when I am ready to introduce you to your first assignment. You are welcome to this place any time you need to get away and I need you to

familiarize yourself with the perks here and to understand them", Vincent replied.

"It's a long way back, so I need to hurry before my parents think I ran away", Shawn replied.

"Shawn, stand in the center of the room for me. Now, when you supplant yourself, I want you to close your mind," Vincent deeply stated.

The young teen stood in the middle of the room and began closing his eyes, as Vincent guided him.

"Don't close your eyes, close your mind. Softly envision your room in your mind and allow it to flow onto the walls", Vincent stated.

Shawn began to follow the advice of what Vincent was telling him and the vision of the sky on the walls began to turn grey and within seconds, Shawn could see the surroundings of his own room on each wall. It was like he was standing in the center of his own bedroom and a huge smile cracked upon his face.

"Vincent, I can't believe this. Its like I am inside of my own room and it came from my thoughts", Shawn happily replied.

"Now, blink your eyes once and see what happens Shawn", Vincent mentioned.

Without hesitation, Shawn closed his eyes briefly and upon opening them, he felt his surroundings change in an instant. The coolness of the room changed to a much warmer temperature as he felt himself standing in the center of his own room and his mind was racing crazily. Within a few seconds, his mother was calling him from the other room for Supper. For the duration of dinner that night, Shawn stared at his mother with a look of anger and confusion. Taking notice, Shawn and his mother spent the remainder of the early evening talking about what his clouded mind was thinking.

Shawn and his mother ventured out into the streets of the neighborhood and began to delve into a meaningful talk.

"Shawn sweetie, what's bothering you?" His mother asked.
"Who is Vincent Mother?" Shawn angrily asked.

His mother's face slowly covered with tears as they slowly began falling, while the guilt in her eyes told the story.

"I am so sorry my son. I made a terrible choice years ago and I relinquished everything to save my own life. It was a selfless act that I never imagined wanting to tell you", she replied.

"Mom, do you have any idea why Vincent is using me to get what he wants?" asked Shawn.

"Yes, I do. Please listen to what I am about to tell you, or your life is in danger. I can only help you a little before Vincent realizes it", she stated.

Shawn nodded his head and remained focused on his Mother's words.

"Back in 1972, I was a struggling teenager living in my house and I ran away from home because of my abusive parents. I was so upset how my life was going that I met the wrong people and made some bad decisions. One night I went out on a ride with some apparent friends I had been staying with and the vehicle was stopped outside of a convenient store. I was asked to stay in the car while the other three went inside. A matter of a couple of minutes or more passed by and then I heard a very loud popping sound. It repeated over three times and that is when the doors of the car slammed open and my friends were yelling hysterically. Shawn, I had no intentions of hurting anyone that night and the police were chasing us. While our car was eluding the cops, my friends were arguing that Mike was not supposed to shoot the clerk. The plan was to rob the safe and move on without incident. The two idiots up front began pushing each other and the last thing I remember was suffering a loud bang to my head and I awoke in the hospital. The nurse was horrified with the damage done to my face and day and night, I would beg someone to save my life. My parents were never to know I was there and as I am laying there, a dark figure out of the corner of my eye began comforting me. His voice echoed in my ears and he asked if I was alright. It was the first time in a long time that I felt like someone cared about my well-being. The comfort he provided allowed me to heal quickly in the hospital and on my last day there, Vincent proposed a plan to let me keep my life and away from the cops. Since I was going to be properly arrested for being an accomplice to murder when I left the room, I needed an out. Vincent promised me that if he was to make it all go away, he would ask that I obtain the soul of my first-born child. It was the deal I had to make to save my own life and with a blink of an eye, I was back at home with my parents. Shawn, I had no idea this was all real and I pretended it was a bad nightmare. Vincent showed his face again when you were *born, and he promised that you would never be hurt, and I believed him. Shawn, I know the truth about Weymouth and what happened with those kids. I am sorry with all my heart and Vincent made this all possible and I need you to please do what he needs. You are a true blessing and you can't escape what you really are. You now know what happened and I am asking you to please fulfill what he is wanting and let's move on. I sacrificed your needs for mine and I promise someday I will make it up to you. Let's go home and just take this one day at a time, ok,"* his mother proudly stated.

Not one thing was said again that evening as Shawn would embrace and comfort his mother. He was now understanding the true reason for his identity and he was at a crossroad. It was his Mother who sacrificed him to further her own life and he would never have existed without the deal she made with Vincent. Equipped with the knowledge of who he was, Shawn went to bed that night with memories of his entire childhood and did what he could to bury his feelings. His first day as a freshman in High School was a mere few hours away and that part of his life was now encasing itself as a new Chapter.

Chapter 12
Freshman Year (87'-88')

His first day at Masconomet began early in the morning with the first period beginning at a few minutes after 7. Quite earlier than what Shawn was used to, but who cared. The halls of Masco were clean, full of teens and just crazy busy for the first day. First period would begin with History class and as the day would move forward, he would have a total of seven classes including a lunch period in the middle. The same cafeteria that he visited months ago while in Junior High was convenient to find and after a few morning periods, the clock striking noon was obviously a sign to delve into eating lunch. The hysteria behind the groups of classmates coveting each table in the cafeteria allowed him to choose only a couple of options to sit and eat. Holding a tray of food, Shawn caught the attention of a few boys who were attempting to flag him down. He focused on the identity of those wanting him to come sit with them and he realized as he approached that it was a couple of his baseball teammates and others he played against. Placing his tray of food on the table, Shawn said hello to everyone and didn't invite himself to say much. Listening to the others while he ate, he caught on to the names of everyone around him and learned as much as he could about them.

Rich was the shortstop on his team and he was always considered polite and the brain of the group. Travis was the mouth full of braces and had a knack of laughing a lot at others expense. Sitting next to him was David and he was as preppy as they came. Dressed in a long sleeve polo shirt and pants, perfect wavy hair and super polite as well. David was also a player on the Summer Baseball team from Boxford and he was the first to speak to Shawn.

"So, Shawn. Thanks for quitting the team so that we could face Middleton in the Championship. We absolutely had no chance with you on the mound. Where did you even come from?" David asked.

"My father is in the military, so I have lived almost everywhere", Shawn replied.

"Where did you learn how to throw that fastball? Every single time I was up to bat, I was barely able to get a swing on it?" David again asked.

Shawn hesitated to answer the question because the question intrigued the entire table to listen to his answer. The curiosity amongst them all had withdrew his interest and it wasn't the answer they were seeking.

"Ok, the silent type are we. That's fine because you are one of the wicked best baseball players I have ever seen. I hope you join Masco's Varsity team this year because they need another arm", David replied.

"We need another arm like I need a hole in my head. Get out of here David, that was a wicked stupid comment", Andy replied sarcastically.

Andy was the young looking second baseman for the Topsfield Summer team and Shawn immediately didn't like him. It was something about his arrogance and realizing his father was the coach of the Summer team. Andy had a disliking for the way Shawn quit the team, but the new kid in town could care less and Andy took notice.

"Andy, you are an unhappy little guy, aren't you?" Shawn asked.

The table became silent as all eyes were shifted towards the attention of Andy's reaction to Shawn's question.

"I wasn't the one who quit my team, so what's to say you won't quit the Varsity team?" Andy bravely asked.

"Before you and your Daddy go around assuming the wrong things about my situation, why didn't you just come ask me Andy? I was very sick and had to be home to heal. I didn't want to leave the team, but this was out of my control and I moved forward. So, don't open your mouth again unless its to shove something inside of it. I'm done talking about it", Shawn angrily replied.

The mood at the table changed and the others at the table began to see that Shawn was able to stand up to Andy and his pessimism and they liked him right away.

"Shawn, in regards-to your health, we are very glad to have you here and looking forward to seeing you on the football and baseball fields", replied Travis.

"I agree with that statement one thousand percent and glad you are on our side", replied Richard.

Richard Gross was Andy's best friend and he wasn't going to intervene on his behalf, but he knew Shawn was correct. If an illness was the true reason for him to not play, then it was by the grace of God that he was able to come back. Richie was always the guy that everyone liked, and he was an avid football player. When he found out that the freshman team was without a quarterback, he figured the team would run more with him as the running back. The day Shawn walked onto the field on the first day of practice, he exuberated the will to make his team better and respected the new kid immediately.

Lunch that afternoon was the highlight of Shawn's first day because the next few hours would end in misery. Rounding out the final classes would be Science, Gym and English. The classes were horribly boring, and the weight of Shawn's lunch placed him into daydreaming the rest of the school day. Masconomet Regional High School was a palace of sorts with hallways filled with waxed floors, locker doors and an abundance of students. The mixture of Freshman, Sophomores, Juniors and Seniors ravaged the population of the student body and each time the bell rang to end a period, the flooding of the hallways began. Shawn started the day on the 2nd floor and ended it on the far east part of the High School. In total, he would end up walking over two miles in less than eight hours of the day before Football practice began. It was an invitation to his fitness while others complained about the distance to each classroom.

The High School had a large cafeteria, massive auditorium, basketball gymnasium, regular indoor gymnasium and miles of hallways leading to the Junior High School. The school housed all students from the surrounding three towns of Middleton, Boxford and Topsfield and everyone had their cliques to hang out with. During his first day in High School, Shawn spent the day familiarizing himself with this classes and schedule. It was the second day that he would abbreviate his meaning to recon the types of students attending Masco. For the remainder of the week, Shawn studied those around him and the type of behaviors to determine if they were worth becoming friends with. Masco was a school of massive diversity and a compilation of rich and poor and it was the difference which created several cliques. Just like any High School in the 80's in America, the more diverse the community, the more friction and differences that would develop in the schools. Interstate 95 separated the towns of Topsfield, Middleton and Boxford and was also the main highway right beside the High School. The easy access to the school allowed visiting students to have easy access to both the sports teams and facilities. That access could also have its downfalls with school busses servicing a large area that would usually take up to an hour to get students home.

Shawn's recognizance revealed in detail everything he needed to determine who to avoid and invite in his circle. He was able to decide there were several different types of students that seems to cling to each other at Masco and it was contagious. The first group were called the tree smokers or in simple terms, metal heads. These were the teens with the long hair, the continuous smoke breaks, the dark clothing and Metallica T-shirts. Shawn was never fond of these students because they spent most of their time annoying each other or smoking cigarettes which was a terrible habit. It wasn't like the movie *Grease* where smoking was cool. This was a continuous habit that attempted the ways to be cool, but it truly wasn't. That group was mostly responsible for producing pregnancies and drop-outs and the few that excelled in school would eventually hide their talents.

The next group would be the preppy kids and they absolutely dominated the entire school. Where in the world would you see a teenager on a fifty-degree day wear shorts, sweatshirt and a pair of moccasins? If you answered the preppy student as your answer, then you are correct. This group intrigued Shawn the most because they were well dressed, with perfect hair and happened to invest a lot of money into Ralph Lauren clothing. Never in his entire young life did he see shirts or sweaters with (a polo guy riding a horse) stitched onto any clothing. It was clear that this type of clothing symbolized the difference of money for which student's parents had it and who did not. This group also walked through the hallways together and some of them would entertain the notion to join other groups. If you were to see the presence of these students within your sights, you would automatically assume they would grow up to have a successful life. In comparison to the tree smokers, it was a large difference because one would drive a BMW into a gas station while the other would be attending to your vehicle at the gas pump.

The next group Shawn noticed were the alternative group. These were the Sex Pistols and the Cure fans that painted their nails black and grew their hair out with curls galore. The following wasn't as large as the tree smokers, but this was the clique that everyone respected. Most if not all were very smart and the only difference amongst all the groups were their appearance. With each student drawing names of their favorite bands on their book covers with black lipstick, it was the music they preferred the most. Despite the attention, they were the classmates that most wanted around because they were willing to help lead class projects or help others with homework. It was the lunch period that brought most together because the moment you walk into the doors of the Cafeteria, you couldn't miss the four tables garnered in darkness like a Haunted House.

The other groups that Shawn depicted clearly were the Jocks and the Nerds. Just like in the movie, *Revenge of the Nerds,* the clear angst of the Jocks, were to propel their dominance over all the other groups. Masco was no exception according to the movie, but it was mostly a few morons from the Senior class that chose to continue the traditions of becoming pranksters towards the student body. During the first week of practice while school began, Shawn would endure the "Jar" that began with a Senior student. His crazy idea was for members of the Varsity Football team to urinate inside of the glass jar to collect over the season. It was the few brain cells of this linebacker that would eventually lead one of the worst defensive units in Massachusetts history. A mixture of the preppy kids and nerds would invite themselves to play for the football team and it was a good place to be during the season. The jocks commonly wore their jerseys and leather jackets during school, so the teachers and students could classify their school spirit. It was a sea of red and white throughout the first couple of weeks and it was leading up to the first game for Masconomet against North Andover. Signs plastered everywhere indicating support for everyone to attend the football game. The relevance of the team would take a back seat to the most important sport Masconomet fielded. The soccer teams were amongst the best in the entire state and this angered the football community. Masco never had a true chance at a championship in football due to the rumors that the play calling on both offense and defense were terrible. The Athletic department was at its wits end and they were giving the Coach and his staff one last year to produce a winning team.

With the fall sports dominating the school in Soccer and Football, it was the group of the nerds that Shawn took a liking too. These were the kids that wore glasses, picked their boogers and most likely were on their way to scoring a 1580 on their SAT's. If there was a clique that avoided drama by joining the chess club and other unpopular clubs, they were it. Nothing else mattered to them but their brains and their willingness to do what it took to excel at their education. It was the common ground Shawn found throughout all the groups because it was the relevancy of being noticed at school that drove each clique. There wasn't a day that would go by that someone didn't want to let others know of a new shirt or a new car that was given to them. Whether it is the heavy metal idiots or the nerds that walked together in the hallways, they all stuck together like glue.

The choice was quite easy to choose who to avoid and who to approach, but at-the-moment Shawn easily decided to lay low until the football season began. Every class he attended always had some beautiful young woman sitting near him or in front and he chose to focus on his classwork and her perfume. The ability to raise a daughter to look amazingly gorgeous and let her attend Masco was magic to Shawn's eyes. The group that was the most attractive were the girls that chased themselves crazy enough to garner the attention of all the boys. It was crazy to watch the feline in heat teasing the thousands of male cats to dare themselves to approach her. School at Masco was a cycle of constant drama with rumors that swirled quicker than the oxygen they would breath. The girls used the boys and the boys used the girls to a point where the daily rhetoric became a comical certainty. The young women attending Masco were mostly breath taking and it was as if they were all growing on trees of a golden harvest. The interest to befriend as many teens as he could would take its graceful time and his approach to be the comedian and sports star were about to take place. It was the day in the cafeteria a few weeks into Shawn's freshman year that changed everything for a group of metal heads that chose to bully the wrong teenager.

Chapter 13
Reckless Isolation

During the second week of school, the student body was preparing for the upcoming Saturday Football game against their arch rival North Andover. It was a balmy Wednesday early afternoon and Shawn had sat down with his friends for lunch in the cafeteria. The table they commonly settled in was located near the south exit of the cafeteria, farthest away from the hallway. Each day the tables became like seating arrangements for the entire lunch period, so it was always a routine that everyone was accustomed to. Since the boys were centrally located in a position to view all the tables in front of them, they didn't miss the daily interactions. That afternoon was different because the table that accompanied a group of metal heads were bullying another table beside them. They were located to the left of Shawn's table and Travis began gaining the attention of the table. With everyone's eyes focusing on the table near them, it was an orange laying on Shawn's tray that started a massive food fight between the entire cafeteria. The skinny teen wearing a Megadeath t-shirt quickly was yelling in the direction of another teen sporting a Motley Crue shirt. The metal heads had created an issue within their group and the orange's destination found its mark upon the eye of its intended target. Shawn had thrown a perfect strike five tables ahead and knocked the student to the ground.

"Food Fight", screamed a student close by. The moment no one expected reveled a massive food fight by everyone inside the cafeteria. Literally cartons of milk, fruit, trays, and pieces of pizza were seen flying abroad towards everyone that stood in

their way. The one isolated incident created mayhem for the teen and his band of friends took it personal. The fastball that everyone heard in the High School left a remarking impression on the student who was victimized. In a matter of sixty seconds, the food fight was over, but a new fight was just beginning. The tree smoking group of friends that sat with the victim approached Shawn about his antics.

"Hey punk, what is your freaking problem?" one teen from the group shouted.

"What you did to our friend Craig is not cool. How about we all kick your ass", replied the second teen.

Shawn smiled with a grin and began to walk away from the group as if they never existed. One of the teens in the group attempted to reach out and shove Shawn in the back and failed. The weakness of his arms unable to extend against the strength of Shawn's back, caused him to fall forward to the ground as Shawn continued walking away.

"Come back here jerkoff. We didn't say you could leave?" Screamed one of the teens.

Stopping in his tracks, Shawn turned around and began walking towards the four teens dressed in their Heavy Metal cheap t-shirts. Shawn walked up close to the boy on the far left and stared him deep into his eyes.

"I recommend you walk away and take your four sisters with you or this may not end well," Shawn stated.

Taking a deep breath, the frightened teen began to see the glaze inside of Shawn's eyes and they began to turn into a bright blue color. With no one around in the cafeteria except the hundreds of pounds of food littering the floor and tables, all four teens began to take notice. Shawn stood in front of them all and heeded a vast warning to leave him alone and walk away. Whether it was the drugs or the lack of sleep amongst them, they failed to take the hint Shawn had been radiating and declined to leave. The tall well-built teen on the far right appeared to Shawn as the leader of the group and he began to stand in front of him.

"What's your name?" Shawn asked.

"Does it really matter since I am about to knock your teeth out?" replied the brash teen.

"You know, I have had a simple pain here in my back molar and you would save me a dental visit", Shawn replied laughingly.

"You seem pretty confident for a guy who is about to get his butt kicked. Let's go punk", the boy mentioned.

"Kick his ass Dwayne with your boxing skills son", replied the scared teen on the far left.

Neglecting the foolish words from the scrawny chicken of the group, Shawn focused his attention towards Dwayne. Just as the teen with the Slayer shirt was about to attempt a punch, Principle Anderson spoke loudly.

"Boys, Boys. Move along and get to your classrooms now. Put away this childish behavior. Don't you see we are dealing with this mess of a cafeteria already?" The Principle pleaded.

All five of the boys had disbanded and began to walk towards the hallway and looking over at Dwayne, Shawn whispered softly.

"Not a good day to be a bad guy huh Dwayne?"

"We will continue this later, I can promise you that", Dwayne replied.

"Assumptions are the mother of all screw ups Dwayne. I would recommend looking the other direction if I were you. You could stay healthy that way", Shawn directed towards the group. Standing in the hallway in front of the cafeteria, Dwayne began to clinch his fists and looked over at his friends.

"Let's get his piece of crap now", Dwayne whispered.

"Get him", yelled one of the teens.

Shawn took notice that the four boys in dark t-shirts, long hair and dark jeans began running towards him. Instead of embroiling himself into beating the boys all over the hallway, he began to turn around and run down the hall towards the Junior High. With students looking on, the speedy teen ran as fast as anyone had ever seen while leaving the group of bullies to trail far behind. Within seconds of his departure from the front of the cafeteria, Shawn turned right at the first intersection of the hallway and raced through a smaller hallway. Passing a few doors to the classrooms that were still filling up with students, Shawn flew quickly through the double doors that lead into the yard of the High School. Upon seeing the distance of about two hundred yards to the back of the High School, Shawn continued onward. Shawn looked behind him to finally see the tree smoking idiots had keeled over in exhaustion.

"Damn he is fast. I don't think this is such a good idea and I have a bad feeling about this kid", replied Craig.

"Hello, McFly. Are you in there? (Dwayne tapped Craig on his head). *Did you already forget that jerk plastered your head with a piece of fruit? Let's focus here and plan something because I am going to get that clown"*, stated Dwayne.

The entire remaining hours of the afternoon were spent talking about the new kid in school that sparked an awesome food fight and dashed the hallways like speedy Gonzales. The swirling rumors began and spread like wildfire and the once quiet little sprout was now a flower and everyone wanted to speak to him.

It was a wild remaining week leading up to the Varsity football game and the practices revealed something to the coaches that they had been ignoring. Their attention was brought forth to a young freshman Quarterback with the cannon of an arm. Coach Bentley had remembered the brash young attitude that walked into his office weeks earlier. The entire Varsity team took notice and the staff decided to scrimmage the teams against each other. It was a matchup that would strengthen the curiosity of the coaches to entertain the new offense the freshman team was pondering. Considered the rookie team, it was the first time in many years that the starting Quarterback would control the entire offense and Shawn found himself across the line from the starters of the Varsity Defense.

The hour-long scrimmage in the middle of the week presented a huge problem for the Varsity team. A new kid from out of town just lit them up for over two hundred yards and four touchdowns in an offense they found themselves hard to defend against. The anger of the coaching staff that afternoon decided to obliterate the idea that the new offense would work against others in the Cape Ann League that year in 1987. The idea that a young fourteen-year-old inexperienced freshman could come in and implant a successful offense was ridiculous to the staff and they remained contingent to their running offense. When it came time for the freshman team to play their home game Friday afternoon, it was the first time in years that the entire stadium at Masco was packed for a non-Varsity game. The student body had succumbed to the rumors of the amazing arm who stood up to the Varsity team and chose to attend the game. The team of young teenagers who all began the Summer being led by the kid with the talent of a pro would now be following him in the trenches between the hashmarks of the football field.

Coach Swain controlled the defense while his young QB managed the plays at the line in the shotgun position. Shawn never intended on allowing others to understand his complicated play calling, but the signals were easy to relay and understand. The focus of the young man was to watch the defense react to their offensive formations and change the plays to accommodate all running lanes for his receivers. It was a brilliant idea that earlier obliterated the Varsity's defense and would create the same fate against the freshman of North Andover. The game lasted merely over a couple of hours and the result would suffice the crowd in a Forty-two to ten blow out with Shawn throwing five touchdowns and his new friend Richie running for another. The student body had witnessed the birth of a new dimension on offense and they were hoping that it would translate into the same kind of offense for the Varsity.

The next evening would bring forth the Varsity team on the same field where the Freshman team began the festivities. Coach Bentley was ready to bring his wishbone offense against the defending Cape Ann League Champs of North Andover. In the previous year, Masco went on the road against the same team and was blown out of the town in less than a few hours. It was the game plan of the coaching staff to start quickly by taking a page out of the new freshman QB's page. On the first play of the game that Saturday late morning, a long fly pattern by the outside wide receiver would be caught for a long touchdown. It was a complete surprise by the offense that stymied the North Andover defense. Placing eight men in the box to stop the run opened the chance for man to man coverage for Masco and they capitalized on it. Unfortunately, it was the only play of the game that would result in a score for the Chieftains of Masco. The coaching staff went back to the original plan of running the ball and with the scripted plays, the offense had no chance against the stout defense of North Andover. By the time the game ended, the crowd fizzled home and reluctantly had forgotten that their beloved Chieftains lost thirty-one to seven. It was going to be the beginning of a long season for the Varsity team while the young Quarterback that guided his freshman team to eight straight victories was about to lose his position for foolish reasons.

The year had progressed for Shawn quite nicely with his football team at seven wins and no losses and he started to create tension amongst the Varsity players. Masconomet's Varsity team was in-the-midst-of one of the largest losing streaks in the nation and they were just supplanted on ESPN for surrendering over four hundred yards rushing to a running back from the town of Ipswich. It was time for change and the rumors that the Coaching staff would not be returning next season were spreading like wild fire. The Senior Class had plenty of talent at every position, but the coaching staff was terrible at best and it was the freshman Quarterback they all resented. Hatred towards the success of the young man became hasty and it was the incident in the locker room that changed their perception. The Linebacker for the Chieftains Varsity team had enough and took it upon himself to walk up to Shawn's locker after practice had ended.

"Rook, what the hell are you trying to accomplish? You are making us all look bad", replied Greg Haber.

"Why don't you go back to where you came from or I will knock your ass back there", stated the Linebacker.

Pointing his finger into the direction of Shawn's face, he began to inch closer to touch him. Once his finger was placed into the cheek of the young freshman, Shawn grabbed the neck of the muscular linebacker and raised him a few inches off the ground. Struggling to breath after several seconds, the teen let him go as he fell to the ground.

"Don't ever put your fingers in my face or I will end you. Are we clear?", Shawn angrily questioned.

"Are you all listening? I want everyone's attention. I don't care if anyone has a problem with what I have brought to this program. I took the initiative in the beginning of the season to ask Coach Bentley if he would implement new plays into the play book. He refused guys and what do you all want me to say here? I tried and not one of you all season has done anything about it. You can be mad at me all you want but don't point fingers at me and think I won't retaliate. Better yet, I will prove to you all that

I am in the right. I will walk out of this locker room and I won't come back to help you. For all I care, you can each take a drink out of the mystery jar of piss and swallow because I am done with this", stated Shawn.

Shawn removed the remaining pads and practice jersey from his body and left the locker room with his hooded red sweatshirt covering his head. It was the silence of the locker room that dictated the attitude of the football team as they all watched Shawn remove himself. The remainder of the season for the Freshman team was in peril and they would go on to lose the next two games without scoring a single point. The Varsity football team performed as if they had all season with losses in their final three games without scoring one offensive touchdown.

It was the silence of that one day that seemed to bring down the entire team and without a hero, the fate of the program was in peril. The rumors that had progressed over time was now coming to fruition as the entire coaching staff was removed from Masconomet. It all came down to an early August meeting inside of the coach's office that some freshman know-it-all presented the gift that could have uplifted an entire community. The Coach had seriously hampered his legacy by ignoring the creative ideas that easily would have given him several more years of existence as a head coach. The chain reaction that started that day trickled down throughout the team and allowed its best player to walk away from a sports team for the second time in less than six months.

Chapter 14
The Shallow Season

There wasn't a sign of Shawn during the Winter season after that day in the locker room on any sports teams. The Basketball team was reluctant with its own problems at Head Coach and the Track and Wrestling teams both were trenched in several inches of snowy conditions. The young teen basically kept to himself since he had isolated everyone away from him. Week by week turned into months and it was the silence of Vincent that propelled Shawn to visit the water station behind his home. During the snowy season and passing Christmas, Shawn developed a liking to the countless weekends inside of the operations room buried under the ground. Never once considering the thoughts of how dangerous his new toy was to the world, Shawn would embrace its power and develop it to his liking.

A few days after Christmas, Shawn was indulging the freedom of a couple of weeks of school break and spent the entire time enshrined with knowledge. It was the complexity of the room that enticed him to learn as much as he could to control it. Each hour of embracing the electricity of magic that ran through the bones of his body tempted his fate to seek further refuge. When Shawn stood in the center of the fifteen- foot by fifteen-foot room, the controlling by his mind would ignite the visions upon the walls to begin searching for what he desired. In the beginning of school break, Shawn began dabbling with ideas of his High School and what it looked like from several hundred feet above. In an instant, all four walls were presented with a vision from a soaring eagle from far above. The wind blowing fresh air upon his face, it felt as if Shawn was floating above the ground he was standing on and portraying the reality of flying above his school. It felt real and each day that passed, Shawn would try different places in the world to search. Shawn was enthused with the power that he was now embraced with and it was a mistake that allowed him to realize this machine was more powerful than anticipated.

Late one afternoon in early January of 1988, Shawn awoke from a late nap and began venturing down to the pumping station. Crawling towards the room through the tunnels like so many times before, Shawn decided to control the candles coveting the path towards the isolated room. Since he had chosen the direction of the path many times before, he attempted to reach his destination in the pitch dark. The walk seemed endless, but his hand reached the door for what appeared to be the same room. Once he opened the door, the atmosphere appeared to remain the same. Standing in the center of the room, the lights upon the walls were different. Colored in fluorescent green and purple, Shawn began once again to control his mind. Instead of the visions appearing on the four walls, a sudden rush of water could be felt through his body. Shawn opened his eyes and noticed that the floor below him was now isolated into just the small square he stood on. The remaining part of the floor became submerged in water and then started to encircle Shawn under and over his body without touching him. In a circulated motion, the vortex of water created an energy field of sorts in front him. With his keen eyes, Shawn began looking into the vision that started to appear inside of the circular apparition. Reaching out with both hands to his sides, his fingers felt the rush of the cool water as if he was under a water fall. The cold breeze rushed upon his face and the faded space in front of him became clearer, while he envisioned his mind of where he would be in twenty-five years.

The visions were confusing and without any hesitation, Shawn's knees became weak and the blurry apparition soon engulfed his body. Closing his eyes, he felt his body project itself into a time warp of sorts and his skin became painful to the touch. In less than five seconds, Shawn felt the weight of his legs touch the ground as he opened his eyes. Left standing in the middle of a busy highway, he attempted to run as quickly as he could. Unable to determine where he was, he hurried to a sidewalk and noticed a man approaching him with a red sweatshirt and winter cap upon his head. He was jogging with what appeared to be headphones covering his ears. No face to recognize, the jogger paced beyond him in a quick manner without acknowledging who he was. The young teen found his eyes staring at a blinking sign attached to a bank and the date and time on the digital display read March 4th, 2013. How in the world could Shawn have realized that he would be standing in the future? Dazed beyond belief, Shawn appeared to walk around the bank lost and bewildered. Peaking at a parking lot next to the east side of the bank, a crying from a woman was overheard.

"Wow, these cars look really cool", Shawn said to himself.

Twenty-five years into the future culminated a lot of progress, but Shawn wasn't concerned because his attention drew close to the whimpers of a female near him. Able to become transparent, Shawn's body passed through the back door of the young lady's vehicle and he found himself sitting behind her. The woman was very beautiful with long brunette hair and the ID hanging on the rearview mirror revealed her name as Kimberly Meadows. Unable to see him in the backseat, Shawn began to realize that he was invisible while looking down at his hands. Clear as day, the idea that the jogger and his Kim girl were unable to comprehend who Shawn was, scared him. Unaware of his ghostly appearance, how was he able to find himself twenty-five years ahead? The tearful voice of the girl in the front seat began speaking.

"What am I going to do? I can't go on living without him God. Please allow me the strength to get through this. I miss him so much and I need him more than anything right now," Kimberly cried out.

Unsure of what her problem was, Shawn quickly escaped away from the vehicle and walked back to the place he first began. Opening his mind as he closed his eyes, the larger circular blurry space appeared and swallowed Shawn gracefully. Ten seconds would pass before he opened his eyes once more and found himself back in the darkened room with lights of purple and green.

"How the hell did I do that? Yes, that was so awesome. I want to spend more time traveling and figure this thing out for real", Shawn said to himself.

Over the course of the next several days, Shawn would venture into the unknown places from his past and future and he realized that he was only able to travel to places he had already been to or was going to. It was slight downplay from what he wanted, but without Vincent or Sebastian to guide him, he chose to control his destiny. Shawn began learning more about himself and he took the chance to spend time understanding who Kimberly Meadows was. When that second chance arose, something blocked Shawn from visiting the same place. He suddenly thought a glitch in his mind was preventing him from visiting her, but maybe it was another reason. Without hesitation, the School year began once again while Shawn kept to himself. It was the months that passed that opened the new Season of Spring, inviting the chance for Shawn to shine once again. His lesson towards those who doubted his abilities were far and gone and now it was time to enjoy his favorite sport.

There wasn't a hallway in school that didn't catch the attention with the many posters of Varsity Baseball tryouts right around the corner. Shawn knew in his heart that it was an easy process to become the best pitcher the team had, so he made the brave decision to skip the invitation. He was going to revel himself with group of kids who needed him more. The freshman team was the epitome of those teens who were not good enough to make the Varsity and Junior Varsity teams. On the day that tryouts began for the freshman team, many familiar faces put a smile on Shawn's once unhappy grill. The feeling was easily reciprocated as their team now had an ultimate ace to begin winning baseball games. No freshman team had ever finished the season with a winning record according to the coach. On the first day of tryouts, Shawn stood up and spoke to all the players.

"Guys, I promise you that I will give you a hundred percent as long as you give me the same. We can do something no other freshman team has accomplished. What do you say?" asked Shawn

Everyone on the team replied with a positive response and once the first day of tryouts had completed, the team was set to endure a couple of weeks of practice before their first game. For the duration of the practices, Shawn would find himself as one of the favorites by the Coach and he would make him team captain. With a combination of speed and power, the Coach recommended that he be placed second in the lineup to help assist in garnering as many at bats as he could. The respect of the Coach to finally understand who he was, Shawn developed a huge liking to his new mentor. Coach Anderson was a mean old drunk that was heavily overweight and didn't care what others thought of him. It was the combination of his recognition for talent and his bragging of his all-star player that angered the Varsity team.

It was during the last week of practices that Coach Anderson addressed his team and broke the news delighting his eyes.

"Boys, we are preparing today to play the Varsity team in a seven-inning scrimmage that they have requested. Who here wants to go home and admit they are scared?" The Coach asked.

Not one of his players raised any doubts in his mind and as they all began to take the field for a brief practice, the Varsity team began showing up with their uniforms on. The site of the red shirts seemed to be a bit unfair, but it wasn't going to matter because Shawn was going to lead his young men against this formidable opponent. The Varsity team was led by its hard throwing right handers and his face looked familiar to Shawn. The same player who brought the Summer Championship to his Middleton town was also a part of the Varsity team.

"Shawn, you are going to have your work cut out for you against this team and I want you to throw all seven innings. I am asking this of you because everyone else on this team sucks, so please make me proud", asked his Coach.

Shawn disagreed with his coach because he developed a rapport with this freshman team mates and he was about to go up against the Varsity team for the second time this year. The game that became a last-minute decision was to be witnessed by only the players and coaches and the Freshman from Masco were ready. Each player on the Freshman team equipped with a pair of sweatpants and the Jersey that their Coach had provided them, the game began with Shawn on the mound. The cold air coming from the northerly wind would drop the temperature ten degrees from game time to the first few innings. Despite the conditions, Shawn began mowing down one player after the other from the Varsity team. With his fluid motion and array of four separate pitches, not one batter would reach base in the first five innings of the game. Dick Sawgrass was the coach of the Varsity team and his reaction to the poise by the opposing pitcher was priceless. His team down by three runs in the sixth, be began to attempt a change that would lose the faith of his young team. He commanded his first batter in the sixth inning to bunt the ball. The hard throwing right hander pierced the inside of Homeplate for strike one as the batter withdrew his bunt. The second pitch thrown would buckle the knees of the batter as the tipped foul would end up in the catcher's glove. With two strikes, Coach Sawgrass relentlessly asked his batter to swing away. With the pitch count remaining at around fifty-six pitches, Shawn easily released the baseball from his fingers and the cut fastball again ended up in the same spot the first pitch ended. The called third strike invited the batter to the bench and the results for the next two batters would remain the same. The Freshman pitcher had a two-hit shutout entering the bottom of the sixth and with a slim three run lead, the first two batters reached base by walk. The next batter in the Freshman lineup to step to the plate with his two hits and 2 runs scored, Shawn dug into the batter's box.

Coach Sawgrass had seen enough and asked his best pitcher to come into the game. The sight of the pitcher looked very familiar to Shawn with his tall frame and lightning fastball. The sigh of relief by the Varsity Coach would soon turn into a dramatic showdown with Rick Antonio and the Freshman phenom. The result of the last altercation did not end well for the tall pitcher, but he was seeking redemption. This time around he was going to let the past go and seek a way to right the mistake he made before with his two-strike curveball that still hadn't landed. Taking a deep breath, Rick delivered a look back to his catcher while gathering his sign from the stretch. Winding up to set his position on the mound, Rick buckled down and threw his first pitch as hard as he could and without hesitation, he tried his hardest to hit Shawn. The baseball projected itself from the tips of Ricks two fingers onto it's intended target. The velocity quickly gazing upon his face, Shawn slowly reached out to catch the ball with his left hand. In amazement, the mouths of nearly everyone on the diamond stood in shock.

"If you are going to challenge me, lets keep this clean Rick", yelled Shawn.

He threw the ball back to Rick and Shawn dug back into the box waiting for the next pitch. Rick stood in disbelief that some rookie would just grab a ninety mile per hour fastball without flinching a lick. The presence of a supernatural force could be felt by all and they were witnessing the miracle unfold beyond their wildest imaginations. The second pitch delivered towards Shawn left his bat quicker than it arrived as the sound of thunder deafened the silence of the field. The second straight at bat against Rick would result in a homerun for Shawn and there was basically nothing left to prove. The Freshman team would score a few more runs in route to a ten to zero score and it was the beginning of an amazing season for the young players. Upon shaking hands with each other after the scrimmage ended, the Varsity players would indulge their own conversations with the amazing freshman. With available space on the team, they all tried to convince Shawn to join them as their teammates. The same answer was given to Coach Sawgrass resulting in Shawn remaining with his young team. Shawn's choice would result in two separate seasons for the teams from that scrimmage. The fate of the Varsity team would culminate in a state playoff absence for the second consecutive year and a five hundred record. On the other hand, Shawn and his young team would obliterate all the competition in route to a very respectable fifteen wins against two losses. Coach Bentley had gotten the season he well deserved and used his success to retire from coaching. Coach Sawgrass had a team for the next season that would include a pitching staff of both Rick and Shawn and he was delighted to realize that he had his best team in a very long time. Once the baseball season ended, it marked end of the schoolyear and Shawn's Freshman year ended perfectly. It was his imagination anticipating a Summer full of venturing through his past and future, but it was a planned party that would change him forever. The Coast Guard picnic planned for the first Saturday that coming weekend would indulge many to conjoin on a small island where destiny would collide with fate.

Chapter 15
Katie

Saturday morning began early for Shawn and his family because today was the day that the Coast Guard planned a gathering at the oldest light house in the United States. Encased amongst the busy traffic in Boston Harbor, Boston Light was a plateau upon an island surrounded by the water from the Atlantic Ocean. Once the family arrived and parked their truck on the base in downtown Boston, they met up with several others that were waiting to take a boat to the island. Equipped with a smile and his Mother's intuition, a beautiful woman eclipsed the peripheral of an eye destined to fall in love.

"Dad, who is the girl over there?" his son asked.

"Son, that's Katie my boss's daughter. Let me introduce you", his father replied.

Walking side by side to meet the angel he couldn't withdraw his eyes from, his father introduced them.

"Captain, this is my son Shawn," his father mentioned.

"Shawn, I have heard a lot about you and it's nice to meet you. This is my daughter Katie and she is right around your age. You are fourteen, correct?" Captain Banker questioned.

"Yes, I am sir. It is very nice meeting you" Shawn replied while shaking his hand.

"Hi Shawn, it is really nice to meet you as well", Katie replied softly.

Keeping his distance, Shawn never relinquished his eyes away from the gorgeous brunette. She was standing just a shade over five foot with perfect teeth, her hair as elegant as the shirt she was wearing, and hair glistening in the sun. Shawn instantly fell in love with her brown eyes and perfect lips. Graced with the body of an angel, Shawn walked away in the opposite direction to join his mother as the ship began to board. The sight of Boston from the Harbor was a breathtaking event as the several

 ships and buildings from afar set the mood of a million-dollar painting in Shawn's mind. The brief trip to the island lasted mere minutes, but the gathering of one hundred people or more indulged themselves on a very large island with a gorgeous lighthouse encased near the waterline. The rock formations surrounding the island were as if the land was carved to perfection and the few homes located on the island belonged to those preserving the oldest lighthouse

in the world. As explained by the Captain of the ship on the way over to the island, the lighthouse was founded in the mid 1700's and has been a mainstay for the city of Boston. Witnessing her Harbor suffer through the Boston Massacre, she stood as monumental as the Statue of Liberty from New York. It was a symbol that has stood for centuries and the Coast Guard was responsible for the upkeep of the island. Today was the day that the men in uniform would hold an enormous gathering amongst the families of the military and it would last all day.

The events planned for the picnic would involve flag football, softball, music and plenty of food and beverages for all. Shawn found himself listening to all the stories about his Father's job, but his mind was concentrating on the girl that he met earlier. Walking around the island in search of the princess that touched his heart, he peaked around the corner and saw Katie sitting on her knees and painting a heart on a large rock next to the shoreline. Just the slight glimpse of her beautiful curves and amazing beauty was enough to crawl over to where she was painting.

"You are a good painter Katie, what does that heart stand for?" Shawn asked.

Looking up at the handsome boy she met earlier, she replied swiftly. *"I was hoping that this boy I met recently would see it and realize my heart is bleeding."*

Wow, this boy must be special and seems to be very lucky if you ask me", Shawn replied.

"Yes, you are Shawn. Took you long enough to find me by the way", Katie joked.

"Punctuality isn't my strong suit, so will you forgive me?" Shawn asked.

"Just this one time, but you now have to make it up to me", Katie stated.

"Whatever you ask is my command. I am all yours", Shawn replied.

Reaching out to grab Katie's hand, they began to walk side by side throughout the island learning about each other. While the day saw the sun rise from the east and nearly settle to the west, Shawn and Katie were inseparable. They both learned that they lived nearly ninety miles away from each other and the long distance would test their new relationship. Katie was a daughter of a soon to be retiring Coast Guard Captain living in the dunes of Cape Cod. She was starting her second year High School this coming Fall and they both realized they were only one-month part in age. Katie was an amazing painter and loved the same music as Shawn and the several hours they would spend together that day, it took the passion these young teens shared to convince their parents that they were only friends. The teens both understood the ramifications of a love shared between them and Katie did her best to hide that from her Father. Shawn invested the time to gather everything he could about Katie to fall hard for the girl he met early that morning. The ten hours of excitement was more than enough to realize there were two less lonely people in the world and with a few minutes to spare, the two would hide amongst the buildings to share the passionate kiss that bound their hearts together. Staring into her beautiful eyes, Shawn saw the simplicity of the fireworks glaring within her pretty face and soon reached forward to touch her lips. Holding his hand softly, the weight of Shawn pressed up against her chest and the secure feeling of the young man she was falling for gave her the warmth she had long embraced. The first kiss lasted minutes while the warmth of their bodies lasted forever during their embrace. The cool air upon the Harbor invited those back to the boat to set sail and out of each other's company for the evening. The reluctance of their eyes would lock the entire time the ship brought the families back to the base. The glorious lights beaming from the tall buildings of downtown Boston placed a spotlight on the two teens that were venturing into each other's hearts.

Arriving on shore to head home with this family, Shawn gave Katie his address and number to contact him. Calling him from home would cost his parents an insane amount of money, so the relationship would have to be maintained by mail. Quietly leaving their love for each other away from their parents, the strength of a million men could never break apart what had just been earned amongst the lonely lovers. The endless nights of writing Katie throughout the Summer blended in with the responsibility of venturing into his own life and balancing his future and past. Shawn decided to exclude his special circumstances about who he really was from Katie and his focus was to attain her attention. The first month without each other was hard and Shawn spent his days under the pumping station while his early evenings found him on the diamond. Summer baseball had started again, and Shawn entered the Babe Ruth League with a chip on his shoulder. Regardless of what others thought about him, Shawn showed up to each practice and demanded a lot more from himself as an all-star performer in the league. The teams he would now face in the beginning of the summer would consist of towns farther away. The advantage to what he was facing would allow him to further study the different players that eventually played on the High School teams. The other baseball teams began to learn about the teen's ability to take over games. His aggressive baserunning, batting and pitching skills were a rare combination and most opposing coaches has no answer for the talented upcoming sophomore at Masco.

While the teams across the Northshore were planning strategies to keep Shawn at bay, he was being a normal teenager at home while reading letters from his girlfriend. Shawn's parents had announced that they were headed out of town to handle a family member's passing away and he would be on his own for three to four days. Trusting their son to handle himself while they were gone, Shawn was given enough time to inform Katie of a brilliant plan to lure her in his home. For the plan to work, Shawn had to call her from his home phone and the charges for a long-distance call were astronomical. If this was going to remain undetected, he was going to quickly make his point and move forward. Dialing her phone number, the dial tone felt like an eternity while the pits of harmful pain settled in his stomach.

"Katie, it's me baby", Shawn nervously stated.

"Oh my god, how were you able to call me? Never mind, forget I asked you. I miss you with all of my heart Shawn Lee", Katie stated.

"I don't have much time, but can I ask you something. Do you love me?" Shawn quickly asked.

"Yes, I do with all of my heart. What's wrong? You are scaring me", Katie responded.

"Something has come up and I am all alone from Thursday until Monday. Is there any way you can get away for a couple of days?" Shawn asked.

"Call you back in thirty minutes. Love you my handsome man", Katie replied and hung up.

The next twenty minutes were nerve racking as Shawn began pacing around his small home. Without much of a place to walk and unable to leave the house, he nervously prayed with his entire soul that Katie would respond with good news. As the thirty-minute mark surpassed him, Shawn began to doubt his gorgeous girlfriend was able to get away and the negativity angered him.

"This is just my luck. I find a beautiful woman and she just had to be over ninety miles away. Good job dumb ass", Shawn told himself.

As he began to sink more doubts into his heart, the phone rang with a deafening sound. Attempting to pick up the receiver as fast as he could, the phone dropped onto the ground. Fumbling as nervous as Earnest Byner on the Denver Broncos two-yard line, he attempted to gather himself. Shawn took a breath and picked up the phone with highest anticipation.

"Hello", Shawn replied.

"Do you love me?" Katie asked

"Oh no, is everything ok?" Shawn asked frightened.

"Everything is great and just got off the phone with my best friend Becca. I am heading over there in the morning and she knows about you already. You must figure a way Shawn to get me up there to you. If you want me there for the entire four days your parents are gone, then you come get me", stated Katie.

"Baby, I will do what it takes to get you, so be ready. I will call you before I come get you, ok. Love you", Shawn happily replied while hanging up the phone.

Since his parents were leaving the next day to head to Connecticut for a funeral, Shawn made the decision to use his Father's car. The plan was for them to leave early in the morning and he would attempt to drive out a few hours later. During that entire day, Shawn and Katie spoke a few more times about their schedules and the route that was easiest to take to pick her up. The plan seemed easy as Shawn would travel through the city of Boston and Interstate 93 would lead him to Route 3. The drive would be smooth sailing through the morning traffic and onto a town called Braintree. Katie's older friend was able to drive, and she was offering to help her new boyfriend by bringing Katie a little closer to Boston. Shawn packed his Mother's atlas in his bag and placed it into his closet for the trip. The two teens were excited to see each other and the minutes on the clock turned into hours and night approached without warning. The eeriness of the moon staring back into his room painted a brightness for the wilderness to see. It was the surrounding population of all the creatures of the night that protected the disciple of Vincent. The stillness of the night would soon fade from dark to dawn and his parents had already left by the time Shawn woke up.

The plan was finally rolling a long and the young man decided to leave early knowing the sixty-mile journey was far ahead. The nervousness of the young man stepping inside of his Father's 1968 Chevrolet, was previously used to teach him how to drive. Since he was used to the tough clutch in the car, Shawn turned the key and began to leave his neighborhood. Without any recourse and a Driver's license, the young man in love with the gorgeous brunette from Cape Cod was on his way to prove his worth. Living near Interstate 95, Shawn would delve onto the highway during a busy Thursday morning of Boston traffic. It was his intention to finally catch Interstate 93 south and drive through the city of Boston where he would meet up with Route 3. The plan seemed effortless and he would never have to leave any major highways and avoid backroads. His Father's red beast was a smooth car on the highway with a small exception. The exhaust leak below the car's cabin wasn't anything to cheer about, but everything else seemed perfect. Who cared that Shawn was about to spend the next two hours breathing the emissions from his Father's legendary car and possibly passing out. It was the destination that fueled his passion to arrive gracefully and spend the next few days with Katie.

The path leading to Interstate 93 didn't take as long as anticipated passing the towns of Wakefield and Reading. It was the exit that began the next step in getting through the toughest part of his drive amongst the traffic into the northern parts of the city. Katie has previously mentioned that it would have been smarter to venture around Boston through Interstate 95. It encircled the outskirts of the town and Quincy would have led him to Route 3 a lot easier. Since Shawn knew the path quite often venturing into Boston with his Father for work, he chose his memory over the advice of his girlfriend. Katie was the type that allowed her beau to find out on his own and the hours were counting down in anticipation. The bumper to bumper traffic on the Interstate was annoying because Shawn wasn't used to the car's touchy clutch and his legs began to feel weak. Continuously for over an hour, Shawn would disguise the pain he felt in his legs with the pride of his heart. Inching closer through the city of Boston, Shawn needed to leave the next exit to allow his legs to gather the circulation needed to finish the trip. The availability of the next off ramp would lead Shawn and his car to 4th street in South Boston. Once off the exit, he began driving east away from the overpass to hopefully stop at an available gas station or lot. The first opportunity arose at a vacant lot on the corner of Foundry Street and 4th. It was clear that the next light ahead was a busy intersection, so Shawn turned left into the vacant lot and parked his Father's car on the corn. Getting out and stretching his legs, a voice from behind him startled the young teen.

"1978 Chevelle. Son, this is an instant classic", stated the voice behind him.

"Yes, she sure is. My Father's pride and joy", replied Shawn.

The balding gentleman with the large glasses covering his eyes, Shawn looked over to notice a large heavy-set man smoking a cigarette while sitting in an older four-door Buick. The car quietly parked beside the Chevelle, the older gentleman who had spoken, was now looking into Shawn's car from outside.

"What is a young man like yourself doing in my neighborhood?" the older man asked.

"I live north of here and was on my way to pick up my girlfriend in Braintree when my legs were tired", Shawn replied quickly.

"Come closer young man, let me get a good look at you", he asked.

Without a blink, Shawn walked over to the elderly man and positioned himself in front of him. The man with the large sunglasses began to reach out to grab Shawn's shirt and pull him closer to his chest.

"Son, do you know who I am?" he asked loudly

"Let me guess, the tooth fairy", Shawn jokingly replied.

"Look at who we got here Stevie, a fucking comedian in our midst. I like this kid a lot. He's got balls", the older man stated.

Looking back at his partner Steve as to motion him out of the car, the swift looking South Boston muscle found himself standing next to both.

"Kid, you better watch your mouth around these parts", replied Stevie.

"Get back in your car and tell your loving girlfriend that you had a dance with Whitey Bulger and you walked away alive. Got it?" The old man aggressively stated.

Whitey let Shawn go from his grasp and opened the car door for the young teen. Turning the key and engaging the clutch, the old man lowered himself to the open window of the Chevelle. *"You enjoy your day now and I better not see you again",* murmured Whitey.

As quickly as he arrived earlier, Shawn turned his vehicle right onto 4th street from the corner and proceeded to get back on the Interstate where he would continue his plan of picking up Katie. Thoughts of the unknown man were moved relentlessly to the back of his mind while his heart took over his emotions. He knew that he would be able to revisit the recent confrontation from the older man at another date. His desire to rush into the arms of the girl he had met not too long ago was racing in his mind. The remaining part of the trip to Braintree would settle itself as Shawn drove with the greatest of ease. The coolness of the wind against each side of his face from the Boston air would tempt his thoughts of the next few days.

With the trip basically almost over, Shawn approached the Route 3 exit towards Braintree and it would be one more exit remaining before he saw Katie. The Elm street exit was coming up next and it was the plan to meet her at the corner of Elm and Church street. The heart of the teen illegally driving his Father's vehicle on the road took a back seat to his morals as each beat pounded his chest. The excitement glaring in his eyes, the exit was now completely behind him and the gas station located at the corner ended his route. Parking his car at the gas pump, he heard a whimper from the side of the parking lot behind him. In the distance, he looked and saw Katie approaching at a fast pace one step at a time. The embracement of the teens allowed their lips to touch while the peaking of the sun pierced the small space between their bodies.

"Oh my god, you are here. I can't believe this is happening", Katie happily commented.

"Trust me, it was an adventure getting here and I am so glad to see your pretty face", Shawn replied.

The two walked over to Katie's friend and with their calm greetings turning into sudden goodbyes, Shawn and Katie ventured onto the highway system that Boston had to offer. The trip back to Topsfield didn't take as long arriving because once the two had passed the city, the Highway was much clearer. The bench seat in his Father's car invited Katie to lean up against Shawn the entire trip back to his home. The two young teens had found themselves bound to the reluctance of how sudden time would pass, promising to capitalize on every second. Silence between them as Shawn drove through the beautiful scenery of Interstate 95 towards home. The embracing arms surrounding her boyfriend offered solace in a way that he had never felt before. The thoughts of giving in to Katie and explaining to her who he really was began to prosecute his ideas of a pleasant weekend. If given the proper time to evaluate the premise of how he could bring forth this idea, Katie wouldn't care.

The teens had arrived at Shawn's home and with still over a half day left, Katie invited herself into the side door of the Kitchen and into the awaiting sheets of Shawn's bedroom. Shawn closed his door behind him and as Katie began to kneel on his bed, she reached over to kiss him. The feeling of her tongue inside of his mouth would penetrate an innocence that slowly scared him. The sudden nervousness of his knees beginning to buckle would relegate him to sit beside her. The trembling of each other's bodies exuberated the inexperience of the teens and it was the first time they had imagined a day like this happening.

The calm breeze rushing up against the house offered a symphony of silence as the two would lie under the sheets holding each other. The previous few minutes prior to the moment allowed them to embrace gracefully as their bodies would create a heat to sooth the coolness of the room. The time was now and they both reluctantly dared to remove themselves from the positions their bodies lie in. The afternoon crept upon them as each hour passed them by lying in the comfort of their arms. Holding each other occasionally kissing for several minutes at a time, Shawn remained a perfect gentleman without taking advantage of his new girlfriend. It was the security that Katie enjoyed most with the man that she found her heart encompassed with.

"I love you Shawn with all of my heart and I pray this moment will never wilt away. I feel like we are both in Heaven and please be at my side forever", Katie whispered.

"Lying beside you has given me a new reason to live and I am not going anywhere Katie. I am yours forever and I love you too", Shawn replied with his gentle voice.

The teens would lie with each other for another hour as the late afternoon approached them. Unable to really leave into town to show his girlfriend to everyone, they would stay inside for the duration of the evening. Katie took it upon herself to make them dinner with whatever she could find in the refrigerator. The young woman from Cape Cod piqued the interest of Shawn's senses with a culmination of garlic and strong seasonings. The smell was amazing and when it was time to serve dinner, Shawn gathered a few candles his mother hid in the cabinet and set the mood for a romantic evening. Katie was everything Shawn could dream of and it was the conversation that night into the early morning that drew the most interest for each other. It would be realized by both that they were raised in the same type of house holds and given the same sort of life resembling a strict environment.

"My dad would absolutely kill me if he knew I took his car", Shawn stated.

"Oh yeah, I will one-up you on that comment sir. My Father would kill us both if he knew I was staying with you", Katie replied jokingly.

The flickering light from the candles that brightened their faces in the dim lit room shined a new perspective for them both. Katie had finally broken free from her home in a way that shadowed the abuse suffered by her father. Shawn had also taken solace in the form of enjoying the freedom from the grasp of all the pressure against him. He was always supplanted as the hero that everyone looked up to all year and Katie offered him peace. During the remainder of that early evening, the two would sit across from each other telling stories for hours of their past and enjoying the company the conversations brought with them.

With their heavy eyes and calm darkness coveting the entire house, Katie and Shawn took turns taking showers and readying themselves for bed. Upon them ending up in the same position under the sheets as they had earlier in the day, there was a noticeable change. The smooth bodies of both teens were pressed up against each other and the engagement of Shawn's kiss would invite Katie to lay on top of him. The once subtleness displayed by both teenagers would now bring their bodies together as one. It was the ease of Katie that made if very relaxing for Shawn to enjoy making love to her that entire

evening and when both awoke that morning, they found each other wrapped in their arms. Love was thick in the morning air as the pleasant sounds of the forest by his window were reluctant to allow the lovers from sleeping any longer. Shawn opened his eyes to his surprise that Katie was as beautiful as the day he saw her. Her beautiful curly hair and the curvature of her perfect face laying on the pillow beside him withdrew a small tear from the corner of his eye. *"How could something so beautiful be so deserving to him?"* he asked himself quietly.

"Good Morning my handsome prince", Katie whispered.

"Good Morning baby. Did I wake you?" Shawn asked.

"Yes, you did, and I am glad because you are still here. I was so afraid to wake up and be back in my own bed", Katie replied.

Katie's hair smelled of Lavender and her beautiful bare skin became soft to the touch. Shawn began kissing her neck and shoulders as the delight of his lips created a mass of goosebumps all over Katie's body. The gentleness of the young man who held his girl in his arms would present a huge challenge for the afternoon. Would they want to stay in bed all day or would he want to entice his girlfriend to stick to the pre-planned schedule. The day was Friday and Shawn had a game that evening at the baseball field. His friend was going to pick him up to attend the game, so it was decided that the two would arise from the ashes of their cotton heaven and move on with their day. The late morning of breakfast and conversation turned itself into a remote decision to begin explaining to Katie who he was. Since it was only Friday, he had the entire weekend to express to his new love that he was a disciple of Satan and that there was no set plan for him on Earth. Could a conversation be so easily told over a bagel and coffee?

The wits of the teen abruptly made the wise choice to slowly break it gently to his beautiful girl over the course of the next few days. Since his parents were prodigies of the music generation, the family had a large stereo in the living room and Katie immediately took notice. While Shawn was cleaning up the dishes, Katie began listening to the radio. Watching his girlfriend dance in his long-sleeved-button down shirt wearing nothing but a smile, it was the amazing curves that captured his eye. Katie was well beyond her years with curves of a young adult and her amazing body glistened amongst the rays of the sun in his living room. She took a major liking to the hair band era and the sounds of the new album released by Poison excited her.

"See, this is real music and it just get me overly excited", Katie replied.

Turning the music down as Shawn sat down on the couch, she began to explain her fixation on the types of music she enjoyed.

"I love Whitesnake and bands like Cinderella, Poison, White Lion, David Lee Roth. The list goes on and on and I just don't think I could ever live without music", Katie steadily stated.

"Ever since I can remember, my parents played their music non-stop. From country music to rock and roll, you can name it and I have heard it. I am very interested in learning more about this music you like, and I will get the tapes", replied Shawn.

Shawn had been introduced to bands like Def Leppard and Guns N' Roses at school and the music was quite tempting. The age of the guitar and tons of hair spray dominated the decade and the radio made everyone aware of how overplayed it could be. The stereo in Shawn's room had a variety of radio stations that would play the songs from different era's because he had a liking to all music. Shawn's favorite bands were Tears for Fears, Survivor, Europe and he made it clear to his girlfriend that music was the basis for his existence as well. The conversation over music could have lasted an entire week, but the realism that the day didn't want to be wasted, Shawn moved the couple along. The afternoon was spent touring the neighborhood and meeting the boys down the street that happen to be playing baseball in front of their homes.

"Holy crap man, where did you find this girl Shawn?" John asked.

"The sky is raining Angels man, that's all I can say. Consider me lucky I guess", Shawn smartly replied.

The boys were captivated at how beautiful Katie was and her presence interrupted the baseball game they were playing amongst each other.

"Hey, can I play?" Katie asked the boys.

Since Shawn was going to pitch that evening against the first-place team out of Newburyport, he reluctantly played with the boys. Watching his girlfriend manhandle the competition in front of her, she was an angel in disguise. Her knowledge of baseball, music and love were all he needed to find the woman he hoped to spend his entire life with. The huge obstacle of course was the distance and their parents, but who in their right mind at his age could he find perfection wrapped behind the skin of a goddess? Asking himself over and over if he truly deserved her, it was the risk of temptation that followed his true instinct. The baseball game lasted for a while and with the remaining afternoon winding down, the two lovers enjoyed each other's company in front of the television until it was time for Shawn's game to start.

Shawn's friend had arrived to pick him up and with Katie by his side, they were on their way to the baseball field in town.

"Katie, this is Michael. Mike, this is the girl I told you about", Shawn stated.

"Wow dude, you were not kidding about her. Katie, it is an absolute pleasure to make your acquaintance", Mike stated.

"Mike, it is very nice to meet you as well. So, let's play some baseball, shall we boys", Katie directed.

"Katie, have you seen your man play ball?" Mike asked.

"First time and I can't wait", Katie said looking over at Shawn.

The teens were on their way to the huge game against one of their arch rivals. It was the one team that Shawn wanted to beat since he was unable to pitch against them during his freshman year. Sitting on the bench and given a day off, the team from Newburyport plastered Masco fifteen to one, ending their undefeated season at twelve games. For Shawn and everyone on the Babe Ruth Team, this was pure redemption. This was the fourth game of the season as both teams sat on top of the standings. The Babe Ruth league was a substantial platform for most young teenagers that were familiar with the High School Varsity team. Shawn was going to find himself playing for this team until he graduated High School and it familiarized him with

his competition. The faces would become familiar later in the School year, but for now Shawn was focused on depleting the egos of the visiting team. With Katie in the stands, Mike began telling everyone who Shawn brought with him. All eyes were focused on the girl that became their biggest fans. Waving at the boys at the Topsfield bench, the whispers back to Shawn was music to his ears. With an occasional eye looking back at the beautiful woman in the stands, the suddenly shy girl from the town of Cape Cod would lower her head to ease the attention she brought Shawn. She was in full understanding that this was his game and he needed to focus. The view that Katie had in the stands allowed her to envision the type of hero that Shawn was to all the parents and players surrounding her. Strangers in the stands, having never met her, spoke to her about how amazing her boyfriend was. Story after story of how he was the most dominant pitcher to enter Topsfield in a ton of years. The smile from ear to ear enticed Katie to listen to every person who had nice things to say about the man she was in love with.

The game existing before her very eyes had blossomed into a portrait of perfection. The man that won her heart was sending a clear message to the other team that the night belonged to him. The young man wearing the number thirteen jersey was striking out almost every single batter while his few at bats resulted in two triples and a single. The crowd followed their emotions as the final score of eleven to zero graced them with celebration. All were presented with the graces of Shawn's girlfriend and it was the look that everyone gave her which excited him. Wishes of good luck throughout the ball field were presented to each team and later that evening Katie blessed Shawn with the surprise of his lifetime. Dressed in sheets and each other's bodies, Katie made love to Shawn throughout his wildest dreams while the glow of her perfect body was present from the rays of the moon. It was the moment that Shawn had wished upon himself to be graced by the gift of god and his eyes caught the glimpse of a shadow in his bedroom window. Katie's hips swayed quickly over Shawn's lower body and with her eyes fixated on the ceiling above, her violent trembling soon followed by releasing her aggression in a rage of loud moans.

"Baby, are you ok? Did I do something wrong?" Shawn asked.

Unable to speak because of her heavy breathing, Katie looked down at Shawn and touched his face with her finger tips.

"Oh, hell no, you did everything right. Give me a moment to catch my breath", Katie exhaustingly stated.

While Katie had laid beside Shawn, his eyes were still fixated on the feeling that someone was watching them. Unsure of the mystery laying behind his window, Shawn couldn't see Vincent in the distance. Standing in anger watching his disciple and his girlfriend making love, it was time that he began making an example of his young prodigy.

Chapter 16
Headed for a Heartbreak

Saturday morning was the beginning of a long weekend, but someone failed to let the two lovers in on the secret. The rainy storms that morning had failed to awaken them as they laid comatose with nightmares dancing in their heads. The sound of a sudden scream had alerted Shawn to race to his feet from his bed.

"What the hell was that?" he asked aloud.

"Baby go back to sleep. It's early", Katie whispered.

Was the voice in his ear from a dream or was it something else that felt entirely real? The questions in his mind altered the plans he had spent to bring Katie into Boston for a day of fun. Previously wanting to spare her the truth about who he was, he sat calmly watching his beautiful girlfriend sleep. Counting the seconds on the clock in his room, Shawn was more than willing to wait a lifetime to tell her. The opening of her beautiful eyes sank his heart because he knew where the next seconds were headed.

"Good Morning sweetheart, how did you sleep?" Shawn asked softly.

"I had the strangest and scariest dream at the same time. We were saying goodbye at some airport and after the plane I was in took off, I remember a ball of fire racing past me and it just felt so real. I remember screaming and then asking you to come back to bed seconds later", Katie stated.

The look of shock on Shawn's face answered his earlier question and it was the explanation he needed. Despite settling his fears aside briefly, Shawn wanted to share his story regardless of the moment. The next several minutes were key and it would determine if the love they share would last long enough to handle the identity of Shawn's self.

"Katie, it was a dream and I know exactly how it got placed into your head," Shawn stated.

"Stop being silly weirdo?" Katie asked.

"Katie, I need you to listen to me please. What I am going to tell you will shock you and most likely cause you to leave, but I need you to promise that you will take time to comprehend what I tell you today?" Shawn asked.

"Shawn, you are scaring me. Please tell me what's wrong?" Katie nervously responded.

Sitting beside Katie, Shawn looked into her beautiful tired eyes and began telling his story. While Shawn had explained all the tales of his life, the look of happiness changed drastically with concern on his girlfriend's face. Taking only a few minutes to alert the senses inside of her soul, Katie began crying while understanding all the terror that Shawn suffered. The few-hour conversation that took place in his bedroom assured Katie that he had come from somewhere special and was unsure to believe him. Noticing the slight disbelief in her face, Shawn grabbed Katie's hand and walked her to the closet in his room. Covering her with one of his long-sleeve dress shirts, they continued out of the home hand in hand. It was the long walk behind his backyard that Shawn lead his girlfriend to the pumping station and its tunnels.

"Oh my, this looks very creepy. Where are you taking me?" she asked.

Remaining quiet and placing his finger over his lips to silence his lover, Katie continued to follow Shawn through the narrow tunnel. The same walk that he had made many times before was suddenly bringing them both to the door leading into the room. Katie displayed a look of surprise on her face and a hundred questions ran through her mind.

"What is this place Shawn, why is it so dark in here?" she asked in anticipation.

"Stand in the middle of the room with me and please watch", he replied.

Shawn began to use his mind to help Katie believe in everything about him, but there was a problem. The sudden sounds of breathing gave way to the wall facing the couple and the vision  of a face appeared. The grey and darkened beard covered the anger on the face of the apparition staring back at them. His dark hair and mystified blue eyes locked upon the bodies of the two strangers encircled in the small room of four walls. The size of the apparition was about three-foot wide and very life like to the young couple.

"Shawn my dear friend, why did you bring her here?" the voice questioned.

"Vincent?" Shawn asked.

No reply was made towards his question, but the eeriness of the room was drawn to the evil caricature placed on the wall.

"I brought her here because I want her to see me for who I really am", Shawn stated.

"I want her to leave this room, so I can have a word with you", replied the voice.

Nervously walking towards the door, Katie complied with the terror upon the wall.

"I will be right on the other side of this door", Katie mentioned to Shawn.

Once the door closed behind Katie, the voice didn't waste time in shamefully disregarding the pain that Shawn was bringing to himself.

"You are to immediately send the girl back to where she came from", the voice boldly stated.

"I love her though. How can I just walk away from her? Can I please keep her?" Shawn asked with purpose.

Katie stood on the other side of the door in shock wondering what was happening. A small noise behind her brought her attention away from the door and in the direction of the long tunnel.

"Hello, who's there?" She asked loudly.

The snarling noises Katie had heard indicated to her that something was watching her. As her eyes attempted to focus through the darkness, a set of blue eyes began staring back at her. The sight of the eyes looking into her soul crippled the heart beat within her chest and Katie fell to the ground.

"If you bring her here to me, I will make sure she gets back to her home. You are forbidden to acknowledge the existence of this creature any more. Am I clear?" The voice asked.

Walking into the tunnel through the door, Shawn looked to see a shadowy four-legged wolf standing above Katie while she lied on the ground.

"Get out of here", Shawn yelled.

The black wolf suddenly ran in the other direction while Shawn reached down to pick Katie up from the ground. Katie was passed out and he began walking towards the door into the room where he was commanded to return her back. Her soft hair brushed against his face as her head lay on his chest while carrying her. Shawn set her down in the middle of the floor and walked backwards away from her in disbelief. The apparition upon the wall remained and began looking down on the girl laying on the floor. The face hovering above her began to disappear upon the wall as the vision of the beach amassed around her. The fluctuation of the area focused on the setting of a two-story home sitting closely to the beach. The picture was breath taking and Shawn's eyes looked back down as Katie had disappeared and onto the frame of the vison upon the wall. Her beautiful life seen sleeping on her bed of pink satin and white pillows, Shawn was at ease.

"She is safe my son and we are to never speak of this treachery again", the voice loudly stated.

The visions of Katie's home disappeared from his sight and the room remained darkened with exception to the lit candles flickering with anger. Shawn walked towards the tunnel with a dejection that his life was a mere memory in Katie's mind. The love that he had endured the last couple of days was now gone. The long and lonely road back to his home was clearly a reminder that he was relegated to living a life of loneliness forever.

"This is so unfair, why me? I have done everything I have ever been asked to do and I get this? This is crap", Shawn told himself.

Walking with a poor posture and his shoulders shrugging slowly, Shawn failed to notice the set of eyes walking beside him. The feeling of wetness tapping his fingers on his right hand, Shawn looked down to see his best friend walking beside him.

"Sebastian, where have you been?" Shawn asked.

The blue eyes amongst the darkness appeared to feel sad for Shawn and Sebastian was allowing him to realize the beast was there for him. Katie was gone and there was nothing Shawn could do to hide his feelings and it was something Vincent was going to have to deal with. There was no way in the world that Shawn was going to allow anything or anyone to detour his heart. It was the long walk back home that Shawn decided he was going to keep his feelings hidden because he eventually knew Vincent was going to come calling for him. The plan was to physically show no remorse for losing Katie but allow his heart to bleed internally, preparing itself to mourn the victory hiding its true purpose.

Chapter 17
Failure

The next few days before his parents were to arrive home, Shawn ignored the ringing of the phone. He knew Kate was calling, but he wasn't prepared to defy the command given to him. With misery closing in on his shallow heart, Shawn decided to delve into his Father's closet. The several cases of Bud Light beer containing twelve cans each, he decided to begin drinking them. Regardless of the awful taste of warm beer, Shawn witnessed his parents at times drinking their sorrows away. Just as the third can of beer found its way deep into Shawn's stomach, the ringing of the doorbell came to fruition. Answering the door without a care in the world, John and his brothers had ventured from their home to check on their friend.

"Guys, want a beer? I have plenty to pass around", Shawn stated.

"Shawn, what is wrong man? You look like absolute shit", John abruptly mentioned.

"Drink them up boys before I bury each one inside of my misery", Shawn laughingly replied.

Without any hesitation, David and Joey were the first to pop open the tabs on their cans of Bud Light. John would follow suit, but his complaint of the temperature became annoying to everyone listening of his rambling.

"Drink the damn beer and shut up for Christ sake. Its just beer and these are all on me", Shawn replied.

The countless gulps of alcohol consumed that morning by the boys would make Alcoholics Anonymous members jealous. Standing in the living room of Shawn's house were a collection of underage boys from the neighborhood deciding to follow an older teen unwise to the complications of consuming an abundance of alcohol. It wouldn't be the first time in an American household that several teens made bad decisions, but it was a first for these idiots.

"I have a great idea since you are some mega athlete at school. I am sick of hearing that shit about you, so I dare you to ride your ten speed down the hill?" John convincingly dared.

Barely able to walk with his stomach full of the warmness of the unsettled beers, Shawn called him out on his challenge and asked the boys to join him. Since apparently it was follow-the-leader day, Shawn jumped on his ten speed and dashed down the hill towards the boys' house. The group collected their bikes and Shawn had previously thrown a case of beers in his book bag to bring with him. They all decided to venture over to the gate of the abandoned missile base as the younger brothers followed. Climbing through the gate like they previously encountered, the boys all continued to consume the beers like water while their fate lie ahead. The pathway towards the southside of the base led them all to the unchartered waters of the lake as they stumbled steadily through the forest. The reservoir was massive in size and the younger boys began to throw loose rocks as far as they could into the water. The skipping game was a popular choice for any age and it was the rock thrown by little Joey that landed him into hot water. The distance of the light rock that projected itself towards the east hit a small wave and collided with a young child who was close by. Knocking the little tyke to the ground, his Father took notice and became angry. Observing the original spot where the rock came from, he began yelling at the top of his lungs while walking fast towards the group of teens and boys.

"Who the hell threw this rock and hit my kid? Someone better answer me before I knock your punk asses out", yelled the angry man.

Unmoved by the anger of the parent that failed to chase the group of boys' away, Shawn began to speak up.

"Listen you mute. Go back to your kid before something bad happens here and you will regret it. Little Joey here accidently threw the rock in the wrong direction and let's move on from it", Shawn boldly stated.

"So, it was this little shit that hurt my child, huh?" the parent asked.

Reaching down to grab little Joey in anger, John tried to defend his little brother against the rather large man. Standing a few inches over six foot and anchored with a stocky build, John was unable to protect his brother because he was pushed down to the ground. Joey started to gasp for air as the parent began choking him with one hand while holding him off the ground.

"Let him go", Shawn yelled.

The group of boys standing a few feet away from the man felt the air drop a few degrees with sounds in the distance of thunder crackling the skies. Within seconds, the young teens were blown backwards in an instant. Knocked to the ground, the brothers gathered themselves and upon looking up at Shawn, he remained standing with their brother Joey cuddled behind him. Shawn looking down on the parent who had threatened them, appeared to have an invisible chokehold upon the neck of the man on the ground.

"How the hell is this possible", John whispered.

"Please stop, I am a Father", cried the older man.

Looking up at the teenager who somehow created the energy to knock him down was staring back at him. The blinding light beaming from his eyes and his controlled breathing could be seen piercing the skin upon his chest. No comprehension could explain what happened, but several minutes later, the drama disbanded back into the woods and away from the lake. The defeated parent hugged his child to never speak of the event again. Shawn and his friends deciphered the reasons over the next few days of what happened, but not one of them spoke about it. The forbidden tale of that day would burn deep into their hearts and Joey never again doubted the older boy who saved his life.

The entire Summer of 1988 was spent hanging out with the younger brothers and Shawn avoided the pumping station. Blaming his heart for the failure to keep his promise to Katie, Shawn's bleeding soul would amass the feeling of regret and possibilities. Nothing in the entire world could ever explain who Shawn really was, and it was a calling of sorts to understand the complication of his power. He was a gifted athlete, a fast runner and one very powerful being. Shawn never questioned the logic of who he was until now and he began searching for answers. Spending day after day at home while ignoring the world, everything that mattered failed to exist. Tired of feeling lost and having to let Katie go, he felt as if he wanted to tear the whole world down. Shawn's failure to recognize the dark before the dawn covered the true heart that he was to become. Endless nights of burying the sunlight gave way to the brightness of the moon and nothing changed. The nights were just as lonely as the days and Shawn was unable to erase the memory of Katie and her beautiful face. Envisioning the truth that Shawn was to live his entire life without the young girl that captivated his loneliness, He began to look up into the sky.

"Katie, will this faith in love be rewarded as we come to the end or have I missed the final warning during this lie that I live? Is there anyone calling while I see my soul within, as I feel I am not worthy of the life that you give. Are you with me after all? This hurts so much and why can't I hear you? Are you with me through this all and why must I need to feel you?" Shawn tearfully spoke to himself.

The closest to Heaven Shawn felt was at the side of Katie and his destiny broke the foundation that his heart would rely upon. As promised, Shawn agreed that if he was to keep this love together, he would have to remain unforgiven. If there was a chance that he would give Vincent all his soul to keep their love together, then the approach was simple. The foolish days of Summer ended with the shape of the pencil embracing the fingers that surround its fate. The few-sentence note, written on the back of a blank envelope intended for the eyes of the stranger from Cape Cod. Its message was simple, and the complexity of each word dashed upon the paper to signify patience deserving a true meaning. The temptation began with a mere phone call to the young woman who deserved more than she had ever given. Her subtle voice would enter the mind of the forgiven thoughts of a raw innocence as John would repeat the words Shawn had written down.

"Katie, I have a message for you", Shawn's friend calmly stated.

"Please close your eyes and drive away the clouds that hides our light. This pain left behind must find its way to escape our lives cause, I don't want to fall or let you go. Our love has left me hollow and I am with you until the end. Please continue to keep your smile as we both shall set this Earth on fire together", John silently spoke.

"Thank you for calling and please tell him I will be waiting", she replied.

The signal to the phone suddenly went blank and it was the moment Shawn needed to fill the emptiness in his heart. Never again would he allow anyone or anything to disturb his heart, leaving it shattered and worthless. His focus was to patiently await the intentions of his place in the world while hiding his demeanor remained stagnant. His pain was buried deep enough to keep it away and it would no longer defeat him.

Chapter 18
Sophomore Year (88'-89')

Awaking from a sudden nightmare relegating Shawn to his normalcy, it was the thoughts of the teens back in South Weymouth that pierced his emotions. The darkness of the forest would betray the intentions of its meaningful purpose and Shawn would encounter the same dream for the last week of the Summer. The morning began like any other for it was now the first day of School in early September. Six in the morning came early and he had already been used to it since he faithfully was never a late sleeper. Slipping into a new pair of jeans and t-shirt, the bus ride to Masco helped Shawn escape away from the lonely Summer. Upon his arrival, it was new friends that had greeted him from his long and lonely road. The Sophomore year at Masco began with a reluctance in his mind while thoughts of Katie never escaped his thoughts. Questions from every student about the girlfriend attending his baseball game riddled the hallways of the school. The constant reminder ignited his cause to fight for what he believed in and it was a welcoming of sorts. The fire deep within a will to defeat those that had attempted to break his soul. The group of boys that previously ended his meaning were never going to escape the wrath that Shawn wanted to bring upon them. The thoughts of relentless pain began to fade away with the sound of an eerie voice.

"Oh my God, he is upon you. Your soul is his, you belong to him", the young girl spoke aloud.

"Ignore her, that's just Amanda being herself. The school won't commit her. I am Keith and it is nice to meet you", the smaller teen greeted.

The homeroom class that morning monitored by Mister Oliver was the constant invitation to the twenty students after first period for the remainder of the year.

"Keith, I am Shawn and I am not worried about that girl", he replied.

Amanda moved to the middle of the classroom while keeping her eyes on the evil surrounding Shawn. Amanda was the girl that everyone disliked because of the way she dressed and presented herself as an opinionated outcast. Somehow, Shawn found her interesting and he would silently listen to everything she said during the year because he thought it would someday become helpful. As the school bell rang, Shawn's schedule brought him to the classroom down the hall into Math. His favorite subject would have to take a sudden backseat to the fireworks presented to him with a few unexpected visitors.

The door to the classroom had opened and it was the summons by the hall monitor in request to have Shawn report to the Assistant Principal. The walk downstairs to the front of the office was a place he had very rarely visited. While sitting in the lobby, Shawn was approached by a shorter older man with grey hair.

"Shawn, I am Assistant Principal Lucy and I have a few people that would like to speak with you in my office", he stated.

Following the older man to his office, Shawn was beckoned to sit down in the chair positioned in the center of the room. Surrounded by cloudy windows, books and the smell of a burning candle, Shawn noticed the four adults standing behind him. Leaned up against the wall, Shawn's attention was brought forward with the words of his Assistant Principal.

"Shawn, it has to come my attention that you aren't playing Football this year. Is that correct?" he asked.

"I have no intentions of playing for any coach with a misdirection for his players", Shawn replied.

"May I have this one Norman?", the deep voice behind Shawn stated.

Sitting beside Shawn in the large chair next to him, the older gentleman brought his attention to the young student.

"Shawn, I would like to introduce myself here. I am Jim Hugh and I am the new Head Coach of the Varsity team. I saw your tapes last year running the Freshman offense and I was very impressed. Have you played organized football before?" Coach Hugh asked.

"Nope", Shawn stated briefly.

"Can I ask why you quit the team last year after seven games?" The Coach asked.

"Nope", Shawn again replied.

"Can I ask why you didn't try out this year?" he asked.

"Nope. Are we done here Coach?" Shawn asked.

The Coach reluctantly answered and stared at the young student in front of him and shook his head in disbelief.

"Son, you have the rawest talent I have ever seen on tape and you expect me to believe that you don't want to run my new offense?" The Coach asked.

"Coach, I respect your honesty here and I am just not interested", Shawn painfully replied.

The Coach stated to Mister Lucy that he was done with the meeting and while Shawn was instructed to return to his classroom, the gentleman remained in the office of the Assistant Principal.

"Norman, what do I have to say to this kid to get him to direct my offense?" Coach Hugh asked.

"I warned you that he was a dark horse and I am not surprised here. He is a wreck loose and it could blow up in your face mid-season because he is a quitter", Mister Lucy stated.

"I know this program isn't expected to do well with the garbage I have in front of me, but at least we have a chance with this kid as my Quarterback. God Damn it, back to the drawing board I guess", Coach Hugh angrily replied.

Upon leaving the office of the Principal, Shawn ventured down the hallway and decided to skip class. Not one thought crossed his mind about joining the Varsity team because it was clear that his success brought friction amongst the team. Baseball was going to be his release and he needed to keep his mind busy with Katie solely grappling his heart. Without hesitation, Shawn ended up walking outside of the school and onto the side of the campus that faced the Cafeteria. The cool morning comforted the bright sun rising slightly from the east. The Junior High was within reach and Shawn continued walking towards the south west corner of the conjoined schools.

"Shawn" the voice stated in his mind.

"Who is that?" Shawn replied.

Maybe he had hallucinated the thoughts of someone calling him, but it appeared to be coming from the woods next to the field where the girls field hockey team played. Curiosity was most definitely killing the cat as Shawn ventured with exuberance towards the hidden forest. Reaching the edge of the tree line, Shawn focused on the scenery of trails in front of him and began walking deeper into the abyss. The tall trees were attached by ropes and hanging lines and appeared to have

been placed there by Masco. The mystery surrounding the slight fog hovering above the ground gave way to memories of Weymouth. The tightening of Shawn's fist encased the anger deep inside his heart and it was the figure standing in the distance that detoured his emotions. The darkness of the forest shading the sunrise embarked Shawn's curiosity to seek the identity of the hooded character within his sights. Facing the opposite direction wearing a red-hooded sweatshirt over its head, Shawn called out.

"Hello, can I help you. Are you lost?" Shawn asked.

His echo reaching deep within the forest, the being stood still without a movement from its body. The sudden rush of adrenaline and nervousness ran through Shawn's body as he crept slowly towards the student. The creepiness of the forest released its symphony of noises from the chattering of bugs to the wind blowing the branches of the tall trees above. The unsettling thick smoke began to hover above the ground as Shawn found himself within an arm length of the hooded student. Reaching to grab him, the figure turned around and the sight of two bright eyes within the hood knocked Shawn to the ground. The terror ran through Shawn's body as to see the similarity inside of the sweatshirt looking back at himself. The burning smell of raw flesh crisp in the forest air while the memories of that day in Weymouth came rushing back.

"It's time Shawn", the voice stated deeply.

The remaining words spoke quietly in Shawn's mind as to remind him that it was an extended invitation to seek vengeance against those who had harmed him. The being reached out with his fingers of burning flesh and pointed at Shawn lying on the ground.

"Go", the voice stated.

Without a blink of his eyes, Shawn stood up and began venturing away from the forest. The rushing of his pace to get back to School propelled him to start running to his next class. Just as he had approached the doors of the Cafeteria, the bell ended the second period. The look of exhaustion and terror brought Shawn to his next period of Science class. Mister Heck was a sight to see for the students because he appeared to look like a cross between Abraham Lincoln and the Lucky Charms elf. The small stature of the teacher provided the room with a vibrant array of chemicals to hide the bad odor the little man had spewed. His religion apparently had removed the word deodorant from its category and all students attending would suffer its fumes. Class began like normal with the teacher reading an except from the Science book that morning. The voices began to chime inside of Shawn's head as if they were rushing to get his attention. Looking behind him, Shawn saw the eeriness of the clouds hovering over the Football stadium in the background. The darkness created an unexpected storm of rain and lightning that swiftly engulfed the school.

"That rain is awfully loud, don't you think", Shawn asked the student sitting next to him.

"Dude, what are you talking about?" The student asked back.

"Are you being serious right now? The rain outside, you can't see it?" Shawn asked.

"Whatever your problem is this morning, maybe you need to go the nurse's office", he jokingly replied.

In a state of confusion, Shawn turned his head towards the door of the classroom and the hooded figure from the forest was staring at him. Closing his eyes, Shawn avoided everything around him and placed his head down on the lab table. The voices becoming heavier and deeper while the lightning in the background became louder, Shawn screamed, *"Stop"*.

"Mister Lee, can I ask you why you are yelling in my classroom?" Mister Heck asked.

Shawn suddenly lifted his head up from the desk and the giggling of the students brought an embarrassment to his nature. Breathing heavily, he looked behind him and the field was bright under the rays of the sun as the voices disappeared.

"I am sorry sir, I need to go to the Nurse", Shawn replied nervously.

Walking out of the classroom as the door shut behind him, Shawn felt alone and scared. He looked to his right and then peaked to his left and not a sound was heard from afar. Attempting to pinch himself from a possible nightmare, he was unable to awake. Realizing that everything was not beyond his imagination, he attempted to figure a way back to the pumping station behind his home. Unphased to walk the several miles to his home, Shawn ventured out into the student body parking lot located on Endicott Road, and began walking east towards the town of Topsfield. The road home he followed was also catching the attention of several pairs of eyes as Shawn's silhouette disappeared into the distance.

The bully of the High School caught the attention last year of Shawn's blunt attitude and it was pay back time. Dwayne and several of his friends had kept a close eye on Shawn all year awaiting the right time to exact their revenge. The time was now and equipped with a friend's car, Dwayne, Jody, Craig and their older friend Matt jumped in and drove onto Endicott Road in search of the teen. Matt drove his car while Dwayne observed to locate the target the boys were seeking to destroy.

Chapter 19
The Bully's Demise

The search for the student they began to follow, disappeared in the shadows of the trees hovering the road. The disgusted look upon their faces felt wasted away because they planned for an entire year to exact their revenge. Mile by mile driven, Matt became exhausted and wanted to turn around and return to school.

"Hell, no you aren't Matt. We are going to find this prick until it takes all night. You think he is going to get away with what he did to us last year? We may never have this chance again", Dwayne replied.

The drive brought the young men to the intersection of Washington and Boxford roads. Unable to determine which direction they would head, Jody recommended that since Shawn was a baseball player, maybe they should head towards the field.

"How do you know so much about his punk, huh?" Dwayne asked.

"Who the heck cares how I know, you want to find him, right?" Jody replied.

Matt turned his beat-up green Volvo to the right to maintain his course on Washington Ave. The posted speed limit on the road was thirty miles per hour, but the drive felt like they were walking while all four boys were on the look out for the teen. Frustrated from the length of time it was taking to locate the student, the pinned-up anger to capture Shawn was growing.

Meanwhile, the pursuit of danger inching closer to him, the voices quickly had him running towards the direction of the town of Topsfield. Shawn had sped through the long road leading to the same ball field that looked familiar to him. Standing on the side of the field near the bleachers, Shawn began to take notice of a red sweatshirt lying on the end of the bench. Walking towards the article of clothing, a note written on a small index card atop the clothing read, "Put this on". Looking around to see if anyone had placed it in the very spot he found it, Shawn placed down his book bag and placed the sweatshirt over his head. The space was comfortable and efficient, and once it settled over his body, the hood collapsed over his head. Shawn began to walk towards the same mound that he would frequent over the Summer and began to stand upon it.

Matt had followed Jody's advice and took the road that lead to the baseball field. Arriving along the large tennis courts, the Volvo parked in the lot that faced the back of the baseball field. Dwayne took immediate notice of the sweatshirt wearing jerk standing in the middle of the field. All four of the teens exited the car and walked toward the back of the trunk. Matt released the hatch and reached inside to grab the two bats and tire iron laying on the bottom of the trunk. Dwayne grabbed one of the bats out of Matt's hands and Jody reached for the tire iron. Craig had pulled the knife deep within his front pocket as each teen began drifting towards the ball field.

"Have you guys noticed the drop of temperature out here. Damn it is starting to get cold", Craig stated.

"Shut up you idiot, let's get this stupid ass once and for all", Dwayne angrily replied.

All four bullies were dressed in their lazy black shirts and black jeans and with all of them looking around, not a soul would witness the massacre they were about to perform. Approaching the backstop of the baseball field in their hi-top sneakers, the eyes of the wicked kept focus on the teen. Arriving upon the grass next to the third base line near home plate, Dwayne and his friends spoke.

"Hey asshole, this is the end of the line for you. We have you surrounded, and we don't plan on letting you go so easily this time".

Clinching his right hand over the bat with an angry grip, Dwayne looked to his right and left and asked everyone to spread out further.

"We aren't letting this fool get away so easily this time", Dwayne replied.

The bluish sky above the town quickly succumbed to dark as the approaching clouds brought the look of night over the confrontation on the ball field.

"Dwayne, I don't feel good about this", Craig yelled.

The wind across the field began to swirl heavier and faster while the temperature had steadily dropped. The warmth of the sweatshirt engulfed over his body, Shawn noticed the boys across from him. Without pause, he stared back at the weapons that were closely surrendering themselves to his will. Breathing slowly, an evil smile cracked upon his face with the acknowledgement of the dangers facing the four bullies.

"Do you hear that?" Jody asked while his teeth chattered in the cold air.

"What the heck is that snarling?" Matt asked.

"Both of you bitches shut up and concentrate. Let's go after this punk now", Dwayne demanded.

Taking a step forward into the dirt of the baseline, the sounds of growling began to pierce the cold air. Unable to avoid the noise through the loud wind, Craig turned around and the several sets of eyes in the darkness of the woods next to the field began to concentrate on them.

"Dwayne, what the hell is that in the woods? Oh my god, are those dogs?" Craig nervously asked.

"Oh shit, rabies!" Matt screamed.

The others turned around with one foot in the dirt and observed the appearance of the same eyes Craig witnessed.

"What the hell is going on here?" Dwayne asked.

Turning around to face their fate, the boy on the mound was no longer alone. A large white wolf stood beside him with glowing blue eyes with large growling teeth.

"Guys, we better get out of here. This can't really be happening", Craig insisted.

"I am calling bullshit. This is some type of hallucination or something", Dwayne replied.

Dwayne took slow steps gracefully towards the mound, keeping his eyes on the teen. The other boys stayed behind shivering in pure agony while the breeze swept the dirt over the ballfield. The visibility amongst the infield was less than a few feet and Dwayne followed the glowing eyes of the beast. The approach was swift and when he finally arrived in front of the mound, Shawn had completely disappeared. Frustrated and angry, Dwayne turned away from the snarling wolf and just as his head was completely facing the opposite direction, he stood face to face with the daring eyes of the teen under the hood of his sweatshirt. Visibly frightened, Dwayne remained frozen like a deer in headlights as Shawn removed the hood from his head. In pure angst, Dwayne was staring at a being that did not appear to be Shawn and worse. The hair was burned and singed to the top of his skull, his once formed face was now completely melted. The smell of burning flesh raced through the nostrils of the teen standing in pure agony. What appeared to look like Shawn was another form of terror that Dwayne wasn't prepared to see. Attempting to hit the demon with his bat, he reached behind with all his might and followed through with his swing. The powerful thrust eventually landed on the side of the demon, but the thud created by the friction collapsed the grip Dwayne had and released the bat. Falling to the ground, the bat landed away from its captor and Shawn reached out to grab Dwayne. Lifting him up a foot off the ground, Dwayne begged to be released.

"I am sorry, please let me go." Dwayne said in fear.

The demon looking into the bully's eyes from below, he began to speak, *"My pleasure"*. The voice was muffled and struggled to present the chords together for Dwayne to comprehend. Dwayne fell to the ground and without hesitation, his friends ran as fast as they could to the car and drove away. Avoiding the terror in the rear-view mirror, the boys disappeared away from the field in a matter of seconds. Breathing heavily and scared out of their minds, the terror of the ordeal horrified them.

"We never talk about this day ever. I don't want to even acknowledge this ever happened. Agreed?" Dwayne said.

The dust began to settle over the field and the darkness remained as the silhouette rushed behind his perception. The feeling that something behind his shoulder had arrived, Shawn turned around.

"So, not playing well with others I see?" Vincent politely asked.

His mind racing over the entire confrontation with his bullies, Shawn deciphered the entire dramatic sequence that led up to this exact moment. The more power he could unleash, the smarter he became. Not acknowledging what Vincent asked, the feeling that something of a higher power invaded his thoughts.

"Son, your beautiful mind is on the right track and yes I did manage to get you to this very spot. For you to become more powerful my young disciple, you are going to have to spring confidence in your limits. Envision every moment as if it already happened and make it your own", Vincent stated.

Walking together with Vincent's arm around Shawn towards centerfield, he quickly joked with the teen.

"Great job back there by the way. We just need to work on your appearance because you are god awful ugly right now", laughed Vincent.

"Where have you been? Why did you allow Katie to be removed from my life?" Shawn asked in a hurry.

"All in due time my young friend, all in due time", Vincent replied.

"She doesn't need to be around you right now because you have a much bigger purpose to tackle soon. Focus on your getting back into school and living your life and we will revisit her later", Vincent explained.

Dejected with a frown on his face, Shawn placed the hood back over his head and with a blink of his eyes, he and Vincent were standing back in the room under the pumping station.

Chapter 20
The Hollow Caricature

The familiar setting of the isolated four walls brought a comfort back to Shawn's emotions. The last time he stood in this room was to face the breaking of the union between himself and Katie. Pulling his hood away from his head, Shawn's face had brought itself back to normal as the tips of his fingers ran themselves across his skin.

"If we are going to bring this room to full use Shawn, you are going to have to concentrate harder. Each day that passes brings you much closer to your destiny and the power will be unimaginable", Vincent stated with purpose.

The flickering candles upon the walls were providing the only light to see the seriousness that fed into the wise words from Vincent's rhetoric.

"If we are going to bury this world and its beliefs, we are going to have to get you up to speed here. Do you want to understand the full power of what this room has to offer Shawn?" Vincent asked.

"I am ready to learn Vincent", Shawn replied.

Over the course of the last several months, Vincent kept a close eye on Shawn from a distance and realized that his pupil was much closer to becoming ready than he first anticipated. The fire deep within him was begging to be released exacting the moment of revenge buried beneath his skin.

"I have a few questions to ask and not sure how these words will come out, but I want to give it a try?" Shawn asked.

Hesitating with the mind set to combine the questions into a gathering of important information for himself, Shawn proudly spoke.

"Am I able to teleport from this room to anywhere irrelevant to myself or the past? In other words, can I teleport where I want? Secondly, what are your true intentions for me? The bully looked into my eyes and I felt as if I could see myself and I was totally burned. How can that be? Thirdly can we compromise somehow a few visits to my girlfriend without you getting upset? Vincent, I somehow found myself in the year of 2013 by accident and I ran into a young woman by the name of Kimberly. Why is she important? Lastly, who are you really? I know you aren't the Devil, but can you clue me in on your identity", Shawn asked with purpose.

The hesitation in the enclosed air of the room depicted a classroom of matching wits and Vincent set the mood. The color of the candles turned to a dark red and the darkness allowed the communication to be easier understood. The chilled bones of his disciple were stronger than ever before, and it would take an eternity to scare him away.

"First off, let's get your mother to switch to decaf coffee because you talk way to fast. All jokes aside, Shawn, I am going to explain more than what you have asked because you have impressed me beyond any of my wildest premonitions. Your senses are becoming stronger and you seem to be wiser than I

anticipated, so to answer your last question, yes. If you want to place a caricature of who I truly am, then how about this?" Vincent stated while the front wall viewed a picture.

"Not the best picture in the world, but this was after I was cast out of Heaven. You can call me anything you want, but my former name could darken the entire room as I was looked at differently while in Heaven. I did everything I could to get a few of the angels to defect with me and I have spent the remaining time here on Earth looking for disciples to help me", Vincent answered.

"Vincent, you are the Morning Star. Otherwise known as Lucifer, but it is really you?" Shawn again asked.

"Nothing gets by you, does it. That a boy. As for Kimberly, you are not to ever meet her Shawn. For each decade that passes, I choose disciples like yourself to run the Earth as Angels and her fate will soon meet my demands when the time comes", Vincent stated.

"Shawn, do you really know who you are?" Vincent asked.

196

"I am a young man in the flesh standing before you", Shawn replied.

Chuckling with laughter, Vincent kindly reminded him who he was with the vision of the forest that saw his life come to a sudden end in the lost trees of Weymouth.

"Hold up, are you saying I am dead?" Shawn asked nervously.

"No, my young friend, you are very much alive. You are on this forsaken Earth because I deemed it so. The moment you lost your life that cold afternoon, I granted you the gift to roam this Earth forever", Vincent replied.

"You are alive because of the pact your Mother and I made many years ago, as you already are aware of. I was to watch over you in hopes that if that day would ever come that you would move on from this Earth, I would take you under my guise and allow you to be an Angel", Vincent explained.

"Is this why Katie is not allowed in my life", Shawn asked.
"As I previously stated, you are picking this all up without much help from me. Shawn, if you continue to see Katie, she will eventually fall, and it will be at your expense. Do you want that for her?" Vincent asked.

"Is there any way I can prevent that from happening with what you have given me"? Shawn asked.

"Shawn, let it go. As for your bully, he saw the true caricature of who you are. You are going to realize that you possess the evil I have passed down into your soul and you are going to wreak havoc on many others, while living as a human on Earth", Vincent furtherly explained.

Shawn clouded his judgement enough to attempt to hide the feelings in his heart over Kate. The question that Vincent avoided gave Shawn hope that there was a chance he could keep Katie in his life without hurting the fate chosen for her. The fallen angel standing before him, Shawn began to see the purpose of his demise in the forest because it was situationally staged. It was always the plan of Lucifer to bring Shawn to his demise and it was going to take the will of his newly found power to break free. The failure of such a plan could doom Shawn forever, so he had to conjure up a plan with patience to save himself.

"The power of this room that is solely yours will give you the path to place yourself anywhere you choose to be Shawn". Your recent ventures to your past secluded you only to the timeline of your life because of your inexperience. Now that you are honing your powers within your expanded mind, you will notice the lengths to which you can go. Tell you what, lets try a destination and see if your mind is strong enough to get you there", Vincent demanded.

The faith of Shawn's mind was seeking the benefit of his new expansion as he stood in the center of the room. With Vincent slowly disappearing from the area, he began closing his eyes. The faint sight began to dim the candles upon the wall as the visions of a forest began to appear. All four walls captured the area that Shawn once found himself lying beneath the ground. His mind wanting to tempt nature, Shawn used the room to venture into the current position of the resting spot that once took his life. Concentrating more with his mind, Shawn was able to transport his body to his own burial site. Opening his eyes, Shawn felt the south wind brushing up against his face. The peace of the forest blossomed sounds of birds and creatures as Shawn stood in awe. Everything that Vincent told him clearly allowed him to understand that this could have all been avoided. There had to be a contingency to release himself from Vincent's grasp, but Shawn wasn't ready.

"I am going to have to learn all I can in order for my unknown plan to work", Shawn told himself.

Kneeling on the dirt beneath his feet, Shawn placed his fingers an inch into the soft gravel. Slowly reaching down to his soul, Shawn softly spoke.

"Shawn, I know you are down there, and I promise I will work on getting this life back. I need help and I will find it somewhere and get myself back. I promise", Shawn whispered.

The strength of his prowess began allowing him to realize that his thoughts were channeled without guidance. He was able to hide his feelings inside of his heart and it would be a library of information for Shawn to seek so that he could conjure his escape.

Standing to his feet, Shawn closed his eyes and once they had opened, he stood back inside the room where he decided to call it a day. Tired and broken over the events leading him to this moment, Shawn had to report back to school the next day. Without any sign of Vincent around, he began to gather his concentration upon the walls and in an instant, Shawn was standing in his own bedroom.

"That never gets old", Shawn told himself.

The evening included the preparation for another day at school and in the next several months through baseball season, Dwayne and his group of misfits avoided Shawn at every turn. The once dominant bully was now playing the victim, and everyone took notice. Random students began spreading rumors that Dwayne Williams and his friends attempted to ambush the younger Sophomore outside of school grounds. It was somewhat another rumor about Shawn that invited people to realize that he was somewhat of a mystery. The incident last year with Greg Holland on the Varsity team was a story of legends and this new rumor was tarnishing the reputation the bully spent years building. Not a soul on campus was willing to confront either student about what everyone was hearing, so the awkwardness was left alone to wither below the halls of the school. The inner circle that once surrounded the bully was now spreading itself away from him, becoming extremely noticeable. Masconomet Regional High School had its temptations and dark side with endless innuendos and there was no escaping its wrath as Dwayne realized. Every High School across America from Boston to Los Angeles had its issues and Masco wasn't any different. The culture of the school located on Endicott Road wasn't aware of the evil walking through its hallways and it was best kept hidden. The end of the decade was approaching, and the summons of an evil was closely gathering momentum on the unsuspecting tri-town area. The fate of many would depend on the mind of a young teen entrapped in an internal battle with himself.

Chapter 21
Shattered and Worthless

Sitting in the Masco library on the last day of school, Shawn was venturing into a column that he calmly put together with collected resources. His first year on the Varsity Baseball team was a success with an undefeated record as a pitcher and a visit to the State playoffs. His essay would be a letter to the local newspaper out of Salem with the subject pertaining to the failures of his coaching staff. Sitting in the corner away from everyone, a young woman slowly approached, and began to sit across from him. Aware of her identity, the young teen with the scraggly hair and pale skin began to whisper.

"I know who you are, and I am not afraid.", she stated quietly.

"That's a good thing to know, thanks for the reminder", Shawn replied.

"I need to know why? Why you?" Amanda asked.

"What are you talking about? Aren't you in my homeroom class?" Shawn replied with a question.

"C'mon, be real with me here. I see right through you and this transparency is easy to see", Amanda stated.

"Why don't you leave me alone. I have no flipping idea what you are talking about, freak", Shawn angrily replied.

"Will you two both keep it down?" The Librarian asked.

Unaware of how loud his response was, other students in the Library peeked over their shoulders to see what the commotion was about. Noticing that Shawn was amongst them, they all focused on themselves hoping that their eyes were unseen. The calmness that morning once Amanda walked away, was strangely bleak. Whispers of many were finding their way inside Shawn's ears and the mass amount of words became a huge distraction. The project in front of him became secondary as his visions throughout the room began to darken. The once bright morning lights peaking through the windows of the massive Library disappeared instantly. Dark clouds hovering above the sky, Shawn looked over at the large panes of glass leading to the front doors of the library. The misty darkness began to appear in the hallway outside of the doors and slowly crawled its way into the Library air. The large room full of books and students were becoming draped with the faded entity surrounding Shawn. Each student sitting in their chairs were now frozen as time stood still, giving the apparition an appearance before Shawn. The massive black smoke floating above the floor appeared to be fifteen feet wide and shaped with wings and blurriness. Unable to comprehend its true form, the smell of clean oxygen sifting through his lungs prepared the entity to enter the body that was meant to receive its evil.

The mass of black cloud and withering smoke slowly dissipated through the small opening upon Shawn's face. His mouth slowly opened, inch after inch the ghoulish appearance of the angel began aggressively forcing itself deep into the teen's gullet. The relentless pain inside of his gut stretching beyond its imagination gave way to a calming feeling once the darkness faded. The stillness within the walls of the Library granted the solidarity for which Shawn had relinquished the darkness inside him. His eyes turning to grey, he began to stand and the sudden pressure inside of him granted an awful scream. Falling to his knees, the heat rushing through his veins suddenly pierced his skin upon his back. Reaching behind him to comfort the pain, his loud screams gave way to his transformation on the floor of the Library. The weary silence surrounding the teen amplified the tearing of his flesh while sounds of horror screamed within him. The pain of a thousand nails piercing his skin released a pain so unreal, he lay upon the floor wishing he was dead.

The heat unbearable, Shawn removed his shirt from his body as he leaned forward on his knees. The two punctures appearing on his back began to open wider with each scream of pain from his mouth. The cool air of the room soothed his aching body while the large feathered objects began stretching away from his back. One last scream gave way to the relaxation of the cool wind, created with the flap of his newly born feathers. Not able to stand, Shawn leaned back on his knees and threw his hands above his head. Stretching as far as he could, his dark wings spread further away from his body and the site of his newly found blackness had brought a new beauty to his eyes. His bright blue corneas found themselves enlightened with the calm darkness in his presence. The sight of the several faces paused in admiration in the corner of his sight, he pushed against the ground to stand up. The weakness of his legs garnered the strength to withstand the new heaviness of his body and Shawn began to walk towards the library doors. Shirtless and brandishing a new purpose, his wings closed behind his back to fit through the small opening into the hallway. While the twenty students remained without movement, an exception was discovered as the young woman who revealed Shawn's identity watched the newly winged-creature walk away. During the entire transition, Amanda's creativity began drawing while she remained hidden from the commotion within the library. The enticement to pencil every detail of the teen standing several feet from her gained momentum once he left the room. With patient eyes, she captured the horrific terror that Shawn suffered through and remained silent through it all. Inept by the evil grip the rest of the students surrendered to, Amanda envisioned this moment in her dreams. Considered an outcast at Masco from most of the student body, her physical appearance scared those who weren't familiar with her purpose. A prodigy of "The Cure" and "The Echo and the Bunnymen" grunge era, the students at Masco were unaware of the music that Amanda likened to the core. The reality that others like Amanda existed in the world and remained to themselves only strengthened the movement. The dark lipstick, black hair, the strange hair-cuts, the torn baggy clothes, the charms and bracelets and the shyness of most would result in becoming an outcast. Amanda was one of those considered to be part of the grunge population and no one understood her amazing talents. Growing up in a house with one parent in the town of Topsfield, Amanda was always secluded and believed in remaining to herself. The young teen began seeing visions once the new kid from Weymouth showed up to school while they were in 8th grade. The entire Summer leading up to her freshman year were filled with nights of dreams unexplained. Unaware of the existing evil, Amanda one day during school hours ventured into the forest next to the Junior High School to secretly draw while skipping gym class. It was the ladder on one of the trees in the course that Amanda found peace to entertain her mind. The boards nailed to the tree lead to a small perch about twenty feet above the ground. The calm breeze rushing against her face, the pencil she held began telling a story of the nature surrounding her.

A few minutes later, Amanda noticed the new teen from Weymouth standing directly below her. Remaining focused on his stance, she saw Shawn staring at another student with a black hood over his head some distance away. Facing the opposite direction from the approaching teen, the hooded figure turned around and Shawn fell to the ground. A slight mumble that she was unable to decipher came from the standing being with eyes of red staring down at Shawn. Cupping her mouth with her hand to keep from making a sound, the shocking revelation was in sight. The demon-like creature with creepy eyes had brought her nightmares to life as she was feeling a bit of Deja vu. She had remembered this exact moment and Amanda from that day on would envision the terror surrounding Shawn and his aura in the hallways.

With no sight of Shawn, Amanda gathered herself and began to walk into the hallway. Just before her arrival to the double doors, the sounds of the teens behind her drew away from their minutes of silence. With everything back to normal, Amanda reluctantly chose to chase the winged angel throughout the school because it was more than likely he was nowhere to be found.

The next morning Shawn's eyes awoke with the sound of the loud alarm. It was Saturday morning, and while he would usually sleep in a couple of hours, his biological schedule began to change. The previous day was a complete blur and the soreness from his back evidently presented a complication. The appearance of his bare back in the bathroom mirror visually saw two small slits below his shoulder blades. Painful to the touch, Shawn draped his t-shirt over himself and disguised his shock. Venturing out to the pumping station, Shawn noticed a drastic change. His once easy entrance to the room he spent many of his days was now locked. Apparently, someone recently had visited the area and relocked the door leading down to the tunnel under the ground. Feeling shattered over the pain creeping through his body, Shawn began to examine the lock with this hand. With one quick tug, the large lock broke into several pieces falling at Shawn's feet. The strength built up inside the growing teen was multiplying and he was learning more each day about his gifts. Upon entering the tunnel, Shawn wisely closed the door behind him and focused his energy on entering the room with a purpose.

The curiosity of yesterday brought Shawn to a point of trying to examine the events of his pain. All he remembered was studying in the Library and then waking up this morning. The confusion settling in with his mind, he began to process the location of the Masco Library and the exact time he lost consciousness. Upon the walls of his room, the sight clouded with the blackness of a large figure, Shawn witnessed himself suffering the wrath of an evil unexplained. Looking closely behind the apparition, Shawn noticed the appearance of small wings upon its backside. Raising an eyebrow, Shawn was particularly interested in understanding why an angel would be visiting him. To Shawn's surprise, the blackness covering most of the room had begun to grow smaller as it disappeared while he saw himself falling to the floor. His memory began remembering the exact moment when he was overtaken by the demon and suddenly both his mind and the picture on the walls began to coincide.

The significance occurred when Shawn began to transform into the angel with large black wings. While the transition occurred, Shawn noticed that a young woman with dark curly hair was seen penciling a piece of paper from behind the book case close by. Her sparkling eyes gave herself away while Shawn delved into the emotions surrounding the young woman. The projection upon the walls began to tell the story of someone who was sure that Shawn was no longer himself. That secret was going to remain hidden until he needed to use it for his advantage, but in the meantime, explanations were needed in understanding the entity that remained in his blood. The night that Sebastian and his friends visited him in the back of his yard seemed long ago, but this occurrence felt different. The blatant intentions of this dark evil imposed its controlling will forcefully and seemed more contained. With the truth still lingering for him to understand, it was Vincent who decided to set the record straight.

"The time has come my son", the voice stated.

The silence of the room was awakened with the deepness of Vincent's voice as he appeared on the forward wall in front of Shawn. His face like that of a large caricature, he began to explain the purpose for why he needed him.

"Surprised to find out that one of my Angel's visited you yesterday?" Vincent asked.

"Honestly, no I am not surprised. I am befuddled without explanation Vincent. What is going on?" Shawn asked.

"I told you before that this process was going to take time to develop and in learning everything about yourself, don't you think that you are ready to fulfill your destiny?" Vincent asked.

"See this from my side. You indirectly involve me into a brutal confrontation that results in my painful death. You than decide to reincarnate my body for the sole purpose of letting a bunch of wolves rape me with their gauntly eyes. Abolishing my girlfriend back to her home was the worst part of all this, and then you summons the ghostbusters to scare the crap out of me while I am trying to get an education at this snobby High School. I am beyond grateful that I was able to expose the bullies for who they were and teaching them a lesson. Where I am having a problem now is the destiny part. Is it really my destiny to take a royal enema from a ghoul who is scared to show his face? What the hell was that anyway?" Shawn asked.

"That is why I love you my son. You always find the comedy while also living the drama. You were visited by an Angel that I did not summons, like you mentioned. That spirit came from above and I need you to realize that we are always going to be in a war", Vincent replied.

"You mean Heaven and Hell", Shawn stated.

"Oh, my dear boy, its much bigger than that, but you are on the right track. For every death on this Earth there is a birth and that is the cycle all of humanity lives by. Some great mind many years ago learned that every action causes a reaction and he was right. Every sin tempted by humanity is opposed by an act of kindness and so on. I chose to remain on this side of fate because for the balance of life to remain in perfect harmony, I was to instill evil while goodness existed", Vincent explained.

The look upon Shawn's face was priceless and he had no reason for understanding why he was chosen. His Mother had her issues with Vincent, but he needed to delve into that historic day when they met. What was the confrontation that caused Shawn's life to suddenly adrift away from the good that he wanted to offer? Since his life was basically scripted in the eyes of a deal made years ago, Shawn was bound and determined to place a wrinkle in time that would eventually free him from this evil grasp. It was only a matter of luck and unfortunately, Shawn was running out of that.

Chapter 22
Fate of the Se7en

Vincent began to instill his teaching and knowledge of who he was to his young disciple. As the many days progressed, Shawn would spend countless hours learning about the many faces of evil, the rules of engagement and the fury of power he possessed. It was important that Vincent groom his disciple to follow the script to a tee, because if at any point the attention of Heaven would be taken for granted, a complication would arise. The evil thoughts buried into Shawn's memory were imposing a will to allow him to comprehend the difference between reality and kindness. During the entire several-day process, Shawn would understand that it was a mere importance to pose his will on others. Acts of kindness were reluctant to his balance of evil and Shawn was to entertain his fury upon the unsuspecting towns surrounding Masconomet High School. The hive of madness articulated a presence of wickedness in his new disciple. The process of harmonic evil was now complete and while the summer existed, it was time to relinquish his demeanor onto a group of individuals awaiting his arrival.

"You know what you must do, so this is all on your instincts son. Don't hold back and make me proud", Vincent stated.

Shawn took a deep breath as the image of Vincent faded into oblivion and the room turned into emptiness. This specific night was planned for weeks, and for obvious reasons to Shawn. The visons of crooked wings and voices of surrender allowed Shawn to visualize his destination and he disappeared into thin air.

The Summer of 1989 at Weymouth High School began with its annual student party in the forest near the Junior High. The several year-tradition collected the attention of several students celebrating another year gone by. The expected head count would grow larger every year, and this was projected to be one of the largest gatherings. Zachary Alexander's older brother Gregory was in the class of '89 and this was their graduation party. Several friends of Zach were in attendance and the forest was a microcosm compared to the many other parties being held all over the country. This specific gathering signified the celebration of men and women leaving the area of Weymouth to pursue other projects in their lives. The woods near the Junior High had become a stage of several hundred students that were unaware of the consequences arising from the ashes of the abyss.

Ten o'clock that evening came and went in a hurry as some students dissipated towards other parties in town. Kegs of beer and loud heavy metal music blared through the echo of the forest. The several hundred students in attendance slowly dwindled down to twelve as Zach, his brother and several friends remained behind. The warm evening struck past twelve and Gregory lifted his cup of beer above his head to a toast.

"To the young man who suffered a most deplorable death a few years ago at this very spot. That day we became men will now come to fruition as we move on in search of better lives. I love you guys and we will always be brothers. Cheers to you", Gregory loudly presented.

The others sounded off with their cheers after Greg's statement, while Zachary walked over to the spot that Shawn had died. The permanent burn mark in the ground was a mystery to all the students, but a sour reminder of the loss of life to a young innocent boy. Unzipping the zipper to his shorts, Zachary began urinating on the ground.

"Take this you jerk-off", Zachary laughed aloud.

The sounds of laughter from the other boys became muffled in the slight fog that appeared from beneath their feet. The density became thicker and thicker as the seconds turned into minutes. The eerie feeling of the forest began to display the howling of wolves in the distance. Unphased by the reaction of the forest, the boys began discussing the events that unfolded a few years ago. The bragging of the murder of their fellow student garnered the attention of an appearance within the dark shadows of the trees. The several sets of blue green eyes started to appear one by one behind the tall figure. The darkness overshadowed the appearance of what looked like a person looking back at them.

"Who is there? What are you doing here? This is a private party", yelled Zachary.

"Get the hell out of here before you get your ass kicked", Gregory screamed.

"Yeah. Want to end up missing you piece of shit?" Chris Vincent asked.

The figure in the dark slowly appeared closer to them as the fog surrounding their feet at the ground they stood on. The once bright moon looking down on the opening of the forest was now covered with dark clouds and flashes of lightning. The temperature in the air was steadily dropping and the chill in the air began the chattering of several sets of teeth. The harmony of buckling knees and chattering jaws echoed through the trees as the being crept closer to the fire that gleamed in the eyes of the frightened boys.

"Greg, what the hell is that thing?" his little brother asked.

"I don't know, but this must be a dream or something", Greg replied.

The focus of the boys remained on the apparition's shadow as it slowly began to reveal itself. The darkness surrounding the presence began to enlighten the color of grey into a redness in the eyes of those watching.

"Is that a red hooded sweatshirt that thing is wearing?" Rob Pennington asked.

"Hold on here, is this a fucking joke?" Greg asked.

"This isn't funny at all. Reveal yourself now?" Zach asked.

The coldness of the air began numbing the limbs of the teens as their t-shirts and shorts became less protective. Nature's elements began encircling the spot where the remaining teens stood as the hooded creature stood silent. Gregory reached into his front pocket and grabbed the large knife that he always kept close to him. The cold fingers of the graduate could barely feel the small metal object as he gripped it as hard as he deemed

possible. The moment the knife found the cold air away from his pocket, the loud growling shook the nerves of the boys standing nervously close to each other. Turning around, the appearance of an angry white wolf with large teeth stared back at them. The chills of the air relegated the nervous eyes of those in the wolf's path to stand perpetually frozen.

"Greg, there is a wolf staring at us with creepy blue eyes", his little brother frantically whispered.

Greg failed to respond as his lifeless fingers let go of the knife as it fell beneath the thick fog onto the ground. Frantic of the growling wolf looking through their souls, the boys all stood closer as if they were huddling to remain warm.

"Gentleman", the voice behind them stated.

The voice caught the attention of the teens as they slowly turned around and what they saw frightened them even worse. The appearance of words wanted to creep out of the bully's mouths, but nothing escaped their foolish minds. Confused and bewildered, the shaking of their bodies relegated each teen into a weightless feather floating in the night.

"How is this possible? We killed you", Gregory replied to what he saw.

"This is insane, pure madness. Are we in a nightmare?" Chris Pyles stated.

"I saw you die, what the hell is this?" Zachary asked.

The figure standing before them had previously removed his hood as Shawn revealed himself. The pure look of horror on the faces of those who murdered him were miraculous. The thick fog slowly simmered closer to the ground as the appearance of several blue eyes approached closer behind Shawn. The teens standing close to the fire huddled into a small group were now surrounded by the black wolves eager to strike. The area's light illuminated by the fire was slowly beginning to fade and it was the thought of the boys that irony had come for them.

"We are sorry, ok. We are sorry and please forgive us", Zachary stated.

"Fuck that, you deserved to die you son of a bitch", Greg yelled.

Cracking a smile upon his face, Shawn reached down to his waste line and began removing his Sweatshirt above his head and from his body. The bare chest of the young teen chiseled to perfection was now gathering the attention of the teens. Shawn began to kneel on one knee as the harmful screams of the trees began to sway back and forth. The transformation began to mortify the eyes of the teens looking down on the appearance of the boy who they once killed. The slight fog covered Shawn's face, but the teens were witnessing the small punctures of what appeared to be tree branches crawling away from Shawn's back. The silent pain that withered beneath the veins of the angel kneeling before them, his large wings began to unfold. The arms of a thousand souls began embracing the barks of the trees once again, while the boys cried out.

"What the fuck is that?" Greg yelled.

"Oh my god, we are going to die", Zachary equally yelled.

Attempting to run away from the angel-like creature in front of them, the growling of the surrounding wolves grew louder. Unable to escape, the boys began crying and begging for their lives as the evil amongst them grew stronger. Shawn began to stand and with his dark wings before him, his legs began to float above the ground. His body levitating ten feet above the teens, he spoke with aggression.

"Today is your day of reckoning. My death symbolized the fate of seven lost boys who reluctantly failed to understand their full destiny upon this broken path. Did you think you could murder an innocent boy and assume that this day would never come? Your foolish pride is now your demise and I will bring upon thee the wrath you once brought me", Shawn stated.

Reaching towards the sky with his dark wings spread away from his body, a wave of gravity reached through the area around them as a bolt of lightning struck the fire next to the huddled teens. The sky emptied its anger onto the small spot of flames and distinguished the only light used clearly see their surroundings. The sudden loss of vision turned into a darkness that presented a challenge for the fate of the seven boys in the forest. The eyes of the beasts amongst the dark allotted the screams of innocence as Shawn allowed his four-legged creatures to avenge his death. The electric field of mist surrounding the area insulated the loud screams of terror as the sound of tearing flesh, broken bones and gurgling blood lasted for several minutes. The grunting of his creatures fed upon the fate of the seven boys who sealed their lives with a toast towards the immortal sins of their beleaguered Gregory. The cries of the innocent fell on deaf ears as the commotion upon the darkness was greeted with dead silence. Gregory, Zach, Chris, Stephen, the two Rob's and another Chris had met their fate and would forever remain lost within their own souls. The clouds above slowly moving aside to the rays of the full moon, the macabre scene created by the wolves was in full sight. The slew of body parts had reminded Shawn that his actions led to the demise of seven young men. Startled, the presence of evil inside his eyes began to slowly bring a compassion towards his deeds. The wolves began walking away into the distance as Shawn remained levitated in the forest comprised of death and vengeance below. The moonlight above reminding him of the essence of his true power and with a blink of his eyes, he felt the wrath of his path back to the room under the pumping station. Exhausted and feeling worthless, Shawn slowly limped his pride back to the house. The thoughts ran through his mind thinking he would rejoice over the vengeance he just accomplished, but it wasn't meant to be. Sick to his stomach, Shawn spent the next couple of days hidden in his bedroom and away from the world.

Tired of feeling lost and wanting to let go of his horrific memories, Shawn buried the sunlight for the next several days. Imperfect and shattered, he would discover the Weymouth Seven were missed by many. The mystery of the forest soon brought forth the attention of the nation and Shawn stayed silent. It was the memory of his beautiful Katie that prevented him from tearing the whole world apart. Cold and crippled without the love of his life, Shawn would spend the days inside of his room contemplating the idea to get her back in his life. The idea that having her by his side was not enough, while he wanted everything she strongly offered. The premonition of the next school year would regard Shawn living his life as normal as possible. If that was going to remain true, it would have to start with the Summer. The great divide between the shallow world that Shawn had created, and the rest of the planet were to align perfectly. To remain forgiven in the eyes of many, Shawn would spend the upcoming months going back to becoming a normal teen.

Chapter 23
Junior Year (89'-90')

The Summer of Baseball in the town of Topsfield gave the area an outlook on the upcoming Masco team they were going to see. With Shawn and his teammates besting all who dared play against them, Topsfield would finish the season with no losses and the chances it would carry over onto the Football field were slim to none. Jim Hugh was in his second year as the Varsity Football Coach and representing one of the worst programs in Massachusetts history. He was determined to change the culture and it began the day into the first practice. A familiar and new face was amongst the players and the smile on Coach Hugh's face indicated that Shawn had finally arrived. Absent from the year before, Coach Pugh would spend the first two weeks of double session practices implementing the offense that Shawn displayed two years prior. The strength of Masco was their speed, heart and the arm of their new Quarterback. For Coach Pugh to eliminate the doubters, he supplanted Jeffrey Wilks as the former QB and placed him as the Wide Receiver. His speed culminating with his ability to break tackles would give the team a true slot receiver. The idea to break away from the terrible Nebraska style wishbone offense attracted Shawn to the Varsity team. Equipped with a smaller Defense and quick Offense, the team prepared over the rest of the Summer to validate its place in the Cape Ann League.

Shawn's Junior year began quickly as the Summer came to an end twice as fast as the previous years. Rumors began to swirl the football scrimmages revealed Masconomet was on the rise. Coach Pugh held interview after interview with questions of his accomplishments with the new Offense. The common answer would result in the eyes of the entire Northshore area watching the first game against North Andover. Considered one of the largest crowds in Masco history, the entire stadium and track area were filled with students, media and out of towners wanting to see the new results. The game beginning on a Saturday late morning, would result in a couple hours of entertaining dazzle from Coach Hugh's team. The Chieftains of Masco celebrated their largest victory in over a decade with a fifty-two to seven score. The Offense took a back seat that afternoon with a smothering and confident Defense that scored three touchdowns of their own. Amassing over four hundred yards in the air, Masco started their year off perfect and it would culminate into a season of accolades and seven wins against two losses. The last game of the season would be a home game against Ipswich on Thanksgiving Day. The team that gashed the Chieftains Defense the previous few years was now upon them and it was a battle of two of the best teams in the league.

The early morning snow seen outside of his bedroom window presented a beautiful challenge as Shawn awoke early on this Thanksgiving Day. The site of the hard-falling stickiness brought a cheer and joy he hadn't felt since Katie was in this very room. His mother knocked with grace and peaked her head inside the door.

"Son, its time to get up for the big game darlin. I have an amazing surprise for you", his mother responded.

The weather didn't chase away the anticipation as the stadium filled with the entire student body cheered their team. While

Shawn prepared to warm up with his throws on the sideline, a voice slowly grabbed his attention.

"Shawn. Shawn Lee. Hey. Shawn", the voice yelled loudly.

The gentle voice ran chills through his body as his eyes couldn't dare fool him. The face that Shawn died many times over to see once again, was now staring at him from beyond the fence. The sudden adrenaline that ran through his body, mustered the courage to collect himself and run over to his Katie.

"Oh my God Katie, what are you doing here? How did you get here?" Shawn asked.

"My father and I saw you on the news and I begged him to bring me here. Are you mad?" Katie asked.

"No, never. I wouldn't dare be upset with you", Shawn replied.

"Shawn, there are so many people here. I am so proud of you", Katie mentioned.

Shawn crawled over the fence separating the two lovers, and they embraced each other. Tears falling from Katie's face, their lips locked with a passion that warmed a spot beneath their feet as they stood in the snow. The few onlookers that paid attention to the star quarterback near the fence saw their hero deeply in love. It was the first time that his circle has been penetrated by others vision and it was a welcoming feeling. The entire student body in the stands on Thanksgiving morning envisioned Shawn's feelings and it began a cheer that spread onto the field.

"*Now go win this thing*", Katie stated to Shawn.

"*Yes ma'am*", Shawn replied.

Watching Shawn walk towards the opening of the gate and towards the sideline, Katie was approached by a few girls wearing cheerleader uniforms from Masco.

"*Are you Shawn's girlfriend?*" one of the girls asked.

Katie smiled in the direction of the bench Shawn was sitting on and looked over at the girls, "*Nah, I am just going to marry him someday*", she replied.

The excitement and look of surprise on the girl's face's brought quick claps from their hands and jubilation advanced throughout the crowd.

The eyes of the school watched gracefully as the Masco Chieftains endured a battle lasting over a few hours. Back and forth with touchdown after touchdown from each team, the scoreboard on the field could barely keep up. The Defenses of both Cape Ann League teams had fought hard to withstand the onslaught of the two best Offenses in New England. The Ipswich Tigers dressed in their Clemson Orange fielded the most provocative running game in the entire country. Shawn and the Masco red and white countered with their own passing attack that caught the attention of the Boston area. By halftime, the

24-20 score didn't indicate the quantity of yards amassed that early morning. The multiple turnovers by each team prevented the score to add up even further, while play continued. The snowy conditions worsened, and the inches of white powder continuously stuck to the ground, causing issues with the holding of the football. The beginning of the second half allowed Ipswich to flourish in the inches of snow covering the Masco field. Two straight touchdowns generated a 33-24 lead that quieted the aggressive crowd. Visibility was at a minimum and the Masco receivers were having issues with their footing in the deep snow. Noticing the game plan wasn't working, Shawn brilliantly came up with a plan to detour the Tigers Defense.

"Coach, why don't we begin attacking the seams of the field instead of the out routes we're are running", Shawn suggested.

Shawn asked for a marker board and began drawing up the situations for Coach Hugh to see. His mindset was to spread out the Offense while the Tight Ends and Jeff could fly up the seams of the field. It was a brilliant idea to turn five-yard pass plays into a lot more.

"Absolutely brilliant Shawn. Let's do it", the Coach replied with angst.

Catching the attention of the Offense, Coach Hugh allowed Shawn to implement the changes and the first play worked to perfection. The team lined up with two tight ends and spread the wide receivers away from the formation. Shawn drew himself under the center and what appeared to be a running play, turned into a fifty-yard gain down the right hash of the football field. The tight ends became more heavily involved and the game film that the Ipswich Defense has previously studied was now irrelevant. The confusion on Defense the rest of the game allowed Masco to tie the score up with less than two minutes remaining at forty a piece. The drama would soon unfold as Coach Pugh called for an on sides kick. The unfolding play upon kickoff drew ire and surprise from the crowd, but would it work? The often, brilliant Kenneth Fulton and his barefoot approach helped supplant his leg just perfectly as the ball traveled the necessary 10 yards. The kick heard around the world landed in the arms of the Masco special team's player and Masco had just over a minute to score and win the game. The pressure was on to begin the final drive on their own forty-yard line. With sixty yards until pay dirt, Shawn concocted a plan to gracefully wear the clock down. He knew his defense was tired and would more than likely surrender a touchdown, so he focused.

Coach Pugh allowed Shawn to control the game the entire second half and he wasn't changing his position. The first play was an option to the left of the field and as Shawn began pulling away towards the line, he pitched the ball to Richie and he was able to gain four yards. With second down and ninety-five seconds and counting on the clock, Shawn called an audible. He noticed the defense placed nine men in the box in front of him, so he changed the running play. Noticing the two safeties were hugging the line of scrimmage, it was an all-out blitz that was arriving. Fifteen seconds surpassing off the clock allowed Shawn to adjust his team to place three wide receivers on the right side of the field. In a bunch formation, Shawn received the football in the shotgun formation and immediately threw the ball towards the direction of the three receivers. Jeff Wilks had stepped back as the play began while the other two receivers around him began blocking. The receiver screen worked brilliantly as Jeff's quick speed placed each yard behind him. The culmination of thick snow and the speed of the Ipswich cornerback caught up with Jeff and he was knocked out of bounds at the opponents twenty-yard line. Within field goal range, Shawn would bare witness to the birth of his mastery of the football game. The quick change of play gained thirty plus yards and put his team into position to end the battle of titans. The first play from the twenty-yard line resulted in a dive up the middle, resulting in a two-yard gain. With the clock running itself down to fifty seconds, Shawn hesitated. Thinking that this could result in a forfeiture of his mind, he decided to call a play at the line that would hopefully jar the defense. Calling an audible away from the running play, Shawn motioned the running back to the right side of the field. The call would be very gutsy, but the quick screen to Richie would most likely succeed his legs to running through the blocks placed in front of him. Instead, the play call suggested that Richie catch the ball and place his hands of the laces of the football and deliver a pass to the other side of the field. The awaiting quarterback would find himself wide open and the receiver of six points dashed beyond the end zone and into the arms of his team mates. The home crowd erupting with celebration and yelling, the score pinned them seven points better than their opponent. With forty seconds remaining, the team would have to rely on their defense, and Coach Pugh had a recipe brewing.

Taking a page from Shawn's playbook, he disguised his Defense from his normal 4-3 scheme to a cover 2. Not known for its popularity, the Defense now placed a two deep safety cover to prevent any passes from reaching behind them. Unaware of the disguise, the Tiger quarterback reached back and threw a deep pass in the middle of the field into the awaiting arms of the safety. The interception sealed the seven-point win and the cheers from the crowd could be heard from the surrounding towns. With over nine hundred yards of offense from both teams combined, it would entice the Boston area to recognize the game as the best of the year. Clearly without seeing a loser from both teams, it was evident that Masco's eight wins weren't expected when the season began. The talk of the area was the High School from Topsfield that took a team with one of the worst records in the country to League Winner in 1989. The emphasis focused on the coaching changes the year prior and it was also attributed to the new attitude brought upon the football field. Masco was highly regarded as a powerhouse in its football program and visiting teams took notice for years to come.

Enjoying the accolades that came with victory, Katie and Shawn visited the home of Mike Hilliard for the after-game party. The entire football team met the woman that captured the heart of their star quarterback and they realized how amazing she was. Intelligent and exuberant, the other girlfriends attending the party magnetically drew to her. The guys telling their stories of their vantage points of the game, a sudden jealousy developed between Jeff and Shawn. The two all stars of the Cape Ann League were experiencing a rift in their temporary friendship. The season was to begin with Jeff as the starting quarterback, but Coach Hugh thought otherwise. The jealousy that came with the eight wins was attributed in the media towards Shawn and his electric arm. Quietly, Jeffrey developed a hatred for Shawn and it finally blew up during the party.

"You know what, I should have been the quarterback of this god damned team", Jeffrey yelled loudly.

His friends attempting to calm him down, Jeffrey grabbed Shawn by his shirt and nearly ripped his entire collar off. The torn clothing exposed a marking that his teammates noticed on his back. The small slit appeared to be partially bleeding and they all assumed Jeffery had cut him.

"Its just a wound I received on the field guys, its fine. Seriously", Shawn replied quickly.

With Jeff visibly angry, the team pulled the two together and both shook hands after several minutes. The heat felt inside of Shawn's palms, hallucinations of death and evil ran through his mind as he pulled his hand away in fear. The emptiness felt throughout the living room, Jeff immediately apologized and asked Shawn to understand the moment lost.

"I am sorry, I lost my head there. I wanted the success that you helped us attain and I was sort of jealous", Jeff nervously stated.

"Jeff, are you kidding me right now? I wouldn't have done it without you. You and many of these guys staring at us right now are why we are champions. This was not about any one person, it was about our team", Shawn swiftly replied.

Cheers and claps from the guys yelling the words Masco repeatedly brought together a bond that excited the beginning of Shawn's Junior Year. That night at Mike's party symbolized that Masco would win together as a team and lose together also. The fear kept within Jeff's mind was now a part of his conscious and it was because of the man he hated deep inside. Shawn and Katie would abruptly leave early from the party and since she was able to stay with Shawn's parents that evening, they waited for their ride. Unknown to Shawn, it was secretly agreed upon by their parents that Katie would stay at Shawn's house over Thanksgiving weekend. The snow-flakes falling from the evening sky upon both of their faces, Shawn whispered in her ear. *"I love you and yes I will marry you someday"*.

"How did you know I said that?" Katie asked nervously.

Shawn smiled at her and the sound of the horn revealed that his mother had arrived to take them home. The couple would embrace in the back seat of the car while the motions of the roads lead them to the house they called home for the weekend. From late Thursday through mid-Sunday, the two love birds didn't once speak about her abolishment from the Nike Village the last time she visited. Without words, the two would just snuggle for an eternity while Shawn's parents left them alone. The energy between the teens reminded his parents of what they were like when they first met, and it brought a welcomed electricity throughout the home. The conversations on each evening spoke of the love for her boyfriend with her parents. The excitement that her parents were welcoming him with open arms was more encouragement to fight hard for this relationship.

Chapter 24
Poison of the Angel

Cuddling each other through that Thursday night, Friday morning came quickly, and Katie turned on the television to watch the morning news. Boston WHDH7 was reporting the story of the missing seven teens from Weymouth, intriguing Katie. She had heard the story a few times before, but this was much different. The names of the missing teens had been heard before and she slowly remembered what Shawn once told her.

"Shawn, wake up. Baby wake up now", Katie frightenedly said.

Arising from his deep sleep, he opened his eyes and the site of the Forest in Weymouth on his television startled him.

"What's wrong?" Shawn asked.

"Look at me Shawn and you tell me the truth. Did you have something to do with disappearance of those boys?" Katie asked with purpose.

Taking his time to answer her question, Shawn breathed deeply and began to speak.

"I don't know honestly. I heard about them over the Summer and I ask myself each day if I had something to do with their deaths. Katie, I am scared", Shawn cried out.

Holding Katie tight, she gripped him with the security that he had missed, while the truth buried inside of him was never going to be relinquished. The thought of losing her again would nearly defeat his purpose to live, so he played dumb. The nightmares of the boys he had removed from this world stayed far away from his thoughts. Both teens watched the remaining story on television and the sorrow deep inside him felt nothing for the bullies. The demise was a proper exit wound that boiled the poison inside of his veins, and the new angel attempted to figure out a strategy to break his bond with Vincent. Thanksgiving weekend turned out to be the most comforting for Shawn as he spent it loving Kate all over again. The two would spend the days watching the snow storm cover the hills of the Nike Village. The strong bond built their hearts closer together and upon having to leave him once again, tears of pain secluded the lovers with endearing patience. Broken promises given to Katie about the boys from Weymouth gave way to solemn words of romance. The distance between them grew once again and Shawn began to focus more on the remainder of his Junior year.

The School Year of 1989 turned over into the decade of the nineties and the whispers of Shawn's girlfriend ran wild through the hallways. How could a bad boy like himself land such a gorgeous young woman? The innuendos of Masco were unbearable to most, but Shawn was preventing any drama from detouring his promising Year. Armed with a long-distance relationship in Katie and the baseball season approaching, there was nothing that could go wrong in Shawn's eyes.

The long cold winter was still upon the town of Topsfield and as Shawn sat in the cafeteria one afternoon studying, a loud screaming blared inside of his ears.

"Help me please, someone help", the painful voice yelled.

Shawn heard the voice from outside the cafeteria as he focused his eyes through the double doors facing the parking lot. It appeared to his eyes that two boys were dragging a female into the woods. Running towards them, Shawn yelled to get their attention.

"Hey, what are you doing over there. Both of you stop", Shawn yelled.

Approaching closer, he saw Amanda curled into a ball on the ground as the two boys were looking down upon her. The sounds of gargling spewed from the area where the boys were standing, as they began noticing Shawn standing close. The look of emptiness inside of the eyes of the two perpetrators gave way to the blackness releasing itself from their bodies. Their dilated pupils slowly coming back to normal, as they both fell limp to the ground.

"Amanda are you ok?" Shawn asked.

"What the hell were they? What the hell is going on?" Amanda repeatedly asked.

"I don't know and lets just get you back to the cafeteria", Shawn implied.

The trembling of Amanda's body as Shawn carried her to the doors of the cafeteria could be felt in his arms. Her head resting on his chest, Shawn whispered in her ear. *"Everything is going to be alright, you are safe with me".*

Amanda feeling the beating of his plastic heart against her weary temple, she felt safe knowing he was the same angel from the Library. Sitting Amanda down at one of the chairs at the table, Shawn had a million questions.

"What were you doing when they grabbed you?" Shawn asked.

"I was doing homework near the football field when those two idiots began citing weird phrases from their mouth and began grabbing me", Amanda replied.

"Can you recall what they were saying Amanda? Think really hard about it", Shawn asked.

"Shawn, it was a bunch of stupid mumbling. Let me think. Ugh, I can't. Hold on, I remember something strange. One of the boys began talking to the other in a weird dialect", Amanda stated.

"Dialect? Was it a different language?" Shawn asked.

"No. Hold up, I got it. I was just studying this last period with our Spanish class. Let me remember?" Amanda patiently asked.

"Take your time. Just concentrate", Shawn mentioned.

Grabbing a pencil from her book bag, Amanda began writing down what she might have heard from the boys that abducted her. Slowly rekindling the words, Amanda began writing phrases in her head as they translated themselves with her pencil. She remembered that the voices were of Spanish origin and from the very start, the words became clearer as she pronounced them over and over.

"Shawn, I almost have it. The last word I am having issues with, but hang on here, I am literally drawing a blank", Amanda said.

Literally a few seconds later, Amanda finally was able to crack the dialect between the two boys and it made no sense to either Shawn or herself.

"Even angels have their demons? What the hell does that mean?" Shawn asked.

"Beats me, but we need to figure this out before they attempt to grab someone else. I noticed you looked at the two guys real funny. Why?" Amanda asked.

"Let's meet after school. We need to go over a lot and I rather not discuss it here", Shawn mentioned.

"My mother is never home, and my dad isn't around anymore, so my place is good. Meet me at the student parking lot near the football field side after school, I park towards the back.", Amanda quickly responded.

The day quickly went faster than anticipated as Amanda drove them both to her home a few miles away from the school. When Shawn walked in behind her, the house was immaculately clean. The living room and dining room were spotless and as Amanda gave Shawn the tour, they eventually stopped in her den. Stacked with tons of books throughout her small library, it appeared that someone had been looking for very valuable information. Atop the desk near the doorway lay a large open book revealing the pictures of demonic symbols followed by scriptures. With most of the writing appearing to be in Latin and Arabic, Shawn sat down and took a closer look.

"Shawn, ever since I met you, I have had these horrific nightmares that don't allow me to get much sleep. Terrible visions of demonic beings and hell on earth burning in my mind. It sounds stupid, but I have spent the last year collecting as much information as I could learning about these dreams", Amanda stated.

"Tell me everything you know Amanda and I promise to let you know all that I know", Shawn politely stated.

"The day I met you in 9th grade, that same night I remember my first dream. I was walking in the woods by my house here and I

was greeted by a red hooded figure with no face. It stood there saying nothing and the dream kept living itself for a few weeks. Not one confrontation until I decided to approach it a little closer. That is when the red evil eyes started to peak through the hood. I screamed so hard that night, I woke my mother up. From that night on, I frantically had so many nightmares I began drawing them", Amanda mentioned.

 Walking over to the shelf near the window, Amanda grabbed a large book and placed it in front of Shawn. She began turning pages and stopped at a few specific sketches. Shawn's eyes lit up at the horrific ordeal that Amanda suffered. Drawing after drawing of the relentlessness that she suffered at the hands of the evil inside her mind. Not sure how Amanda became entangled or entrapped inside of these horrific dreams, Shawn had a hard time tying his life with hers.

"Amanda, what do these dreams have to do with me?" Shawn asked.

"Give this a second here my friend, this is about to get interesting", Amanda replied.

Amanda turned the pages of her large book of drawings and the pictures were of an evil that Shawn had never seen. The next page turned over placed him beyond the floor of the room they were standing in.

"What's wrong?" Amanda asked.

"Amanda, where did you get this picture from?" Shawn asked.

Fearing her answer, Shawn motioned to Amanda that she needed to remain quiet.

"Don't tell me. I already know, because I feel him here in this house", Shawn replied swiftly.

"Shawn, I need you to listen to me very carefully. I am going to show you a picture of someone that I think you might be interested in", Amanda promptly stated.

Holding his breath and wanting to close his eyes, it was the similar curves of the picture that broadened his focus. The slight dampness forming in the corner of his eyes enlightened his heart to a point of breaking.

"Amanda, how can this be? Look at me god damn it, woman! What the fuck is this all about? Is this a joke?" Shawn angrily asked.

Tears falling from Amanda's eyes, she began to speak and attempted to hold back her true feelings.

"Shawn, I have seen Katie in my dreams for the last several months. When I saw her at the football game, I knew I had seen her before. I don't understand why I see her, but she is always standing by the door of a large house. The picture of her is

always of black and white and she never says anything with this blank look upon her face", Amanda replied.

"I am sorry for yelling and I know you are trying to help, but I have heard about this same dream. Katie always told me that her favorite song was "Heaven" by Warrant and if you listen to the few first sentences in the song, her dream sounds eerily similar", Shawn replied quickly.

"Amanda, the picture of the guy you drew, when do you normally see him in your visions?" Shawn asked again.

"Ever since the day in the Library when I saw you", Amanda replied.

"In the Library. What do you mean? The day I transformed?" Shawn asked.

"I was there Shawn and when everyone else around me remained frozen, I was able to clearly see everything", Amanda said.

Holding his forehead against his hands, Shawn stared down at the picture that just happened to be on the next page. The only  person that could have drawn a picture like the one he was looking at, was someone who had witnessed his transformation. Not understanding clearly how she was involved, Shawn asked again

.

"Amanda, I need you to think here. How the heck, were you able to see me that day while others couldn't?"

"The only person that knows is Vincent and I need to learn how to break from this grasp", Shawn replied to his own question. *"Amanda, you earlier had this book out over here that was presenting pictures and scriptures. What were you in search of?"* Shawn asked.

"You are going to think I am crazy, but I am onto something and I need you to be transparent for a second. What if you were created on this Earth to help this evil spirit do his dirty work. I have no idea why I was able to see you that day in the Library, but it freaks me out every time I think about it." Amanda jokingly replied.

"What if we are approaching Armageddon and you are the key to its beginning?" she continued to ask.

Shawn began to slightly understand Amanda's purpose, but could she be helpful for what he was looking for.

"The demons know you are onto something, that is why they attempted to eliminate you today. What I can't figure out is, why can't you seem them, but you saw me?" Shawn asked.

"Let's not revisit that bullshit again please. That was an ordeal I want no part of again. For a second there, I seriously thought I was going to die. So, thanks again for being my angel. Shawn, I have always known there is something special about you, but everyone in this god damn school thinks I am full of crap", Amanda stated.

The clues were relentless for the two to see, but Shawn was unable to pin point the reason for Amanda's existence in his life. He knew that if he could put the similarity together, she could be very useful.

Chapter 25
Journey of the firefly

Amanda had spent countless nights gathering books and information so that she would be able to understand her visions. It was always her intention to get Shawn to see what she had been envisioning, and now that he was in her midst, it was time to bring everything to the table. The coffee pot was brewing ahead of a long night and the cups of Joe they were facing would only delay the inevitable. Amanda placed the large scrap book of drawings onto another desk in the room, uncovering the book Shawn had moved earlier. Looking down at the open book, Amanda noticed the confused look upon Shawn's curious face.

"Don't let this stuff boggle your mind my friend. I've been studying these books and their meanings since that day in the library. Apparently, a few hundred years after the birth of Christ, seven men encountered what appeared to be a serpent. One of the men approached the kind beast and the human-like snake began speaking. It offered salvation to the men who were seeking solace towards the upcoming months of a cold winter. In exchange for its protection, the men would owe him their souls. Two of the men agreed and the others hesitated because they just needed

medicine to heal their wounds. Unable to agree, the serpent took notice and banished them to a cave for the next 300 years. The souls of the men would remain trapped and give the serpent a being to transform itself into.

The story continues when a farmer many years later discovers the cavern the seven men were buried inside of. On the wall were scriptures of the dreams and nightmares they would suffer in terror. Reading here, an angel in black wings would visit them offering an opportunity to end their days so the serpent could reign upon the world. The nightmares continued until they were visited by another form of evil. The callousness of this presence wasted no time in burying all seven men alive inside of the cavern. The discovery by the farmer proved that the death of the seven men had recently happened with fresh graves upon his feet. The

drawings of the men on the wall could never have been those who had fallen. But, by another hand and it says here that the signature of all the drawings were

left blank", Amanda cited.

"I recognize this face", Shawn said while turning back to the first page.

Shawn looking startled at the pictures, it appeared that Vincent had been consistently going through time seeking victims to

240

take advantage of. Unclear, he began listening to Amanda and attempting to comprehend the information she gathered.

"I am assuming the serpent was responsible for the drawings because it doesn't make sense. Throughout history...."

"I am going to interrupt you Amanda. I know what's going on here. It has come to me now. The signs of the page here after the serpent show a circle and several objects in the center. This is the sign of an evil spell not of Satan, but of some type of ritual. That same picture is located at the Nike Site by my house", Shawn stated.

"Yes, that makes a lot of sense. What you are saying is that these symbols on the walls were used to draw spells to protect them from Satan?" Amanda asked.

"Exactly, but why is he trying to prevent me from seeing Kate?" Shawn asked.

Turning the pages quickly in front of Shawn, Amanda landed on a chapter that she knew by heart. Reading the chapter several times, it spoke about how to defeat Lucifer and his reign of terror on Earth.

"See Shawn, don't you get it. Lucifer is still angry. Cast down from the falling skies of Heaven, all he ever wanted was to cast doubt on society. The moment you show fear or show a sign of being afraid, he has you. Those are signs of giving strength to his powers, but you found a weakness. Your love for Kate and

the ability to keep Vincent away has shown that you possess a powerful hold over his evil", Amanda replied.

"Damn, that makes all the sense in the world. The weekend we were together, I didn't hear from him. Amanda, you are a genius", Shawn stated.

"I know", Amanda smartly replied.

Standing in the doorway by the entrance to the living room, he began to peak at the television that had been left on. Shawn noticed a large abundance of small lights flashing from bugs on a nature channel Amanda had on previously.

"Amanda, what is that on television?" Shawn asked.

"You never seen fireflies before? They are called lightning bugs around these parts, but the males flash a signal for the females to mate with them. Talk about romantic, but you don't see them around these parts until springtime", Amanda joked.

"Sounds like a ton of love in the air", Shawn laughed.

"We need to hammer out a plan here because Katie is going to need my help soon Amanda", Shawn mentioned.

While Amanda continued looking through her book, a question suddenly came across her lips. *"Shawn, how did you ever get mixed up in all this anyway?"*

The silence from Shawn as he stared outside of the window surmised the entire evening. Not withholding the truth from Amanda, he began to sit down in the chair facing the desk. The long story that began in the evening would entice Amanda's knowledge throughout the night. By the time Shawn had finished his story about his mother and Vincent, the sound of the birds began chirping outside of the window.

"Shawn, I have a few ideas that may help, but I am going to need time to develop them", Amanda stated.

"I need to get my ass home before my parents lose their minds", Shawn replied.

Amanda drove Shawn home that early morning and the rest of the weekend was used to study the angles in which both teens would implement ways to help Shawn. Amanda would crack the books as much as her tired eyes could handle and the ideas would have to wait as she fell asleep at her desk. Relegated to learning the entire life of Shawn earlier, Amanda became susceptible to her visions. The flux of information gathered inside of her memory allowed her senses to relax while she lay asleep and vulnerable.

She awoke quickly to hear her mother arrive through the front door. Walking by the entrance to the Library, a tall man with wavy dark hair followed her mother closely behind. Without any words, the face that turned around to look at Amanda had a look of pure evil. The dark clothed man placed his index finger over his mouth to silence the thoughts of the teen. The piercing left eye of the stranger glowed into bright red as the two adults disappeared down the hallway. Seconds later, the loud screams of her mother scared the nerves inside of Amanda's body.

"Mom, Mom. I am coming", Amanda yelled at the top of her lungs.

Running down the hallway, Amanda felt as if her legs were moving, but her body went in slow motion. Unable to get to her mother's bedroom fast enough, the screams turned into silence as the hallway turned pitch black. Frightened to move, the sounds of the walls surrounding her in the hallway began to crumble. Wanting to drop to her knees, the voice within her spoke.

"Amanda, come to me", the deep voice stated.

"What do you want? Leave me alone!" Amanda yelled.

Standing silent in the dark, Amanda felt a slight tap across the back of her neck. Panicking violently, Amanda began trembling with terror while her toes became numb. The dim light piercing her eyes an illumination of several faces upon a grisly wall

suddenly appeared. The fear in the eyes of the many souls plastered on the wall sent chills throughout each cell in her blood. The sounds of gagging and the failure to breath murmured loudly before her eyes. Frightened with fear, the illumination disappeared, and a calm silence rang over the chilling air. Amanda noticed the temperature around her began to drop quickly and

the frost covering her breath invited the sight of an evil she never saw before. The appearance of a scary female with whiteness in her eyes and stitches covering a large scar on her right cheek and forehead, Amanda began screaming profusely. Staring at Amanda without one word to say, the pure evil needed no communication to bring out the terror inside of the frail teen. The inviting evil welcomed the horror as fuel to its creepy nature. Feeding off the panic of her silent tears, a slight resemblance arose in her clouded mind. What appeared before her struck a common feature that Amanda noticed within several seconds. She wanted to open her mouth and scream her name, but something deep within relinquished her of the five letters upon her lips. Feeling lost and lonely, a huge part of Amanda wanted to comfort the broken woman staring back at her. No longer afraid, Amanda began to portray the evil as a sign to understand its purpose.

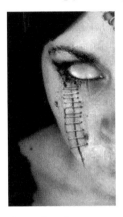

"Why are you here"? Amanda asked.

Silence returned with a vengeance and her efforts were falling short. Feeling exhausted, Amanda took the moment to understand what complications arose and to study them. The clock ticking in her brain, she knew that Katie was the girl standing in front of her, but why? Her resemblance to the teen she met at the football game was a sign that the two were supposed to meet for this very purpose.

"Are you Katie?" Amanda politely asked.

The sudden movement of the creature as she attempted to speak without her mouth, startled Amanda. The look of confusion on the face of the young woman turned into fear and then she disappeared. The frantic cries of help could be heard throughout the darkness and Amanda couldn't pin point the source. Slowing her heart rate and breathing calmly, the noises created less confusion through her body. Taking each second at a time, the sounds of the crying of babies could be heard on each side of her ears. The symphony of deathly screams began to rise louder and louder, yet Amanda remained calm.

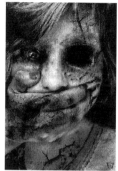

The smart tactic to allow the evil to surmise the position of its control over her fell without anticipation. The reluctance was not welcome as Amanda wanted to fully understand the vision she found herself inside of. She realized that Katie was reaching out to her, but why? The acknowledgement of the creature to its own name helped create the bond that existed between them, though was it enough? Katie was trying to communicate, but how was she able to? The questions were all saved into Amanda's memory and just as she was able to calm down, the terror began again. The dim light ahead for Amanda to see gave way to the frightening appearance of her own face looking back at her. The gripping hand covering her mouth, her face missing an eye and the eerie similarity to Katie presented a dread that pushed her fear to the limit. Amanda was staring back at herself and unable to help. The smell of fear and the feeling of pain inside of her heart, she was unable to understand the compromising position her reflection created. What was it trying to tell her? Amanda couldn't think fast enough hoping the apparition would stay in front of her long enough to decipher its purpose. Just as the vision began fading into darkness, Amanda was face-to-face with an unimaginable fear that literally sank her soul beneath the earth. The vision suddenly took place upon a wall that appeared before her eyes.

The distant appearance from far above, she saw two men standing further away from each other. As the picture became clearer and the vision drew closer, Shawn was standing in the road shirtless in between two larger buildings. Opposite of where he was standing, a dark-haired man that appeared to follow her mother earlier was staring Shawn down. Dressed in a suit and wearing a long coat, the sudden movement between the two caused a catastrophic sequence that set the entire area under fire. The pulse of the explosion could be felt inside

 Amanda's bones and her visions were turning into premonitions. The site of the meeting between Vincent and Shawn would possibly create a cataclysmic war that may destroy the demographical area of Topsfield. Amanda knew she had to act quickly, but she wanted to make sure she was able to help Shawn and not hurt him. Amidst the controversial visions that appeared before her, the vision again soon faded into the darkness. Pitch black and cold, crying sounds of a baby began protruding the ears of the young female. The helpless whimpering lasted minutes and then the appearance of a strange vision Amanda never expected. The still face of a baby covered in what appeared to be flies flashing a bright light from their bellies. The image made no sense to the keen intuition that the smart teen had presented. As quickly as the image had shown, it faded into the blackness it originated from. Tired with exhaustion, and the feeling of emptiness within her body, Amanda fell victim to her heavy eyes and suddenly woke up with her head leaned on the desk.

The visions were freshly burned into her mind and she knew she had a few choices to make concerning the premonitions. The careless hands of the teen would make a drastic decision that would change the course of Shawn's life and possibly seal his fate.

Chapter 26
Careless Gravity

The drops of bombs falling into her cup of coffee, Amanda reluctantly felt obligated in making the phone call that could change the fates of everyone involved. The riddle inside of her visions prepared her obtuse mind to solve the fractured puzzle. Instead of following her immature reasons, Amanda would calmly relax that morning while sifting through her research. The long night had left her exhausted and while the temptations of revealing the unknown would reach as far as the opening in her mouth, the words would remain vacated from her lips. The expectations of what she accumulated in the previous evening needed clarity before she would assume their intentions. For no reason, Amanda couldn't figure out why she was mainly involved with the connection between Shawn and Vincent.

"He had mentioned before that I was unable to see most of the apparitions, but why could I see them in my dreams?" Amanda hinted to herself.

The unexplained bothered Amanda and she promised to investigate long enough before revealing what she knew. The key concerns were helping Shawn break free and then understand her involvement. The two had a collision course lying ahead and would it be in her benefit to understand the result? The snowy day had trapped Amanda in her home as the weekend brought a couple of days of relaxation. Since her Mother had been out of town on a business trip, being alone was welcome and needed. Amanda Schmidt was a prodigy of two parents that barely knew each other. She was given up for adoption, but her mother changed her mind and raised her on her own. The Father was kept unknown as he disappeared to never be heard from again. Amanda's mother did everything she could to protect her daughter from anyone and everything. The young girl from age three through today was always special in her own way. Able to translate her visions onto her drawings caught the attention of her teachers. Both positive and negative, the relationship with her therapist the last ten years grew stronger for Amanda. Transforming her ability to become more articulate in her details, her therapist helped her channel the aggression into magic. For over ten years Amanda's visions became relatively more graphic until the stranger from Weymouth arrived. Amanda stopped seeing her Therapist to concentrate on the macabre of events that surrounded her. The visions of death and strange premonitions grew larger and more in detail as each day passed. The day in the Library watching Shawn's transformation had previously drawn itself in a vision week's earlier. If these premonitions were becoming true, Amanda didn't have much time to sit and wait for other visions to appear. They were becoming more violent as each day passed and the confrontation of fire could possibly mean the end of existence as she knew it.

Meanwhile, Shawn woke up with a massive headache and failed to realize the snow outside had accumulated high enough to cover his window. The morning started bleak as his parents left town the night before to visit family in Connecticut. He was alone and left to ponder the conversation with his new friend Amanda. A morning filled with a few bowls of lucky charms, the smile cracking upon his face during memories of Katie, relegated Shawn's boredom. Not a soul in site outside during the brief Winter storm, a knock at the door invited Shawn's reluctance. John and his brothers were wanting to enjoy the temptations of the snow and asked Shawn to endure the events with them. Inviting the boys inside, he noticed little Joey having issues with his garments.

"Dude, who the hell wrapped you up like a croissant?" Shawn asked.

The brothers laughing at the questions, Joey nearly cried.

"Oh stop, it's no big deal little guy. Let me help you here", Shawn replied.

With memories of little Ralphie's brother from the movie *A Christmas Story*, the aggravation turned into laughter. Little Joey's mother was a bit overprotective of her youngest son and didn't want any of his boys getting sick. The few minutes Shawn spent throwing the necessary clothing on to endure the cold had passed, and the boys found themselves on several sleds. The ideal path to take would have been sledding down the large road leading from Shawn's house to the bottom of the hill. The impact of the salt and dirt on the road made it nearly impossible to enjoy the ride, so an alternative route was chosen. John noticed that behind Shawn's house was a steep decline leading through the woods. Without caution, he placed his plastic round sled onto the thick snow and began leaning forward. The quick trip lasted several seconds, but the adventure was wreck loose and care free. Missing a few trees by mere inches, the path John created with his sled implanted a direction for the others to follow. Joey and David both followed quickly as the trail became more permanent for the boys to enjoy. The ride entailed like a roller coaster, the steepness of the decline pumped adrenaline into the boys with a slight hint of dangerous. Equipped with a metal and wooden sled, Shawn followed as well, and his momentum carried him further than the previous landing spot of the others. Able to break through the small barrier, Shawn unintentionally created a longer path the boys would endure. The climb upwards to the top of the hill became tiring for the boys, but Shawn noticed that his new path led close to the concrete walkway nearby. The same walkway that began at the middle of the downward road near John's home was discovered. The walk was longer, but much easier to handle as the boys would spend the entire morning enjoying the rides.

Simultaneously on opposite sides of town, the unfolding events that would occur near the same time was about to begin. Joey had borrowed the metal and wooden sled and attempted to create a new perspective to impress his brothers. With a long running start in the deep snow, Joey approached the awaiting sled with full speed. Jumping on the sled belly first, Joey quickly grabbed the rails to steer the massive wooden rails beneath him. The speed unimaginable to his handling, Joey started screaming as he approached the end of the embankment. Racing faster than a baseball out of his own hand, the sled crashed through the pile of snow as the rails of the sled grabbed the icy concrete of the pathway. Screams turned to laughter as Joey gained full control while guiding the massive sled towards the downward trail. Since this was his first time, Joey was unable to stop because he saw Shawn use his feet to control the distance he would travel. Scared to use his hands to stop his progression, Joey prepared for the crash ahead. The trail led to a structure that appeared to him as a small shack. With his screams attracting the others to follow Joey on the same path, the abrupt crash placed Joey aside of the fence blocking the doorway to the small wooden shed. Waiting for his brothers to arrive, Shawn and the rest of the boys approached Joey by foot. Attempting to say something, Shawn withheld any communication with the brothers about the pumping station they all just discovered.

"This is the water station for the neighborhood", stated John.

"I have heard it late at night making noises, but never really cared", Shawn replied.

David began walking around the fence that encased the large pipes and saw the entrance inside of the shack.

"Hey guys, I found a door", David stated.

Circling the opening, the boys contemplated walking through the door.

"I don't think this is a good idea", Shawn replied.

"Screw that", little Joey aggressively responded.

Joey opened the door to the shed and both boys walked inside, while Shawn and David remained outside.

Across town, Amanda spent the few hours that morning drawing the importance of the visions on her pad. The faces of the premonitions danced on the sheets of paper as if she had been directly with them. The perfection of the details remained quite important to understand the relevancy for what they stood for. The difficulty became unmeasurable when penciling the face of the baby in her visions. The irony of flies crawling on its face puzzled Amanda, but there was a significance that needed to be drawn out. The several pages of material Amanda drew that morning began to help her prioritize her thoughts.

Assessing the similarities, Amanda began to see a hidden pattern she withdrew from her mind. The silence withdrawn from Katie's face resembled an irony with Amanda's reflection. For some reason, Amanda began to assume her thoughts out loud.

"What if Katie is suggestively remaining silent while I am being forced to be quiet? What does that mean? C'mon Amanda, get it together here and figure this out", Amanda said to herself.

Attempting to furtherly think of the possibilities, it finally came to her hours later. The visions weren't meant to scare her away from the situation. They were meant to send a message and the idea that Shawn would understand the purpose for Amanda's involvement would remain confused. Katie was the key because she was silently reaching out to Amanda to provide insight. Still not able to fully comprehend the visions, she knew enough to reach out and call Katie. The attempts to figure out her phone number were resolved the night before when Shawn left his wallet on Amanda's desk. The phone number written on a blank business card, the dangerous fingers of destiny reached out to the lover of her new friend. The dial tone lasting a mere few seconds, the gentle voice of a female answered.

"Hello, can I please speak to Katie?" Amanda asked.

"Hi there, yes this is Katie. Who is this may I ask?" Katie replied.

"Katie, my name is Amanda and I am friends with your boyfriend. Do you have time to talk for a while?" Amanda kindly asked.

"Sure. What's this about? Is Shawn ok?" Katie asked.

While the girls began affiliating themselves with their new conversation, Shawn and the boys were knee deep in snow and seeking shelter inside of a shack by their homes. Joey and his older brother John noticed the small window upon the wall was providing the only light for them to see. A chair and a small desk were pinned up against the corner and the room was close to ten feet by teen feet in diameter. With enough room inside for the four boys, David and Shawn remained uninterested. Joey looked beneath his feet and a hollow sound erupted as he placed pressure upon the floor.

"Hey guys, something is under this mat", Joey insisted.
John pushed his little brother out of the way and removed the mat from its position over the floor. The small door encasing half of the floor has appeared to be an entry way into the ground.

"Shawn, come look at this", John yelled.

Comprehending what had already been there, Shawn acted in surprise to the sudden appearance of the door.

"What the hell is that?" Shawn mysteriously asked.

"It looks like a door numb nuts, open it", David mentioned.

"Wait a second. What if this is also under water like the other place was on the old base?" little Joey asked.

"Let's find out", John replied while pulling on the door.

The large creaking sound from the hinges echoed beneath the ground and the darkness below hindered the boys' vision.

"How far down does this go?" Joey asked.

"David, go down there and see what's down there", John roughly asked.

"Fuck no, you go down there", David aggressively replied.

"You scared little girls get out of my way and let me look", their little brother replied.

The younger brother was always the curious one of the family and it didn't take much for him to delve into trouble. Laying on the ground with his stomach, Joey placed his head inside of the opening. The dampness offering a smell of dirt and gravel, Joey was unable to clearly see anything inches beyond his eyes.

"I can't tell if this is a deep hole or just a cave. I just can't see anything down here", Joey yelled while his echo pierced his ears.

Lifting his head to catch his breath, Joey placed his head below the ground one more time. His angst was determined to find the gall to show his brothers that he was the reason for its discovery.

"Hold up guys, I hear something down here", Joey whispered.

Unable to hear their little brother, John reached down and questioned his light words. Joey lifted his head out of the hole and repeated his last comment. While, the discontent of his words fell on deaf ears, he placed himself back inside and his eyes suddenly came within inches of another set of eyes.

Amanda and Katie began their conversation with shared personal experiences with Shawn. For Amanda to win her trust, she was going to open the door to their newly found friendship.

"I am calling you to inform you of some information I have come across in the last couple of days about Shawn", Amanda replied.

"Who is this again may I ask?" Katie asked.

"My name is Amanda and Shawn and I became friends recently and we need to seriously talk", Amanda kindly repeated.

"You are classmates I assume", Katie suggested.

"Katie, did you know your boyfriend is kind of special? What I mean is, did you know he possesses an assortment of talents no one else does?" Amanda asked.

The hesitation on the phone from Katie suggested she had no idea what Amanda was talking about.

"From your silence, I am assuming you are unaware", Amanda suggested.

"Amanda is this some type of joke? I am seriously hanging up here." Katie frantically stated.

"Please don't hang up Katie, Shawn is in serious trouble", Amanda spewed.

The silence on the phone again indicated that Katie was at a loss for words or headed for a heartbreak. The breathing on the phone meant that she hadn't hung up, but Amanda began assisting Katie, so she could muster her sentiments.

"When you stayed with Shawn a couple of times, did you notice anything strange? Katie, you don't have to answer", Amanda mentioned.

Hesitating for a few seconds, Katie silently acknowledged that Shawn was different.

"Yes", Katie replied.

"Katie, Shawn is in serious trouble and ever since he arrived at school here, strange things have been coming across my visions", Amanda said quickly.

"Visions? You are a psychic?" Katie nervously asked.

"Nothing like a psychic dear. I just have nightmares that turn into premonitions. I had them severely when I was a kid, but they were confusing. The clarity began when Shawn appeared at our High School. For the last year or so, the visions made no sense, but recently I am beginning to see a much brighter picture", Amanda stated.

"Amanda, what does this have to do with me?" Katie rudely asked.

"Shawn and I recently collaborated over my visions and we both agree that the mystery surrounding him will soon become more uncontrollable. Well, during one of these visons recently, you were in them Katie", Amanda slowly mentioned.

"What the hell are you talking about? Bitch don't call here ever again. You are crazy", Katie yelled while the silence on the phone turned into a dial tone.

The early indication to Amanda was that she just made a terrible mistake and had no idea what to do. Weary and nervous, Amanda jumped into her car in her Pajamas, and began driving towards Shawn's house.

"Well, that didn't go as planned", Amanda mentioned to herself.

Little Joey looked down into the darkness below him and the eyes of terror were looking back upon him. Joey attempted to remain quiet as the bluish eyes suddenly blinked quickly. His heart rate beating faster inside of his little chest, he was barely able to collect his words. Scared and frightened, Joey's ears began hearing the calmness of the dark turn into loud growling. The heavy breathing from the dark air, the younger brother lifted himself away from the opening in the ground and pushed  John aside. Not saying a word, Joey ran out into the snow screaming his head off. Falling over several times head first into the deep snow, Joey found the path to the top of the road and ran home. The screams fading into the cold air alerted the remaining brothers that something evil scared Joey. Closing the door as fast as they could, the remaining boys dispersed for their home as Shawn remained behind.

The ringing of Shawn's home phone fell on deaf ears several minutes later and Katie was unable to speak to him. Her mind loaded with furious thoughts, Amanda was slowly approaching the final hill where Shawn's neighborhood was located. Pulling up in the snow-covered driveway, Amanda exited her vehicle and frantically knocked on the door of the small home. With no answer, Amanda attempted to remember some of the things Shawn said to her previously.

"When I am not home, I normally spend my days below the pumping station behind my home", Shawn said the night before.

That exact statement ran through her mind and she began to venture towards the side of the house. The thick foot of snow along side the fence of Shawn's backyard slowed her walking, but she was determined. Her mind racing in hopes that she could locate Shawn, her patience paid off as she approached the edge of the forest. The open trees and several footprints indicated that others were recently at the same spot. Looking below at the steep decline, Amanda noticed a snowy trail leading through the row of trees and brush. Searching by the area of the fence, she noticed a small circular yellow sled leaning up against the house. Walking back to grab it, she suddenly placed it on the ground near the cliff's entrance. Her body covered in last night's pajamas and a winter coat, Amanda took the plunge down the hill. The feeling of the cold path beneath her, the chilling breeze whispered alongside her rosy cheeks. The numbness of her face proved secondary while attempting to discover his location. Reaching the end of the path, Amanda's eyes focused on the small green-colored shed. Noticing the footprints in the snow, she followed them to the entrance of the gate surrounding the building. Aware that Shawn mentioned he used to hang out under the shack, the clueless intuition of the teen was attempting to understand how.

Peeking around the corner of the fence, the doorway leading inside was already open.

"Hello. Shawn?" Amanda asked out loud.

The only sound in response to her calling for Shawn were the wind-blown trees and the flapping of the door against the fence. Her curiosity brought the teen inside of the shack and she noticed a large door leaning sideways against the wall. Below the leaning door appeared a dark opening in the concrete floor. Looking closer, Amanda noticed the darkness became susceptible to a few lit candles along the walls. The small ladder leading from the top of the floor to below, Amanda enticed herself to crawl beneath. Thinking she had lost focus her mind began to unravel as her feet landed on the ground. The soft feel of the earth enclosed by walls of dirt, the tunnel provided little sight as she began walking. The dim light allowing her to see a few feet, while the sounds of something behind crept closer. The feeling of chills reaching through Amanda's spine granted her the option to look behind her. The appearance of a large black wolf slowly came in her sights. Unafraid and keeping still, Amanda looked back at the beast with an effortless pause. The darkness of its hair upon the wolf's body shaded its blue-green eyes. Silence followed for a few seconds before the beast began to show it large teeth. Growling louder with saliva falling to the ground, the wolf began to walk step by step towards the teen with caution. Praying to herself, Amanda knelt to the ground and knew she was trapped without knowing what was behind her. Feeling as if the wolf was going to attack her, she closed her eyes in fear and held her breath.

Waiting for the beast to attack, Amanda immediately opened her eyes to the emptiness weighing in front of her. The black wolf had vanished into thin air, and the feeling of wetness began to subside against her left ear. Reaching back with her hand, the texture of a dog's nose had pressed itself against her fingers. Amanda's heart began beating profusely as her head turned around. The appearance of a beautiful white wolf came closer to her face. Rubbing its head against Amanda's hands, the gentle beast reminded her that it was the reason for her safety. The eyes of blue deep inside the wolf relaxed Amanda and a smile cracked upon her face. Relinquishing her boundary, Amanda stood up and followed the wolf. The walk lasted several minutes as the pathway inside of the tunnel lead them to a closed door. Amanda attempted to turn the handle with ease as its resistance gave way to the demands of her strength. The door slowly crept open with Shawn standing on the other side and the surprise of Amanda's face placed a fear through his body.

Chapter 27
The Noose

The look of anguish in Amanda's eyes set a fire through Shawn's awaiting heart. Without words, the reprehensible damage radiating from the look upon her face set in motion events that felt like his own personal Armageddon.

"Amanda, please tell me you are here to give me good news?" Shawn asked.

"What makes you think I have good news my friend", Amanda smartly replied.

Shawn noticed Sebastian walking behind Amanda as the wolf sat beside him. The look of guilt stricken in the eyes of his protector, he began nodding his head.

"So, its safe to assume you both have been acquainted", Shawn asked.

"Amanda, this is Sebastian and he is my protector", Shawn insisted.

"Well, apparently he is mine also because I ran into one of your other friends outside of this door", Amanda mentioned.

The look of disgust draped the face of the man who was beside himself. Staring down at the ground, the questions were insisting on getting answers. The form of communication had already placed the doubts for Sebastian's involvement, but why?

"Shawn, before you assume anything here, Sebastian protected me from another wolf that appeared to be black. He seemed so angry at me and I really thought he was going to attack me, but Sebastian scared him off", Amanda replied.

"I am not mad Amanda, not in the least. I am trying to understand what happened and why they approached you? Doesn't make sense to me why they keep coming. Were you able to assess the information I gave you?", Shawn asked.

"Shawn, when I dropped you off, I came back home and somehow fell asleep. My visions are now getting stronger and I am afraid to really coincide with you the reality I am sensing lately", Amanda furiously stated.

"Just tell me what you know?" Shawn asked.

Standing inside of the room where Shawn was attempting to check on Kate, the conversation with Amanda was taking a very sour turn and the lights upon the walls were beginning to dim.

"Katie appeared in my visions Shawn. She is in real trouble", Amanda stated.

"Problem is, I had a nightmare last night as well and I believe you. Do me huge favor and close the door behind you?" Shawn asked.

"Amanda, whatever you do. I need you to be still and not say one word", Shawn stated.

Looking down at Sebastian, the beast knew exactly the next move Shawn would make, so he placed his paws down on the concrete and looked upon the wall. With the lights beginning to dim once again, the four walls presented a blurry vision. Within seconds, the location of the room was focused on Katie's house in Cape Cod. Frantic, the sounds of crying and falling tears were amplified inside of the room.

"Why god, why? Why are you punishing me with this torture? Why can't I find a normal guy for once in my freaking life", Katie yelled out while laying on her bed.

Immediately halting the vision upon the walls, Shawn looked over at Amanda's smirk.

"Oops, was that my fault?" Amanda jokingly asked.

"What the fuck did you say to her Amanda?" Shawn hatefully asked.

The angry vibrance from Shawn's voice transformed the lights on the wall to a reddish color and Amanda took notice.

"Shawn, I swear to you I didn't do anything with malice. I simply called Katie with the intention of warning her", she frightfully replied.

Before Shawn could ask her how she knew the information to get a hold of his girlfriend, she pulled out his wallet.

"That explains my next question. So, what did you tell her?" Shawn asked.

The sadness appearing in her eyes, Amanda became reluctant to explain the words in full detail.

"Damn Amanda, you just ruined my life. Don't you think about these things before doing? I am not happy about this at all", Shawn replied with anger.

"Shawn, I am sorry", Amanda painfully replied.

Turning around to open the door, Amanda walked out and headed down the tunnel away from Shawn.

"Sebastian, follow her and make sure she makes it out of here fine please?" Looking beyond the four walls, Shawn placed his hands over his eyes in disgust as he took a huge breath.

Unaware of the damage Amanda may have caused, he rushed through the door and up the tunnel to his house. Unclear of his thinking, all that mattered was to get to Katie as fast as he could before she made up her mind. The flurry of snow falling from the sky delayed his quickness, but the patience was soon running out for the teen. His vision blurred, he slowed his pace enough to dial the numbers on the telephone as it shook violently in his hands. The sound of the dial tone louder than anticipated, the beating of his heart rapidly awaited. The nervousness evident with his heavy breathing, the sound of Katie's voice soothed his ears with her simple greeting.

"Hello, Shawn?" Katie asked.

"Katie, are you ok? I need to talk to you please?" Shawn asked impatiently.

"What's wrong babe? You don't sound like yourself?" Katie asked.

Before Shawn replied, he began to slow everything down in his mind before opening his mouth.
"Honey, did you get a phone call from a friend of mine?" Shawn quietly asked.

"Yes. What the heck was wrong with that freak? Why did she even call me?" Katie asked.

Careful with the next set of words, Shawn evaluated in his brain the phrase that would suit the conversation. Hoping that he could detour the situation, Shawn started to recite the version his heart wanted Kate to hear. *"Babe, Amanda is a bit different and she claims that she can see visions. I don't believe her, but I did ask for her help in something I was researching. She felt what I was involving myself in could get in between us, so she reached out. I apologize"*, Shawn remorsefully stated.

"It's totally ok and thanks for calling me", Kate responded.

"You sure you aren't mad at me? Something inside my head thinks you are hating me", Shawn insisted.

"Why would I be mad? I have the best boyfriend in the world and my parents are urging I go with them here in a few minutes to lunch. Can we talk later please?" Katie asked.

Shawn responded to Katie's demand and hung the phone up. Sitting inside of his own daydream, he couldn't understand what he saw minutes before the phone call with Kate. Amanda had stormed off for a good reason simply because it was possible that what they both saw was treachery.

"Why in the world would I see something that really never existed? Whoa, hold up. Vincent wanted me to visualize what he needed me to see to separate Kate and I. Makes perfect sense", Shawn told himself.

The occurrences with Amanda and Katie started unraveling before Shawn's eyes and Vincent was most likely behind each ploy. Collecting himself in the kitchen of his home, Shawn revisited the earlier conversation with Amanda the day before. Reluctant to understand why Shawn was entangled with the evil that swallowed him, he forcefully withdrew the negativity over it all. The few seconds of comprehension had him realizing it would become wasted energy to worry about the inevitable. What was meant to be would happen and he decided to let nature run its course between Katie and himself. The remainder of the afternoon was spent attempting to contact Amanda with a deserved apology. Once the weekend was over, Shawn and Amanda would rekindle their friendship and keep an eye out on each other throughout the end of the Winter.

The visions never left Amanda as they began to increase with more volume and intensity as each night passed. The horror left Amanda with physical scars and her heart felt as if she needed to endure them to protect her friend. Feeling bad, Shawn offered to stay with her on some nights to get her through the premonitions. Afraid to share her experiences, Amanda kept from Shawn the severe consequences that were going to eventually face him. It was only a matter of time before Shawn would have to confront the noose that may eventually end his days on Earth. Amanda felt compelled to relive each night, in relation to understanding her vantage point of the ordeal facing Shawn. His battle was only about to begin, but she was doubting the time the confrontation between Vincent and himself would realize. Since the start of Winter, the engagement with her nightmares correlated a path of wanting to help solve the mystery. Once a timeline was worked out, she always ended up with a fork in the road that created friction with her theories. The more resistance built inside of her mind, the more antiquated Amanda became. Feeling tireless and alone, she seldom shared her thoughts with anyone typing her an outcast amongst the Masco alum. Her friendship with Shawn meant the world to her and while he began the baseball season their Junior year, she felt incredibly distant.

Chapter 28
Of Beauty and Rage

Liberating his will on the opponents of the Masco Varsity Baseball team, Shawn delivered countless strikeout after strikeout with his immaculate array of pitches. The first few games that began the season ended in lopsided wins for the Chieftains against inferior teams. With Cape Ann League play beginning, Shawn was at odds with his baseball coach. The team's star pitcher was purposely omitted from the lineup for the upcoming season. Equipped with power in the middle of the batting order, the Masco Varsity team had a huge hole in the sixth spot of their lineup. With Shawn consistently being the best hitter on the summer team three years straight, it was easy to conceive his presence in the Varsity lineup as one of their best assets. With his omittance, Shawn confronted Coach Sawgrass and the hour-long meeting that coincided after, wouldn't change his mind. Unable to convince his Coach, Shawn was relegated to becoming his best pitcher for the 1990 year. With his 2nd best pitcher on the decline with his skills, Coach Sawgrass relied on Shawn to propel his Varsity team throughout the Season. Focused solely on his pitching, Shawn mastered each batter with a surgical skill that only a doctor could deliver. Understanding his position with the team, Shawn embraced his purpose while the offense struggled against the much tougher teams. Several losses occurred through the season with lack of hitting from the Masco offense. Pleading his case, it was the game of all games that transformed the team into a one of the most talked about teams in the state.

The warm Saturday on this beautiful May morning placed two of the best teams in the league against each other. Topsfield was the setting for the battle between Masconomet Regional High School and North Andover. Considered a huge rival in other sports, North Andover made it a consistent habit of beating the baseball team several years straight. During his sophomore year, Shawn wasn't available to face the team from the western part of the area. Aware of the capabilities Shawn presented as a pitcher, the undefeated record meant nothing to the massive hitters comprised in their lineup. From top to bottom, North Andover fielded a team that had only lost one game all year. With the hype surrounding the game, several college and pro scouts were in attendance as the two giants squared off. The five-foot ten pitcher equipped with a glaring fastball started the game with a three-pitch strikeout. If it was any indication to the home crowd of how the game would end, the first inning provided a tasty side sample. In a surprising move, the injury to their short stop before the game allowed the Coach to insert Shawn as its 5th batter. Leading off in the second inning, the pitcher with the perfect first inning laced a double down the third base line. In position to take the lead, Masco would fail to convert with their next three batters. Considered one of the best pitchers in their league, Morgan Adams would mow down the bottom half of Masco's lineup with ease.

Despite the failure to bring home their first run, the pitching duel lasted through the top half of the fifth inning. In the bottom of the same inning, Jeff Wilks struck out for the 2nd time and Ken Nazareth reached base on an infield single. With one out and Shawn approaching the batter's box, fate delivered a curveball that would eventually land on the opposite side of the outfield fence. The homerun would give Masco a lead they would never relinquish while their pitcher would surrender just one hit throughout the game. The pure dominance of North Andover would be talked about for weeks and the pressure for Coach Sawgrass to implement his rising star into the lineup fell on deaf ears. High School baseball saw its share of streaks within their batting order and it was evident others on the team wanted Shawn in their lineup. Unclear for his motivation, Dick Sawgrass would lead his team into an epitome of shameless losses. The Masco baseball team would limp into the State Playoffs with losses in their final two games. Rumors and innuendos of a lost season due to their coach's inability to understand his own team, Shawn lost all respect. Leading into the first-round playoff game against Hamilton Wenham, Shawn met with his Coach one last time in his office.

"Coach, I am done after this season. No longer will I be playing for Masco sports", Shawn stated.

"Are you moving away with your family?" Coach asked.

The brief hesitation accosted the words that Shawn was wanting to release from his mouth, but his heart relieved his anger.

"Coach, if you are here next season, I will not play for you ever again. These terrible six losses were preventable, and I blame you for our team's failures. How in the world can a coach place one of his best hitters on the bench and not see that his team needed a spark? We barely scraped by a few games with one run here and two runs there. Because of your incompetence, I had to beat North Andover myself and it wasn't supposed to be like that. Coach, you are letting these boys down with your demise and I can't stick around to watch it anymore. I will give you these playoffs, but never again will I play here", Shawn replied as he walked out of the office.

The look of shock remained on the Coach's face as his best player had decided to choose his own gall over the team's. Coach Sawgrass decided that during the playoffs, he was going to show his star pitcher who was boss and with the first two games behind them, the third-round opponent would be a familiar face. Salem High School was the returning State Champion and Masco's team was set for one of their toughest battles in many years. Facing the second-best pitcher statistically in the State, Coach Sawgrass decided to skip Shawn in the rotation and implement the one pitcher that struggled all year, Rick Antonio. With a measly record of three wins and three losses, Shawn's former nemesis got the call to pitch against Salem despite his record. Injected with a new confidence, it was the first two innings that Rick was able to barely escape, but the luck of the Irish came to an end. The tall Senior delivered an array of batting practice pitches that served more like an appetizer for the Salem hitters to devour. In total, several runs would cross the plate over the next few innings and Masconomet would return home with a sour loss to absorb. Coach Sawgrass again demonstrated his lack of leadership with his failure to provide better coaching for his team. Shawn's career as a High School pitcher with Masco was soon at an end, but the temptation to seek retribution was just beginning.

The failure of the baseball team sent shockwaves throughout the school from the Senior class to its Junior High. The expectations fell far below from the year before and it was apparent it would take years to build another winning team. Regardless of the season's outcome, Shawn would entice the voters to capture the years best pitcher award in the Cape Ann League. With his resounding ten wins and zero loss record in both the regular season and playoffs, the remarkable accomplishment meant nothing without a State title. Shawn decided to not receive his award rather just move on away from the team coached by a man who equated into someone who was over his head. Insisting that his Coach had ruined their season, Shawn would finish the school year with intentions of never returning. The plan was to transfer to Danvers High

School where Shawn would progress their baseball and football programs with the acceptances by the teams Coaches. With the permission from the State to accept his transfer, the plan was in motion to combine the already talented team of Danvers with a new leader. The Football program was coming off an eight-win season and with Shawn as the new QB, a State Title was imminent. The Baseball team was returning its entire Junior class that finished with thirteen wins and a State Playoff visit. With Shawn heading the Pitching Staff and Offense, the team from a town over would project themselves as leaders to win the State Title.

His Junior Year winding down to the last few days, Shawn stood at his locker that early Monday morning sulking about the playoff loss. Rumors throughout the hallways of the class of 1991 spread like wild fire with Shawn defecting to another school. The many who liked him and to those who feared his friendship started to walk up to the teen with condolences over his weekend turbulence. Standing with his back pressed against the locker door, he looked over to his right to view the beautiful faces of the girls who had secretly been his biggest supporters. Who would have thought in their wildest dreams that the amazing blonde Shawn first saw in the Cafeteria in 8th grade, would secretly be one of his proudest fans? Since their Freshman year together, Melanie Harris befriended the new kid in town with her brass and charm. Considered the most beautiful girl in their class by many, Shawn and Melanie would find each other studying in the Library for several hours. The silent comradery between the teens was a mutual respect for those who realized their importance to everyone. Through this friendship, Shawn and Mel's other locker mates took notice amongst their High School years. The amazing Jennifer Ashton who stood barely five foot and was close friends with Melanie, noticed Shawn's aura. The perfect hair and the gorgeous face of the tiny teen radiated through others that surrounded her. Next to their locker was the red headed Alyssa Harrison. Considered a bit of a goofball, her vibrance and laughter attracted an array of friends that would find their interest in Shawn quite intriguing. Alyssa had a reputation of seeking the boys who were part of the Athletics Department since her father was a huge sports fan. That secret was probably the worst kept one over the years, but it was always considered a favorite. Valerie Hicks was the girl that found her locker next to Melanie's. Considered the snob of the group, Shawn realized otherwise how special she really was. Her amazing smile and beautiful straight blonde hair always found a special place in Shawn's heart. Shawn's surroundings enticed many to always see the teen that brought everyone's day alive. The frequent laughter, the countless stories attracting attention or the pictures of Katie for the world to see on the inside of his locker door. The kid from Weymouth was going to be missed by many and hated by most, but his career as Masco was defined as the *"What Could Have Been"*.

Excited to propel a new High School into brighter waters, Shawn began the Summer of 1990 by dismissing his Summer League baseball career for spending time with Katie. With his Father's permission, Shawn would stay with his girlfriend for the first month of the Summer. Deployed on a several month tour in Detroit, Katie's dad would not be at home until the beginning of the following year. With the freedom and trust from her Mother, Katie and Shawn would become literally inseparable. The dunes of Cape Cod would entice the two lovers to spend their afternoons in one another's arms. Fueled by the love they shared together, Shawn ignored the warnings he had been heeded in the past by Vincent. The heart of the disciple who once spent countless hours learning the ways to spread his evil, was now in defiance of the greatest power south of Heaven. Regardless of the possible consequence, Shawn was in his own peaceful atmosphere surrounded by Katie's warm embrace. The Summer days were followed my countless hours of making love through the night as the bodies of the teens encountered a magic never felt before. The enlightenment of Shawn's beautiful blue eyes captivated Katie to realize she had found the man she needed for the rest of her life. His charm brought her immediate peace and she had never felt this safe in her entire life. The plan to attend the same college was in place inside the city limits of Boston as Shawn was intending to sign his letter of intent with the Golden Eagles of Boston College. Aware that he would prove himself as a walk on for the Football team was a challenge. The program was on the rise with Tom Coughlin as their Head Coach and he was known to be a huge disciplinarian. The scholarship to play Baseball would supplant Shawn as one of the starting pitchers, but the Athletic Director and Head Coach wanted to also place his bat in the lineup. They were aware of the friction with his High School Coach, and when they saw Shawn put on a hitting display at the Massachusetts Bay State Games last year, they found their new Right Fielder. Examining the few games that Shawn did start at Masco as a hitter, his thirteen hits in twenty-two at bats were noticed by the Colleges in the area. The upcoming season would predict as an explosive one for Shawn by his peers and the change of scenery was needed.

With their futures aligned for the next several years, Katie's mother convinced her daughter that she and Shawn could live in the apartment close to the campus in Chestnut Hill. The motives appeared perfect and another year of school had to be survived before their college experience could begin. With their Senior Year ahead, it would take a miracle for them to survive without each other. Premature plans were met with anguish but the old saying of *"No Pain No Gain"* would prove that the two teens were well on their way to happiness.

While the two teens in Cape Cod were making plans for their future, Amanda had spent the entire first part of the Summer at her home. While Mom was obviously worried about Amanda's social atrophy, she was quick to point out the obvious. The studies were most important to her in life, so she left it alone. The clear reason to decipher the code entrenched in her visions was to solve it quickly. Each day passing as Summer began, the nightmares became more increasingly hostile. The day after school ended, Amanda began experiencing the hallucinations within her day dreams. When the minutes of the clock turned into hours, the spirits visiting her throughout the night proved ruthless. One late evening Amanda was researching a story in Mexico City of the El Diablo sighting in 1959. The encyclopedia entailed the statements

of the towns people who witnessed the strange individual hanging around. No one had seen him before, but the disappearance of eight young men also caught the town's attention. During the investigation, a sketch of the suspect was given to police in response to the witness statements. Fifteen people came forward with the same description, but the investigation lead to nowhere as the bodies were never recovered. The picture of the suspect caught Amanda's

attention because it looked eerily similar with other sightings connected to missing people in her readings. Her heart racing quickly, she dug up another story out of New York City in 1929. The stock market was on the verge of an epic crash and dozens of stock brokers committed suicide over their losses. What puzzled investigators was the sighting of a gentleman who was commonly known to attract a sense of good luck around him. Groomed well and confident, the gentleman was calm and collective while others were losing millions of dollars of investments. While others perished, this miser was seen eating his lunch at a local café while eight men jumped from a large twelve story building to their deaths. The macabre of death surrounding the peculiar man was the crows that encircled him as witnesses heard laughter as the men died. The story sank Amanda's heart through her chest as she was looking at the same man in both pictures.

Scrambling to find answers, Amanda rushed through her notes and drawings, unable to locate what she was looking for. The similarities of the eight men in all the stories she went over didn't align with the Arabic dialect she had been obsessed with the last year or so. The farmer who found the seven men in the cave was no where near the same recollection of the newer  stories. Hunched with an idea, Amanda pulled out the book that resurrected the old story from the city of Jerusalem. Opening the book to the previous pages she had studied for days, Amanda quickly noticed the two pages that were stuck together. Weary of how she could have missed the pages, they slowly separated from each other and Amanda's eyes were welcomed to an additional version of the story. Closely reading with no interruptions, Amanda would quickly learn that an eighth body was discovered near the burial of the seven men. The tomb that enclosed the men would reveal that a child was part of the escapade that was unable to recognize the young boy as a man. The visiting prophecy offering solace to the men would eventually lead them to their violent deaths. The scripture had more inside that Amanda was attempting to depict. The Arabic writing disguised a clue that she was attempting to discover, but her mind was a mess. The message made no sense and after a few hours, she finally translated what appeared to be the writing of the farmer who discovered the cavern.

"Those shall be blessed by the serpent of black angels will walk through the night of fire for eight days".

The similarity between the number of deaths was no closer to being understood than what Amanda first found, but she knew she was close. The answers had to be amongst the visions she experienced, and she needed to suffer a bit more to provide her the clues to helping Shawn. The visions of Katie were slowly fading away as the appearance of the man in the pictures began to replace her. With each night passing, the closer and closer he would get to Amanda allowed her to realize that something was on the verge of occurring. Her ingenuity was able to create a timeline of sorts aligning the reality with her nightmares. If the calculations were correct, Amanda anticipated that they only had a week before these numbers would collide. Attempting to reach Shawn, the phone at Katie's house would turn over to a machine recording where Amanda left countless messages within an hour's time. Calling one last time, Amanda dialed the numbers on her push button phone and before she hit the number seven, a recollection came across her mind. The number she was staring at finally allowed her the clue she needed. Hanging up the phone, she calmly collected her thoughts and immediately began drawing the shape of a pentagram. While drawing the star inside of an invisible circle, Amanda pulled out the book comprised of the findings along side the cavern where the first seven bodies were found. Reading the Arabic scripture, she comprised the names of those found beneath the ground. Soluzen, Halliza, Bellatar, Bellonoy, Hally', Solomono, Pontaenlu, & Afiato were scripted in exact order. Unsure if they died in the exact sequence the names were made, Amanda began placing the names in side of the pentagram. Coincidentally, the symbol

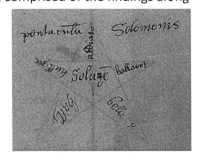

representing the elements of life were also coinciding with death. The pages stuck together provided the remaining pieces of the puzzle. The deaths of the eight bodies were just the beginning and reading further, the pentagram stood for the spirits of the eight in Jerusalem.

The scriptures were fascinating and now able to coincide her visions along with the ancient spells, Amanda was close. The one last nap that Amanda needed was to attempt to use what she knew against the encroachment of the demon that represented hell. If she was right, this could be the last attempt in comprehending the reason behind the necessary evil.

Chapter 29
La Vendetta

Encircling the madness beneath her dreary eyes, Amanda found herself lying on the floor of an abandoned room. The coolness of the air against her frail body, she was unable to locate an exit or a window. With each dream in her previous experiences, Amanda always would recon her surroundings to discover an exit strategy. The empty feeling inside was a realization that her vision was an attempt to entrap her mind. Whatever brought Amanda to this place knew of her intentions and it was more than prepared to confront the teen. The dim lit room began to fall dark as the sounds of laughter echoed against the four walls. The weakened structure began to crumble with sounds of crackling and falling dust as if the walls were collapsing. Fearless and bold, the teen with the brazen heart called out to the being.

"What is it that you want to show me?" Amanda asked.

The deep laughter reaching the chords of scariness, the tone changed to immediate anger.

"How dare you involve yourself with my intentions", the voice stated.

The silence in the darkened room failing to escape the enclosure, gave way to Amanda's heavy breathing.

"Who are you?" Amanda calmly asked.

"Why ask questions you already know answers too?" The voice replied with a question.

"I am not afraid of you", Amanda quickly stated.

The reliance of her gall brought forth a challenge to the presence inside of the room simply knowing it fed on others fear.

"Why do you not fear me?" The voice angrily stated.

Avoiding the question, the lights inside of the room flickered attempting to justify its anger over her refusal to give in. Amanda was more than prepared to isolate the evil away from her soul while gratifying her mind for answers.

"Why can't you show yourself?" Amanda asked.

The dominant approach appeared to have paid off, but the answer she was looking for surprised her.

"Why are you looking for me? What is it that you seek?" The voice loudly stated.

"The spirits of the souls you have affected have reached out to me, I called out for you to understand why.", Amanda demanded.

Standing nervous and cold, Amanda's mind was protected from the being's capability to see through her. Equipped with this sudden formality, Amanda knew the evil being had no idea why she had summoned him.

"Are you aware of the balance of life?" The voice asked.

"Enlighten me for the love of God, I ain't got all night ya know", Amanda smartly replied.

"For a second there, you sounded just as funny as your brother. Amanda, for life to exist, the scales of death against birth must equal each other proportionately. I am the reason death exists and when creation tips the scales every several years, it is I that represents the measure of equality", the voice deeply mentioned.

"My brother? Hold up, Shawn is my brother? How can that be?" Amanda quickly asked with excitement.

Avoiding the question with its silence, Amanda began to realize her involvement with all of this. Shawn's destiny was to cross paths with Amanda so that she could help him find his way. It wasn't Vincent who was responsible, it was something much higher. Getting back to her questions, Amanda quickly spouted off.

"I thought you were an outcast from Heaven. Why are you the chosen one to bring balance to life?" Amanda asked.

"Don't ask things you aren't prepared to listen to the answers to. I have complicated my existence to many and I shall remain vigil towards the purpose of keeping Earth in balance", the voice replied swiftly.

"Than, why Shawn. Why my brother?" Amanda quickly asked.

The silence revered its ugly head as the walls started to cause a crumbling noise while the ground beneath Amanda's feet shifted.

"Look, be angry at me all that you want. Leave Shawn and Katie out of this please and I will surrender myself to you as your eighth soul", Amanda begged.

The crumbling walls fading into transparency, Amanda noticed the inability to see around her. The empty space of blackness surrendered to a silhouette of evil separating itself within her mind. Unafraid and patient, Amanda started to envision the shape of the approaching demon walking towards her. Behind the apparition, a faded light slowly appeared while its shadow encased Amanda's eyes. The appearance of a well-groomed man with a three-piece suit and a pipe in his mouth appeared before her eyes. The chiseled features of his face provided familiar curves she had seen before.

"Vincent, I assume?" Amanda curiously asked.

"At your service my dear, it is nice to meet you", Vincent replied.

Reaching out to shake her hand, Vincent reluctantly felt the aura of Amanda's energy. To him, she was an indifference between Heaven and Hell lost within the powers of the medium.

"You are offering yourself to protect your brother. Does he mean that much to you?" Vincent asked gently.

"He has helped me see more clearly and made me realize my purpose", Amanda replied.

"Amanda, very touching and noble", Vincent sarcastically stated.

Looking deep into Amanda's eyes, her inner strength prevented Vincent from looking for her true purpose. The hesitation in her voice propelled Vincent in cutting the visit short.

"Fate has already decided what happens and regardless of the result, there isn't anything you can do about it", Vincent boldly mentioned.

The embellishment of fire within his eyes created a distance between the two and Amanda was left pondering. The lifeless heartbeat inside of her chest awoke her from a deep sleep and she found herself inside of her library.

"Damn it, I needed to know when", Amanda spoke to herself.

While the plan to gather Shawn as the eighth soul was approaching, destiny was unaware of Amanda. The careless whisper buried inside of Vincent's beleaguered statement would help guide the teen. Aware of the possible consequences, the purpose for her revival gave the town of Topsfield new hope. Amanda lifted herself from the desk chair and while she began peaking down at her drawing, a quick thought came to her. It was the drawing of the baby that allowed Amanda's blind faith the piece of the puzzle she was looking for.

"Could it be that Katie is pregnant? And why does the baby appear to be still-born?" Amanda asked herself repeatedly

Thinking she needed to stay and focus on the clues in front of her, Amanda remained home. Time was running out and she attempted to hurry the unscrambling of her discoveries. Shawn and Katie had no idea of the foreseen danger approaching and it was best to keep the aforementioned under lock and key. Unwilling to give up, Amanda kept at the clues for the remainder of the day.

While his sister back in Topsfield was trying to save his soul, Shawn was in the middle of saying his goodbye's to Katie. She was on her way to the airport to visit her father in Detroit for a

long week and a half. Boston's Logan Airport was one of the busiest in the country and attempting to park was a challenge for Katie's mom. The intention was to see her daughter off and drive Shawn home twenty or so miles north before returning to Cape Cod. Walking hand in hand through the terminals and up through the concourse, the hour delay gave the lovers a couple of hours to cuddle and prepare to be without each other. The sentiments of Shawn and Katie's sensitivity made for a great pair and everyone that knew the two understood the gravity felt between them. Shawn witnessed his parents love for each other help hurdle the small obstacles over the years and Katie was what he had hoped for.

"Baby, I am going to miss you with all of my heart", Katie whispered in his ear.

The glare in Shawn's blue eyes attempted to hold back the tears, but his strength succumbed to her demands. Holding each other as if they were meant to never be apart strangled the fate facing them.

"I am going to miss you too and I will be there when you come back to me", Shawn cried.

The painful look upon her mother's face identified the true reason why she was supporting the man who captured her daughter's heart. Ever since Katie was a young girl, all she ever wanted was to find a good boy to raise a family with. The joy and cheer that Katie had been displaying around the house since she met her boyfriend was exciting and welcome. The joy her oldest child brought to the household was inviting since her younger brother had passed away a few years earlier.

The frightening words over the intercom sent chills down the spines of the awaiting teens. Northwest Flight 255 for Detroit was prepared for boarding and Katie wasn't ready to leave Shawn. Afraid of letting go, they both embraced as if this was the last time, they would ever see each other. The apparent sadness upon their faces fueled the tears of regret and the second calling for her flight separated them. Feeling weak at her knees, Katie was barely able to muster the strength to walk away. One last kiss would allow Katie to release a secret inside of the ears of the man she was bound to spend her life with.

"Congratulations daddy, you are a father", Katie whispered.

The fate of time had placed her on board the flight that was bound for a destination where every second of life remained precious. Sitting at her seat against the window, Katie pulled out the picture of the sonogram. Staring into the life buried inside of her, she placed her head back against the seat and reminisced the amazing life lying ahead. The noise of the engine and the stability of the plane eased itself through the evening skies as Shawn was left behind comprehending his life as a Father.

Chapter 30
Gone Away

Amanda frantically attempted to get a hold of Shawn at his home, but the phone rang with no answer. Able to solve the mystery minutes earlier, Amanda began to assemble a few friends in the neighborhood to help collect a few items. The plan was to join Shawn at his home and equip him with the knowledge to set himself free. Working effortlessly in accomplishing the tasks she set for herself, her mind remained on Katie. In a race with time, the clouds above Topsfield started to roll in with each mile of the town becoming shaded with darkness. The consequences of her actions failing to stop her, Amanda was determined to provide all the resources she had at her disposal.

Upon Shawn's arrival at his home, Katie's Mother wished him well and to see him again in ten days. The pain deep inside his heart would reveal a truth that he was unprepared for. Walking to his backyard under the dark cloudy skies, a sudden noise appeared from behind one of the large trees by his fence. Sebastian poked his head through the small opening by the back gate and whimpered in pain.

"Sebastian, what is wrong?" Shawn asked with concern.

Opening the gate from inside his yard, Sebastian welcomed Shawn by standing on his hind legs and placing his paws upon his chest, knocking him down on his back. Laying in the grass with his tongue licking his face, Shawn embraced Sebastian. The sadness radiated from the wolf to Shawn's heart and the look in his gorgeous blue eyes sensed that something was wrong.

"Sebastian, please tell me what's wrong?" Shawn begged.

His nose staring into the clouds of the sky above them, Sebastian started whimpering louder.

"Is it Katie?" Shawn cried out.

Sebastian leaned forward by placing its head on Shawn's chest. Their eyes would inter twine to assist the teen in depicting the horror willing to unfold. The nightmare deep inside the pupils of his beautiful white wolf propelled him to stand on his feet and emerge before the four walls. Running with a fierce anger, Shawn found himself standing in front of the door at the end of the tunnel in a blink of an eye. The fear rushing through his veins complimenting the small amounts of air released from his lungs, setting aside the upcoming consequences. The mind of the teen who felt betrayed by his mentor encompassed the rage within himself to focus on a certain location. Pacing himself to allow the vision to appear, his eyes would discover a blurry deception of evil that revealed a most unlikely event.

Amanda and her friends were wrapping up the of collection of the tools needed to get over to the other side of town. Unaware of what Amanda was looking for, her neighbors reluctantly cared and did what they could for the quiet teenager. They were close with her Mother and knew that Amanda was quite special in their hearts. Saddled with a large backpack and a heavy glass water jug in the back of her car, Amanda returned into her home for one more item. Walking through the front door and into the library, Amanda carelessly tripped over a small book and fell towards the desk in front of her. Breaking her fall with her forehead, Amanda lie passed out on the cold floor. Seemingly feeling helpless, Amanda woke up in a familiar place.

The eerie coldness upon her face awakened her tired eyes to the brisk fog rushing against her cheeks. The cold forest chilled each breath inside of her body and she began to stand on her feet. The stickiness of the leaves upon the ground crumbled as

she moved, causing the flocking of a few crows above her head. The twilight of the wicked moon seen through the open forest, Amanda felt as if other eyes were watching her. Awaiting the density of the fog to subside, Amanda's eyes fixated on several eyes behind a headstone. Slowly approaching the large piece of rock protruding from the ground, a picture of a skull etched in stone appeared on the front. In the close distance, several wolves were seen surrounding the grave. Unclear for its purpose, Amanda found herself lost in a forest of

compromise and she needed to escape. Looking to her left, the appearance of the trees grew darker as the motionless body of a small boy appeared from the shadows. *"Hello, I see you. Hello"*, Amanda cried out.

The stillness of the air froze nature to its core as she started to notice the chill in the air was colder. Thick smog covering her

breath, Amanda looked behind her and the sounds of faint crying followed the words, *"help me"*. The image of a woman standing near her covering her bloody face, Amanda attempted to comfort her. The energy surrounding the woman was too strong to approach, as Amanda began speaking. *"Are you ok? Can I help you?"*

No immediate response came from the girl, but she turned around to face the opposite direction. Sounds of gurgling and the smell of burning flesh rang through Amanda's nose and the screams of the girl came without warning. *"Help, Help. Shawn, help me!"*

Attempting to help, the tears from Amanda's eyes hit the soft ground below her and the vision disappeared. The silence in the dark forest forgave the sounds of the howling wolves in the distance, and as Amanda turned around, the arm from the fog reached to grab her. Suddenly petrified, the appearance of the

hooded being was attempting to grab something that wasn't there. Lying back on her butt, Amanda looked up and the apparition and the

smoke had dissipated into thin air. Knowing she wasn't going insane; the clues were beginning to add up and she quickly needed to figure them out. Something wasn't adding up, but her thoughts were with Katie. Something was terribly wrong and what if it was Katie and not Shawn that was meant to be the 8th soul. Attempting to wake herself up, Amanda stood up and the bright rays of the moon began to pierce through her eyes. Slowly unable to see, the brightness once before her was now dark. Closing her eyes, she waited a moment for the light to subside in her mind and with a sudden thought, she was laying on the floor of her home.

"Jeez, thank god. I need to get the hell out of here already", Amanda repeated.

With the slight dialing of the phone, Amanda attempted to call Shawn one more time, but to no avail. Throwing the receiver down in anger, Amanda quickly left through the front door and into her car. Looking quickly for the placement of her key into the ignition, the sound of a clicking engaged. Sweating profusely in the Summer night, Amanda's car had a bad battery. Stalled for a bit, she searched through the neighborhood for someone to offer her a jump.

The four walls had placed Shawn inside of a personal hell that he attempted to reveal. The lightened thick clouds covering the stars of the sky, his vision cleared quickly at the sight of a large airplane. The words Northwest were written on the side in bold letters and his eyes began to water. Feeling Sebastian leaned against his leg, the comfort from the beast wasn't enough to slow the heart rate of the teen. Confused and paralyzed, Shawn was unclear of how to appear on a large moving object. He had visited several placed of origin, but never transported to a moving plane or train. Visibly angry and frustrated, the room captivated by the four walls began suffering Shawn's wrath. The smalls cracks appearing in the concrete grew larger as the teen attempted to save his beloved girlfriend.

"Sebastian, I can't get to her. What do I do?" Shawn yelled out loud.

His blue eyes now a dark red, the evil inside of Shawn began to escape his skin. The painful breach of his pores released sweat and blood from his back as the enlarged wings spread across the room. Ripping the remainder of his shirt away from his body, Shawn focused solely on the plane.

Sitting quietly in her chair, the sound of a deep voice raised an awareness in her ear.

"Young lady. Are you traveling on your own?" the man asked.

Insisting that she not say a word, Katie looked next to her and the older gentleman with the well-groomed hair and good looks cracked a smile.

"Whatever seems to be on your mind is troubling you. Are you alright?" he asked.

"I am headed to see my Father, but that the last place I want to be right now", Katie slowly responded.

"We only have one Father, so how do you know this could be the last time you seem him?" The man keenly asked.

"I never really thought about it like that. You have a good point", Katie responded.

Katie looked down at the tray in front of the man and she noticed a drawing on a pad. The picture of a woman had been dressed in a hooded sweatshirt and appeared peaceful sitting down.

"Is that a drawing of your daughter?" Katie asked.

"Oh no my dear, this is someone I am going to miss very soon", the gentleman replied.

"I am truly sorry to hear that, is she sick?" Katie politely asked.

"Something like that", he quickly responded with clarity. *"What's her name?"* Katie asked.

"Her name is Katie", the man quietly stated.

"Really! That's my name too. How funny", Katie happily mentioned.

"The picture is you my dear", the creepy man resounded.

The look of horror on Katie's face realized that this was no coincidence that he was sitting beside her. Confused and nervous, Katie wanted to get the attention of the crew members.

"No need to panic young lady, it will be all over soon", the man stated.

The sudden tears of pain released themselves from her eyes as she began to understand the significance of this moment. Turning away from the dark-haired gentleman, Katie peaked through the plane window to witness a lightning bolt strike the wing. The massive explosion tore apart the right side of the plane as it burst into flames. The chaos inside of the cabin separated the plane in nearly two pieces as passengers unbuckled in their seats were ejected into the air of the night. The opening of the cabin brought a storm of debris and bodies flying over Katie's head. Pinned against the window, she begged for her life calling Shawn's name out.

The cries of the innocent teen reached as far as it could while the winged angel inside of the four walls envisioned her pain. Watching each second count, Shawn began to theorize the simplicity of how to save Katie. If this plan was going to work, he would have to arrive at the same time as Kate before she ran out of time. Looking down at Sebastian, he asked the calm beast to pray for him. Hands over her face, Katie's plane began nosediving and the awful sound of crushing metal and heavy air deafened her ears. Praying to the angel who may never save her, the abrupt wind felt as if it was crushing her face. Appearing to die in an instant, Katie closed her eyes and she felt a set of arms grab her waste and in a quick instant, the sound of silence.

Katie opened her eyes to the delight of Shawn holding her legs and back as she leaned up against his arms. Her eyes full of tears, Katie hugged Shawn as if she awoke from a dream.

"How did you just do that?" Katie asked.

Her eyes wandering as her body felt safe in his arms, Katie spoke again.

"Where are we right now?" Katie whispered in his ear.

"Open your eyes and see", Shawn gracefully mentioned.

Katie listened to his request and her sight noticed they were hovering several feet above in the darkness of the sky. Unafraid with Shawn holding her, they began their decent to the awaiting peace of the Nike Site. The rays of the moon offering the light in her eyes, Shawn placed her on the ground and comforted her. The look between the two lovers as if life meant nothing around them, she spoke.

"What did I ever do to deserve you?" Katie softly asked.

Without words, Shawn's angelic wings offered a peaceful distraction from this most horrible night. Noticing the softness of his feathers, Katie placed her lips on his with a calming desperation. Wanting badly to believe this was a horrible nightmare, the calm winds suddenly shifted.

"We aren't out of the woods yet. I need you to hide behind this wall and do not move until I tell you Katie. I mean it, please don't move. This will be over soon, and I have to face him", Shawn patiently said.

"Are you sure you want to do this. I don't want to lose you", Katie softly whispered.

"Babe, for once in my life I'd like to be sure of what tomorrow may bring. I will be right back", Shawn confidently stated

.

Walking swiftly along the broken path of concrete, Shawn stood in the center of the old Nike Site awaiting Vincent's arrival. The once peaceful sky draped in bright stars was now hazy and covered with a dark madness. Vincent slowly approached the area on foot followed by several black wolves trailing behind him. The showdown of good versus evil was upon the town of Topsfield and Katie did what she could to stay away from the confrontation.

"Shawn", Vincent stated.

"Vincent," replied Shawn.

"So, it appears we are at a crossroad here my young friend. If you had allowed your girlfriend to meet her fate, you would be a free man. Speaking of, where is the young lady?" Vincent asked.

"Vincent, you know that she was off limits. You could have taken anyone else but her. She is the mother of my child and I am asking you to take me", Shawn admirably stated.

"My son, that might entice me a bit here. Killing two birds with a stone from your own personal hell. Let me think for a brief second on your offer", Vincent smartly stated.

Approaching Shawn closer, Vincent looked upon the young man and attempted to see through his soul.

You know what, how about I kill you now and take her later", Vincent quickly replied.

Shawn attempted to grab Vincent and without hesitation, Katie began yelling from beyond her hiding spot.

"No, Shawn please. I don't want to see you hurt."

Katie ran over to where Shawn had been standing while Vincent began to summon the darkness above as sheets of lighting lit up the skies. The violent clouds letting loose upon the fingers from the evil angel, a single flash of karma unleashed upon his awaiting hands. Channeling the energy through his body, Vincent transferred the deadly bolt towards his young disciple. The patience of the electric current found its way though the backside of Katie as she attempted to shield Shawn at the last second. The sudden heat of its strength knocked Katie towards Shawn and into his awaiting arms. Her temperature rising suddenly while her beating heart had stopped without warning. Her skin hot to the touch, Shawn began yelling as the force knocked them both to the ground.

"Katie, no!", Shawn angrily screamed out. *"No, No, No, No! Please don't do this to me, please God"*, Shawn repeated over and over with cries for help.

Holding his beautiful lifeless Katie in his arms, the feeling of a lost love encircled his heart. Tears falling endlessly upon the ground, Shawn attempted to gather Katie as if she was asleep.

"Baby, please wake up. Please. I need you. I can't live without you", Shawn repeated to her beautiful face as he relentlessly cried. Wiping away the hair covering her beautiful face, her dilated eyes began to slowly sink into the abyss of another life.

Shaking Katie to revive her already destroyed heart, the soul of the man who lost his beloved girlfriend became mortified. While her head lay in his lap, he decided to place Katie where she lay and stand up to face Vincent. Blurry-eyed from the tears of pain, he wiped his eyes and began to focus on the hatred for the man who murdered his love. Sebastian appeared before the trees to the left of Shawn and behind him were the packs of white and grey wolves with bright bluish eyes. The army of beasts had arrived supporting Shawn and his plight to stand for what he believed in. Standing feet before each other, Vincent looked back at Shawn with a devilish smirk upon his face.

Just as Shawn wanted to closely attack his counterpart, a sudden transformation took over his body. The sharp pain upon his back began to separate his feathers like a complex argument. Kneeling on the ground in agony, the protruding feathers began to fall one by one towards the ground at his feet. Vincent clearly not understanding the metamorphosis, he watched his disciple's black wings disengage from Shawn. The engagement of pain caused the screams from the teen's mouth to subside with drops of blood at his feet. The moment of truth was now at hand as a sudden power took over the young disciple. Standing up to appear strong, the essence of white tips peaked out of the wounds on his back. Looking behind him, Shawn began to realize his wings were now of a white color.

"How is this possible?" Vincent asked.

Grunting in pain, Shawn attempted to hold in the anger as the feeling of satisfaction jerked his body. The once branded disciple of Lucifer was now the prodigy of a higher power and the look of shock on Vincent's face said it all.

"Vincent, your days on Earth here are numbered and I will relentlessly send you back to hell", Shawn screamed.

Chapter 31
Gods of War

Despite the newly found power inside of his body, Shawn was keen to his broadened strength. Looking back at his beloved Katie laying on the ground, Shawn mustered everything in his faith and began to levitate. His white wings spreading away from each side of his body, Shawn clenched both of his hands together. Floating several feet above the ground, the source of electric power between his palms generated a strength that Shawn pushed away from his body. The light of invisible energy pierced through the body of his adversary, knocking him down to the ground while rolling several feet on the concrete road.

Standing up, Vincent looked back at Shawn. *"Very impressive my young friend, but you better come with more than that"*, he stated.

The darkness of the Nike Site hiding the eyes of the wolves behind Vincent, they closely remained behind him. Sebastian took notice and his army of beasts came to Shawn's side as the stare down began. Looking at his small army, Vincent had some kind words for Shawn.

"Not sure how they got to you, but I plan on making an example for them all to see", Vincent stated loudly.

"Do you hear that God? I am going to remove your new child from this ground he walks on", Vincent yelled to the sky above.

With the flick of his fingers, Vincent raised both his hands towards Shawn and a magnetic pulse exploded towards the young teen's direction. The strength of the wave pushed the winged angel further away from the Nike Missile Base into a massive tailspin hundreds of feet in the air. Slightly discombobulated, he recovered enough to head back down towards Vincent and his pack of angry wolves from the sky. In a hurried rush, Shawn flew fast to where Vincent stood and collided with the man who had murdered his girlfriend. With all his might, Shawn mustered the strength to sink Vincent deep beneath the ground. Attempting to crush every bone in his body, Shawn relentlessly pushed all his power to burying the man responsible for breaking his heart. Stopping with an effortless push, Shawn released Vincent and returned backwards away from the massive hole he created in the ground.

Crawling out of the large hole in the ground, Sebastian pulled him to his feet with his jaws. Weary and broken, Shawn felt as if he wasn't strong enough to keep fighting against the man history called Lucifer. The moment of peace began to open the possibility that Shawn sent the evil being back where he deserved to be. The thoughts to be a little premature, the sudden rumbling of the ground ruptured a light of fire exiting the large hole and engulfing the few buildings near the area. Angry and visibly displeased, Vincent appeared from the walls of fire and made it clear he had enough. Walking towards Shawn, he began to speak.

"I am no longer playing games here. It is time for you to die like your worthless girlfriend", Vincent angrily yelled.

Motioning his wolves to attack, one by one the blackness of the night purged upon its prey. Sebastian and his army met the challenge by intercepting the wildness that blessed its wicked fangs towards Shawn. The violent sounds of teeth biting into skin and fur ravaged the next few minutes. Vincent and Shawn watching the melee between the wolves as Sebastian dominated each black wolf with his prowess and brutality. The Alpha Male disobeyed his creator by believing in Shawn and sticking to his side. Vincent had other plans to end the dominance of his former beast as he prepared a surprise. With a swift whisper, Vincent conjured up the wickedness of his evil and summoned the beast from beneath the ground.

"Alexander, serve me as you may", Vincent boldly commanded.

Crawling from the hole in the ground, the large black wolf was twice as strong as Sebastian and he instantly attacked. Literally destroying the first grey wolf it encountered, it began to search for the teen's protector. The look of evil present in its bright green eyes, the large chiseled teeth obliterated all that crossed its path. Shawn knew that Sebastian could hold his own, but it  was Vincent that worried him. Walking away from the battle of the wolves, Shawn attempted to lure Vincent away from the fight. His apparent control over his new Alpha Male would be less of a hinderance with Shawn in his face. Gripping for what could be an epic battle of Gods, Shawn walked over to Vincent and grabbed the collar from his suit and slammed him against the wall. The blunt force of his skull fractured the concrete in mere pieces. Refusing to let

Vincent go, Shawn grabbed him by both arms and flew twenty feet in the air as he dropped Vincent back into the hole he made earlier. The brilliant distraction allowed Sebastian the time to sneak attack the massive beast. Shawn assisted in grabbing the remaining few black wolves and throwing them down the same hole Vincent was thrown into. The essence of falling ash covered the entire area from the many burning buildings. Seen from miles away, the eyes of the fearless were upon them as Shawn watched Sebastian attack the black wolf.

Taking a large bite into its neck, Sebastian gripped the tough skin of the beast and slammed himself on top of it. Slightly kneeling, the black wolf maneuvered its strong teeth into the lower neck of Sebastian. Puncturing him with ease, Sebastian let out a loud yelp as the bigger wolf took control. Biting him from neck to torso, Sebastian was taking a severe beating and the looks of the other wolves became disheartening. Without hesitation, the other wolves began to jump in to help their ally. The remaining seven wolfs bit and chomped there way to giving Sebastian time to recover. Each bite causing minimal damage, but the quickness of their speed eluded the fatal bites from the black wolf. The several minutes allowed Sebastian to collect his strength and with one crushing blow, Sebastian bit in the back of the neck of the wolf, snapping its vertebrae in several spots. The beast immediately collapsing to the ground, Shawn walked over to Sebastian to check on his best friend. His neck covered in blood, the beast looked up at Shawn and began to speak.

"This isn't over", saying in a very soothing voice.

"You talk, are you fucking kidding me?" Shawn surprisingly asked.

"Focus Shawn, he is coming", Sebastian replied.

305

The sound of collapsing walls from the burning building in the distance garnering their attention, Vincent crept quietly behind them. The angry eyes of the evil serpent cast out from Heaven sought his revenge. Shawn turned around and with a swift punch to his face, he fell back several feet to the ground. Sebastian keeping his distance, he knew this fight was meant for the Angels. The willingness to allow Shawn to learn about himself, fate had chosen to take its course with great uncertainty. Standing back on his two feet, Shawn looked over at Sebastian and repeated with curiosity, *"Really. You can talk?"*

The wolf rolled his eyes in embarrassment and placed his paw over its eyes to ignore his question. With the focus back on Vincent, a sudden thrust from a large concrete object smashed down upon Shawn's torso. The feeling of darkness overcame the angel as he was unable to feel his extremities. The heavy object pinning him beneath the ground, Shawn's head was exposed for Vincent to look down upon. Briefly laying on top of the object, Vincent looked into the teen's blue eyes.

"I told you that you could never defeat me my young friend", Vincent proudly mentioned.

Leaning down to run his fingers through Shawn's hair, he pulled back his forehead to force his eyes open.

"Look deep into my eyes. Do you see your fate now?" Vincent demanded.

His life feeling faint, Shawn looked back up at the eyes of Vincent and saw a bright light against his forehead. The headlights of the car that arrived with screeching brakes, the voice of his friend revived his heart. The look of anger became evident upon the face of Vincent in the bright lights of the car.

"Shawn, I am here", Amanda stated.

Amanda went to the back of her car and removed the large water bottle. Carrying its heavy weight towards Vincent, Amanda lifted the bottle above her head with a loud grunt.

"Remember me asshole. I got a surprise for you", Amanda stated.

Forcing the large jug to smash against the concrete away from her feet, the several hundred flies escaped and immediately started swarming around the area. Hundreds of blinking lights from the fireflies began to flash as it stunned Vincent and the evil surrounding him. The strange phenomenon lighting up the dark sky began to mystify the evil that hovered above the Nike Site for miles to see.

"What is this annoyance bestowing itself upon me?" Vincent asked.

Appearing miscalculated and uninformed, Amanda felt compelled to explain the phenomenon as Vincent looked down upon his hands as he started fading slowly into the night.

"How is this possible, I am beginning to feel very weak. How?" Vincent asked again while falling to one knee.

"What is happening here", Vincent screamed out towards the heavens appearing lost.

"Vincent, you are no longer wanted around here, and you need to leave. Our circle is now stronger and the love we all share will chase all evil who dare oppose us", Amanda spoke out loud.

Looking up to the firefly filled sky with her large cross in hand, Amanda shouted a few words in Arabic as the dark clouds above slowly began to separate. The few seconds of time stood still while a heavenly light appeared through the opening of the sky. The light atop of Vincent's body, he began to envision a heaven above.

"Who are you?" Vincent asked.

The light blinding him, his shadow faded slowly to nothing as his silhouette disappeared in a quick instant.

"What the bloody hell just happened Amanda, how did you do that?" Shawn asked

"I repented the evil surrounding Vincent", Amanda stated.

The fireflies dissipated throughout the forest of the Nike Site rejoicing the harmony of chasing a historic evil into oblivion. The calm silence of the night allowed the peaceful moment to capture itself. In pain, Shawn remained under the object that nearly crushed his soul to pieces. Sebastian and the other wolves began pushing the object away from the broken Angel. With an aggressiveness of a million men, the pillar slowly rolled away and cleared his body. Amanda reached down to comfort him and with her words of grace, Shawn cracked a smile.

"How did you become such a hero?" Shawn asked Amanda.

"Leave it up to the freak at Masco to save your dumb ass", Amanda replied laughing.

Coughing while he laughed, Shawn mentioned, *"Try not to make me laugh, it hurts."*

Shawn looked up at the night while lying on his back, he began to ask Amanda, *"How did you figure this out?"*

"Remember all those painful visions I had to endure? Well, it appears that your unborn son was reaching out to me. He led me to the fireflies and I learned in my research that the lights resemble peace and love and one other strange thing. They also somehow resemble they want to mate. In other words, they are horny and can't hide it. How sexy is that? The sign of love and the peacefulness they share apparently chases away all evil. Ever wonder when you see the lights of a firefly that everything around it seems peaceful? Well, in my books, it also indicated a spell that could send Vincent back to hell. Shawn it was your son who saved you", Amanda whispered quietly.

"You sure you aren't a witch?" Shawn asked with a slight humor.

Gathering more words to muster, Shawn reached out to Amanda in helping him get to his feet. Placing her arms around his back, she helped him towards the body of Katie. *"Amanda, just please walk me over to her"*.

The sound of silence amongst the creatures of the night, the bright light once encasing the evil around Vincent, was now atop of Katie's lifeless body. The shower of golden light hovering above her withdrew the vision of Katie's spirit. The enlightened presence staring into the eyes of the man she loved with all her heart, Katie was now front and center. Holding in her arms what appeared to be her son, Shawn began to cry profusely. Reaching out to touch them, the soft golden skin of his son and Katie melted his heart.

"Katie, I am so sorry I failed to protect you. Please forgive me. Please forgive me for failing you", Shawn cried aloud.

"Shh my handsome man. Jeremiah and I will be waiting in Heaven for you Shawn. We aren't going anywhere without you, please know that. We are in God's hands now and we expect you to continue fighting for the good of man", Katie softy spoke.

Wiping his tears from his cheeks, the soft kiss the two would share would brighten the light around them. The love felt for miles away allowed trees and flowers to bloom with grace and confidence. Reaching to touch his son, he said goodbye.

"Goodbye my sweet Jeremiah. Take care of Mommy until I see you again", Shawn softly mentioned.

The appearance of his beloved Katie and their son flashed bright as the rays of Heaven carried them onwards. Looking down at her lifeless body, the silhouette of her amazing curves faded into the darkness. The wickedness of Vincent and his love for the only woman in his life now all gone, Shawn had no idea where to turn. Looking into the eyes of the beast that had been at his side, Shawn walked over to his Sebastian and gripped him with all his might. The two creatures that shared a common bond for each other allowed Shawn to live beyond his years.

Looking at each other with the grins of wisemen, the words from the beast calmed the man who had withstood the evil of hell. *"I am so glad those wings are gone, you looked ridiculous"* Sebastian laughed.

Walking together, the remaining wolves withered away into the night as Shawn arrived home with Sebastian and Amanda assisting him. Amanda opened the door to his home and guided him to a warm shower and took care of her best friend. Shawn's parent no where in sight, Sebastian took refuge in their bed and dozed off in a well-deserved peace.

"Hey, whatever you do in there, please don't piss on my mother's bed. Thank you", Shawn shouted in pain.

The loud growl in the other room indicated he understood while Amanda sat beside Shawn lying in the tub full of blood-soaked water.

"Shawn, what are you going to do from here?" Amanda asked.

"Let's agree that no matter what happens or where I go, you and I will forever be friends. I love you Amanda and you saved my life. I owe you everything", Shawn cried.

"Ok, ok. Don't be getting too sentimental on me sir. I like your rough edges", Amanda replied.

Comforting Shawn through the remainder of the morning, Shawn would spend the weekend resting his weary head while thinking about his beloved Katie. Laying in his bed feeling defeated, the teen looked at a picture of his girlfriend and spoke to himself.

"No matter what I do in this life, I promise to always think of you", Shawn softly stated.

His sad face looking through patient eyes, Shawn envisioned his life with Katie and their son in the silhouette of the window in his room. Crying at the thought, the tears would crash upon his bare feet as he stood reckless.

The realization came to a clearer picture as his Mother and Father would share with their son the intentions of moving away as the weekend ended. The transfer to Danvers would be unnecessary as the orders for his Father to transfer to a more southern city was appropriate. Accepting his new command in the heart of New Orleans, Shawn would gracefully spend the next few weeks in preparing for a new adventure. With Katie's funeral coming in recent days, the family agreed this was the best option for their son. Heartbroken and ravished with several days inside his bedroom, Shawn reluctantly said goodbye to Sebastian.

"Sebastian, I am leaving in a few days to move away from here", Shawn mentioned as he sat on the ground of the forest.

Sebastian looked up at Shawn without words and his sad eyes responded to his departure. Turning around in the woods, Sebastian spoke.

"You will see me again, I promise. This world needs us, and I have a feeling it will be sooner than we expect. Goodbye Shawn."

Sebastian walked further in between the trees and faded into the distance. Shawn had lost his girlfriend and his guardian in a matter of days and it was time to face his sole purpose in life for he what he was chosen for. Knowing he never had a normal childhood, Shawn felt free of his evil and for the first time, he felt like an average teen. Taking the positivity of his knowledge, Shawn looked upon the sky above him and noticed a large bird and baby close by. Thinking of Katie, he knew that she was taking care of their son in Heaven and knowing she fell in love with a dreamer. Cracking a smile at the two birds, Shawn stood up and walked towards his home without regret.

Chapter 32
Room 138

The beautiful morning that began the last week of his residency at the Nike Site, Shawn ventured over to his friend Amanda's house. His parents allowed their son to drive the car in town gathering his last goodbye's with friends. Sitting down at the breakfast table, Shawn had sadly warned Amanda of his plans to move. Unhappy to be finding out suddenly, she slammed her cup on the granite table and stormed into the Library.

"Amanda, what did I do wrong?" Shawn asked.

"You have done absolutely nothing wrong. I just can't believe this will be the last time I see you for a while. I needed to sit down and talk to you", Amanda replied.

"Talk to me? What do you mean?" Shawn asked.

Amanda grabbing Shawn's hand and leading him into the Living Room, they sat next to one another. Looking into his sad blue eyes, Amanda spilled her emotions.

"Shawn, I love you dearly as my friend and I have endured a lot to appease the happiness around you. I am telling you once and for all that the move to New Orleans will not be an adventurous one for you. You once asked me why I felt so close to you and

why we were drawn together. There is a simple reason for that and I need you to know that I am your sister", Amanda stated.

"Oh. Come on Amanda, it won't be that bad. Wait, what the hell did you just say?", Shawn naively asked.

"Vincent came to me in my last vision and decided to tell me the truth", Amanda stated.

"Oh my god, how the hell did I not see that coming", Shawn surprisingly stated. *"This makes perfect sense"*.

"Vincent is gone for now, but you will see him again and when he does cross your path, I need you to be strong. I saw you as an older man and you looked just as handsome as you do now. You will be needed in this world and just keep to your heart Shawn", Amanda stressed.

"How the heck did our Father not tell us this", Shawn asked.

"Let's leave that up to him to tell us, but this perfectly explains my visions and why I am close to you", Amanda resounded.

Standing up to hug each other, Amanda's phone coincidentally rang from the kitchen. Answering it with a graceful introduction, her tone suddenly sank. Dropping the phone at her feet, Amanda began crying hysterically. With his sister visibly shaken, he reached down to pick up the receiver off the floor and he asked, *"Hi, who is this?"*

"This is Nurse Spencer with the Boston Medical Center. Amanda's mother has been in a terrible accident and she is the point of contact."

"Yes Ma'am, I will get her there quickly", Shawn replied.

"Amanda get your stuff, let's go", her brother directed with importance.

The trip to Boston on Interstate 95 was brief with little traffic to interfere. The silence inside of the car welcomed Shawn with open arms as he looked back at his wounds upon his face in the rearview mirror. Thinking of Katie and his son, Shawn reached over to his sister's hand and gripped it firmly. The song that coincidentally would play on the radio would be Winger's *Headed for a Heartbreak*. The words cutting deep into his heart, the memories of a lost love began to allow the mist of tears to cloud his eyes. The man that everyone knew as a star at Masco was privately a hero to most, especially to his private circle. The hurting of his sister could be felt with her silence and with the exit to the Hospital approaching, he dare not leave her side. Arriving at the hospital with questions and little answers, Amanda found herself in room 138.

Waiting at the door while he gave his Sister and her badly bruised mother some quality time, a whisper from behind him captured his attention. Strangely enough, Shawn walked over to the room across from Amanda's mother where the voice had apparently come from. The door partially open across the hall, the words of his name repeatedly coming from the corner behind the privacy sheet. Unable to make out what the frantic voice was saying, Shawn leaned in closer to hear. His curiosity peaking to recover the riddle from the voice, Shawn grabbed the sheet and pulled it back abruptly. Laying on the hospital bed appeared a man with a shaved head as he lay helplessly sleeping with tubes in his arms. Looking at the paper work upon the clipboard on the side of the bed, the patient's name seemed blurry. Attempting to look closer, the name *"Shawn Lee"* came across his eyes. The look of shock revered him motionless as he felt as he was staring inside of a mirror with ageless consequence.

"What the hell is going on here?" Shawn asked himself.

Attempting to discover the reason for his visit, the words titled *"Coma"* had placed itself under the diagnosis. Slowly leaning in to possibly hear words coming from the patient's mouth, a dead silence rang through his body. Staring into the closed eye lids of the man lying on his back, his eyes suddenly opened. The horrific chills ran through Shawn's body as the patient's mouth attempted to say something.

"Vincent's got her. Please help her, please. The man quietly whispered over and over with a frantic look on his face.

"I tried to help, but she had no choice. Please help her", the patient began crying.

"Wait. Who. What is going on?" Shawn asked several times while looking at the patient.

"Shawn, help her now", the patient frantically replied.

The remaining words having trouble coming from the quivering lips of the comatose patient, he grasped for air. Shawn was desperately awaiting the answer to his question as the arrival of the few nurses on duty came to see him. The sounds of the heart monitor ringing loudly, the man mustered the strength to allow one more word into the crowded air, "*Kimberly*". Taking his last breath, the patient fell into a deep nightmare as the staff attempted to revive the falling soul.

The name from the lifeless man pierced his soul as Shawn slowly felt the raising of the hairs on his arms in a horrific nightmare. Walking slowly backwards away from himself laying on the gurney, Shawn immediately turned around and the vision of the creature wearing the red-hooded sweatshirt looked back at him from the hallway. The mist covering his body, the arm reaching to grab Shawn beyond the door came within reach and the fear deep in his soul began once again. The vision was clear that his purpose was to seek the girl that Vincent chose as his next Angel.

To be continued......

28612047R00179

Made in the USA
Middletown, DE
20 December 2018